Was she destined to lose her soul?

"What do you see?" he repeated softly.

"Evan." She licked her lips. For the first time in her life she forced herself to concentrate on her vision. Despite the fire, the cabin was cold. The breath of the two figures condensed as they spoke, hanging in the air like smoke. Beyond the cabin confines, the wind howled, rattling windows she couldn't see.

"Tell me what else you see."

"It feels like snow." Chill fingers of air crept around her, and she shivered.

"Do you see any people?"

"Two. Male, female." The woman had long hair that she brushed away with a cat's paw. "She has claws. Cat's claws."

"Are they talking? Can you hear what they're saying?"

"Only the woman speaks." And though her voice was soft, its mellow sound stung Maddie's ears, as grating as fingernails across a blackboard.

"What is she saying?"

"I don't know."

"Listen harder. Concentrate on the sound of her voice."

Jon squeezed her hand, running warmth through her body. She licked her lips, trying to do as he asked. Like a radio suddenly tuned, the woman's voice leapt into focus, and she told Jon, "She plans an attack. Tonight."

"Who does she plan to attack?"

"I don't know-" She hesitated.

The woman turned. There was malice on her face, malice in the air, so thick Maddie suddenly struggled to breathe. Jon called her name urgently, but he sounded so very far away. She stared at the woman with the vibrant green eyes until they all but filled her vision, became a turbulent ocean awash with venom.

"You are mine," the woman spat. "Mine."

Maddie screamed, and the dream disintegrated into darkness.

To Kasey,

for keeping me supplied with two of life's
necessities—lots of love and tea.

OTHER BOOKS
BY
KERI ARTHUR

Dancing with the Devil

Hearts in Darkness
(coming in December 2001)

Circle of Death
(coming in 2002)

Circle of Fire

✳✳✳

Keri Arthur

CIRCLE OF FIRE
Published by ImaJinn Books, a division of ImaJinn

Copyright ©2001 by Keri Arthur
Printed and bound in the United States of America. All rights reserved. No part of this book may be reproduced in any form or by any means (electronic, mechanical, photocopying, recording, or otherwise) without prior written permission of both the copyright holder and the above publisher of this book, except by a reviewer, who may quote brief passages in a review. For information, address: ImaJinn Books, a division of ImaJinn, P.O. Box 162, Hickory Corners, MI 49060-0162; or call toll free 1-877-625-3592.

ISBN: 1-893896-70-6

10 9 8 7 6 5 4 3 2 1

PUBLISHER'S NOTE:
This book is a work of fiction. Names, characters, places and incidents are products of the author's imagination or are used fictitiously. Any resemblance to actual events or locales or persons, living or dead, is entirely coincidental.

Books are available at quantity discounts when used to promote products or services. For information please write to: Marketing Division, ImaJinn Books, P.O. Box 162, Hickory Corners, MI 49060-0162, or call toll free 1-877-625-3592.

Cover design by Patricia Lazarus

ImaJinn Books, a division of ImaJinn
P.O. Box 162, Hickory Corners, MI 49060-0162
Toll Free: 1-877-625-3592
http://www.imajinnbooks.com

One

Madeline Smith didn't believe in ghosts. Not until the night Jon Barnett walked into her life, anyway. Maddie drew her legs up to her chest and held them close. Maybe walked was the wrong word to use—his method of movement seemed more like floating.

Outside her bedroom, the branches of an old elm scraped back and forth across the tin roofing. The wind howled through the night, an eerie cry that matched her mood of anticipation and fear. Snow scurried past the windows, silvery drops that glittered briefly in the light.

It felt oddly fitting to be sitting on her bed, waiting for the arrival of a ghost while an early winter storm raged outside.

Only *he* insisted he wasn't a ghost at all.

She tugged the blankets over her knees and wondered if she should stoke the fire with a little more wood. Maybe the heat would keep him away. Or maybe he'd gotten tired of his game and simply forgotten about her. Though she believed the desperation in his eyes was real enough, she just didn't believe *he* was real.

Perhaps he was just a figment of her imagination—a last, desperate escape from the loneliness of her life.

The clock on the mantle began to chime quietly. She turned to look at the time. One-thirty. Maybe he *had* forgotten about her...

"Madeline."

She closed her eyes, uncertain whether fear or the unexpected pleasure of hearing the low velvet tones of his voice one more time caused the sudden leap of her heart.

"Madeline," he repeated. This time a hint of urgency touched the warmth of his voice.

He stood in the shadows to the left of her window. Despite the storm that raged outside, he wore only a short-sleeved black shirt and dark jeans—the same clothes he'd worn when he had first appeared last night.

Tonight there *was* something different about him, though. Tonight he looked afraid.

But he wasn't *real,* damn it! How could a ghost feel fear?

"Madeline, you *must* help me."

She closed her heart to the desperate plea in his voice. What he was asking her to do was impossible.

"I can't." She avoided his gaze and fiddled with the fraying edge of the blanket. "I don't know you—I don't even believe you exist. How can you expect me to leave everything I have here on the whim of a ghost?"

"You must!" The sudden sharpness of his voice made her look up. "All I'm asking is for you to travel across the state, not to another country. Why are you so afraid to move from your retreat?"

Maddie stared at him. He seemed to understand altogether too much about her. No one else had seen her fear—not even her sister, who was as close to her as Maddie ever allowed anyone to get these days.

"There's nothing wrong with being cautious," she said after a moment.

He studied her, amusement flickering briefly in the diamond-bright depths of his blue eyes. "I never said there was. But life has to be lived. You cannot hide forever."

She ignored the sliver of alarm in her heart, ignored the whispers that demanded she ask how he knew so much about her, and raised an eyebrow. "And what does a ghost know about such things?"

He sighed, running a hand through his overly long hair. In the light of the fire, slivers of gold seemed to flow through his fingers. "I'm no ghost, Madeline. But I will be, if you don't help me soon."

Alarm danced through her heart. "What do you mean?"

He walked across to the fire and held out his hands, as if to capture the warmth of the flames. Hair dusted his arms, golden strands that gleamed in the firelight. His fingers were long and smooth and tanned. Lord, he seemed real—and yet, if she looked closely enough, she could see the glow of the fire through his body.

"I mean that I'm stuck down this damn well, and I can't get out. I *will* die, Madeline, unless you help me."

Maddie closed her eyes and tried to stifle the rising spiral of fear. Not for her safety, because she sensed this was one ghost who would cause her no harm. It was just fear of...what? She didn't *know,* but there was something about this apparition that made her very wary.

Perhaps she should play along with him. Surely he'd eventually tire of his game and leave her alone. Or perhaps she was just going mad—as most of her so-called friends had insisted she would.

Yet those same friends had never understood what she was, or what she was capable of doing. Nor had they ever tried to help her.

"Why can't someone else rescue you? You must have friends—why don't you go haunt them?"

"Believe me, I would if I could."

His tone was dry and left no doubt he would rather be anywhere else than with her. *Bad news when even a damn ghost doesn't want to be with you.* "So why aren't you?"

He frowned. "I don't know. Some force keeps driving me towards you. I have no choice in the matter, Madeline. You're all I have."

And you refuse to help me. The unspoken rebuke was in his eyes when he glanced at her. Maddie bit her lip and looked away, watching the snow continue its dance past her window. Maybe she *was* going mad. She was beginning to feel sorry for a ghost.

"Why would you be able to reach a complete stranger and not anyone of real use to you?"

"I don't know."

But the look he gave her was keen, as if he did know but

didn't believe she'd understand.

"If you want my help, you at least owe it to me to be honest."

"Fair enough." He turned his back to the fire, but kept his hands behind him, as if still trying to warm them. "Whatever this force is, it brings with it a sense of danger. And it's connected with you somehow."

He seemed to say an awful lot without actually saying *anything,* Maddie noted. Maybe her ghost had been a politician in a former life.

"That made everything so much clearer," she said dryly.

He shot her a look that was half amusement, half frustration. "Someone close to you is in danger, and somehow, they're drawing me to you."

Besides her sister, the only other person who qualified as being close was Jayne's son, Evan. Neither of them had the sort of power Jon was talking about. No, she thought grimly, there was only one misfit left in their small family unit.

"So how did you end up in the well?"

"Someone shot me when I was out exploring." He shrugged. "I must have fallen into it."

Maddie raised an eyebrow. From what she could see of him, there was remarkably little evidence of a bullet wound. "Then you *are* dead."

He sighed and closed his eyes. "I was hit in the arm. The fall could have killed me, but I was...lucky."

The arm closest to her was a suntanned brown, well-muscled and remarkably free of wounds. His hands were still firmly clasped together, which surely wouldn't be possible if the other arm had a hole blown in it. Maybe it was her ghost who was mad, not she.

"Why don't you just shout for help?"

"As I explained before, I can't take the risk. Someone is out to get me. If they think I'm still alive, they'll just find me and finish the job."

A chill ran through her. "It could have been an accident."

"No."

She closed her eyes at the soft certainty in his voice. "If I come to help you, my life could be in danger."

"How would they know you're there to help me? You'd just be another tourist passing by."

The sudden weariness in his voice made her look at him. His form had faded slightly, merging with the night. Something was wrong, something more than the fact he'd been shot. And she sensed he wouldn't tell her what. "Who do you mean by *they?*"

"I'm not exactly sure. But someone in this town knew why I was here, and they moved pretty swiftly to get rid of me."

"Then tell *me* what town you're in, and why you're there." If he was going to continue haunting her, she should at least try to understand a little more about him.

He stared at her, then shook his head. "How many times do I have to repeat myself before you believe in me?"

His voice held an edge of desperation that made her wince. Yet last night she'd been too busy trying to convince herself he was nothing more than a vivid dream to really listen to anything he said. "You mentioned some town—Sherbrook, wasn't it?"

He closed his eyes for a moment, as if battling to remain calm. "Sherbrook is the name of the inn. The place is Taurin Bay."

An odd sense of foreboding ran through her. Evan had attended a school camp in Taurin Bay not so long ago. Jayne had gone along as cook and chief pot-washer. "That force you said was driving you to me—was it male or female?"

"Male." He paused, eyes narrowing. "Why?"

Evan—something told her it was Evan. Maddie licked her lips and wondered if she should call her sister—or was she just worrying over nothing again?

"Maddie, what's wrong?"

She stared at him blankly for a moment. "My sister has a thirteen year old son called Evan. Both of them were in Taurin Bay last month."

"Damn!" Jon ran a hand through his hair, then abruptly walked forward, stopping only when his knees touched the side of her bed.

He was close, so close. She could see the rise and fall of his chest, felt the whisper of his breath wash across her skin. Could smell him, a faint scent of cologne mixed with hints of earth and sweat. But he wasn't *real,* damn it!

"In the last eight months, sixteen teenagers have been taken from their homes and haven't been seen alive again. In each case, no locks or windows were disturbed. And each time, the teenager was taken on the next full moon *after* their families returned from Taurin Bay."

Her heart leapt. She raised a hand to her throat and tried to remain calm. "Evan is safe at home. This is ridiculous."

"Someone is drawing me here, Madeline. Someone who knows he's in danger. You're the connection between us. Tonight is a full moon. Go call your sister."

She scrambled off the bed and ran to the bedroom door. Then she hesitated, looking back at Jon. He hadn't moved, but his body had faded, losing its shape to the darkness. Only his blue eyes were still bright.

"Go call her," he said. "Then come to me. Save me."

Maddie turned away from his plea, though she knew he wouldn't be there when she returned. She ran down the hall to the phone in the kitchen, turning on lights as she went. Somehow, the darkness seemed too intense to face alone.

Fingers trembling, she picked up the phone and dialed Jayne's number. It seemed to ring forever. Maddie bit her lip, hoping nothing had happened, hoping that Evan was in bed and safe.

"Hello?" a croaky, half-asleep voice said eventually.

"Jayne, it's me," she said without preamble. "Is Evan there? Is he all right?"

There was a slight pause, and Maddie could hear the rustle of blankets as her sister shifted around in her bed. "Of course he is. Why?"

Because I'm a fool, because a ghost told me he may be in danger. "Humor your little sister and just go check, will you?"

Jayne sighed. "Maddie, have you been drinking again?"

Maddie closed her eyes. Whenever Jayne thought she had

a problem, she always asked the same question—even though it had been six years and ten days since Maddie had last had a drink. Not since the fire that had taken her husband's life, she thought with a shiver. The experts had never found an explanation for that fire, though they had theories aplenty. Maddie knew the truth, but she wasn't about to tell anyone— not even her sister.

She cleared her throat. "No. I had a dream, and I want to reassure myself he's all right."

"For God's sake, it's after two." Annoyance ran through Jayne's voice, but at least she was still listening. At least she hadn't yet slammed the phone down.

"I'm well aware of the time. It will only take a minute to check on Evan. Please."

"I guess I damn well better," her sister muttered. "Or you'll be calling all night again."

Maddie heard Steve, Jayne's husband, murmur something about weird sisters, then the squeak of springs as Jayne got out of bed. Maddie grimaced, hoping she *was* just being weird. Hoping Jon wasn't right. She stared out the kitchen window as she waited, watching the snow flurries dance across her yard. Then she heard the sound of returning footsteps, and felt her stomach knot. *Please let Evan be safe.*

"Evan's sound asleep in bed, Maddie." Jayne's voice was a mix of exasperation and annoyance. "And by the sound of it, so should you be."

This time Jayne did hang up on her, but Maddie didn't mind. Jon had been wrong. Evan was okay. She replaced the receiver then thrust a shaking hand through her hair as she sagged back against the wall in relief. Maybe Jayne was right. Maybe all she needed was a good night's sleep—something that had eluded her ever since her world had disappeared into flames.

She closed her eyes, fighting the memories, fighting the sudden need to wash the pain into oblivion with a drink. *That* chapter of her life was over. She would not return, even through memories. And if Jon did come back, she'd tell him to go find someone else to tell his weird story to. She wasn't interested—

not if the cost was to make her sister think she was stranger than ever.

***

His only chance of survival was a woman afraid of life. Jon shook his head at the irony of it and leaned wearily against the cold stone wall of the well. He'd seen the fear in the amber flame of her eyes, in the tremble in her hands as she ran her fingers through her chestnut-colored hair. She was afraid to move from the safety of her home.

And he would die if she didn't.

He smiled grimly and stared up at the pale stars twinkling in the dark bracket of sky far above him.

How he wished he could fly, simply wing his way up out of the well to freedom. But he couldn't even climb with his arm like this. He glanced down, noting his flesh had swollen around the handkerchief he'd tied across his forearm.

Someone *had* shot him, but not with a gun, as Madeline had presumed. Someone in Taurin Bay knew what he was. They'd used arrows made of white ash, a weapon deadly to those with magic in their souls.

He'd broken off most of the shaft, but a section was still embedded in his flesh, and probably the only reason he hadn't yet bled to death.

Oddly enough, he felt no pain. Not now, anyway. Maybe it was the cold. Maybe it was the numbness beginning to infuse his body. Or maybe he was as thick-skinned as many of his friends believed.

He grimaced and closed his eyes. He'd thought about dying many times in his life, but he never thought it would come like this—lying helpless and alone in the cold, cold night.

And yet, in some ways, it was oddly fitting. He'd spent most of his adult life alone, so why not die the same way?

He wouldn't have cared much, either, if he'd had the chance to see his family one more time and explain why he'd avoided them so much over the last ten years.

An owl hooted softly in the distance. He listened carefully, then heard the soft snap of wings, the small cry of a field mouse. If the owls were out looking for a meal, it meant there was no one about to disturb their hunting. And therefore, no one about hunting *him*. Trapped down this damn well, he'd be easy pickings. A day had passed since he'd been shot. By all rights, he should be safe, but he'd learned over the years never to relax his guard.

Had learned the hard way that *should* be safe never meant it *was*.

He toed the water lapping the edges of the small ledge. The water had been his salvation in more ways than one—it had broken his fall and, no doubt, saved his life. And it was drinkable, which meant he wasn't in any danger of dehydration. But it might yet kill him, too. His abilities gave him some protection against the cold, but he knew he was starting to push his limits. His plunge into the water had soaked every bit of his clothing, and now he was so cold it hurt to move.

If Madeline did find the courage to come to his rescue, she might discover nothing more than a five-foot-ten icicle.

Madeline—what was he going to do about her? How could he convince her she was sane and *he* really needed her help? What had happened in her life that made her so afraid?

A wave of dizziness hit him. There was nothing he could do except ride out the feeling. He probably had enough strength left to contact her one more time. If he couldn't convince her to help him, he'd just have to hope that someone in the Circle realized he was in trouble and came to his rescue.

Because if someone didn't, more kids would die.

***

The snow had turned to rain, which fell in a soaking mist. Rivers of water were beginning to run past the house, scouring tiny trenches along the freshly graded driveway. The tops of the cedars, claret ashes and silver birches that crowded the fence line were lost to the mist, and though dawn should have come and gone, night still seemed to hold court.

Maddie raised the coffee mug she held between both hands and took a sip. The wind was bitter, but the wide old verandah protected her from the worst of the storm, and her threadbare coat kept her warm enough for the moment. She couldn't face going indoors just yet. The old house was too big, too full of ghosts...

Except for one.

She sighed and leaned back against a veranda post. She couldn't shake Jon from her thoughts. Couldn't shake the desperation she'd glimpsed in his eyes.

What if he wasn't a ghost, but alive and in dire need of her help?

She sipped her coffee and stared out across the snow-flung wilderness of her yard. In a last ditch effort to salvage her life, she'd bought this house and its untamed three acres six years ago. It had become her haven, the one place she felt truly safe. She had no real wish to be anywhere else. The flowers she raised in the barn she'd converted to a greenhouse made small luxuries possible, and she had enough money invested to see her through the hard times. Even Jayne had given up her efforts to get Maddie back into what she called 'mainstream' life.

Maddie chewed on her lip. The question she had to face was simple. Could she simply stand by and let Jon die?

If she believed he was real, then the answer was no. That was the crux of the matter. Part of her was afraid to believe, part of her afraid not to. She took another sip of coffee and shivered as the wind ran icy fingers across the back of her neck.

Then she stiffened. Something told her she was no longer alone. Slowly, she turned.

Jon stood several feet away, his face as pale as the snow behind him, blue eyes still bright despite the shadows beneath them. He looked like death, and the thought chilled her soul.

"What can I do to make you believe me?" he asked softly.

There was a hoarseness to his voice that had not been evident a few hours before, an edge of weariness and pain that tore at her need to stay safe.

"Maybe it's not a case of me believing you. Maybe it's just a case of knowing I *can't* help you."

He ran a hand through his hair and looked away, appearing to study the silvery drops dripping steadily from a hole in the gutter. "Then you have killed me as surely as those who shot me," he whispered after a moment.

"No!" She closed her eyes. How could she ever survive the weight of another death, whether or not it was her fault? "Isn't there someone I could contact, maybe a friend in a better position to help?"

"My companions live in Washington, and my time is running out." He looked at her. "You're my only chance, Madeline. Please."

Something in his eyes made her want to reach out and touch him. She clenched her fingers around her coffee cup and turned away, knowing she had to react with her mind—not with her emotions, and definitely not with her heart. They had only led her to tragedy in the past.

"Why won't they suspect me?"

"You are...ordinary."

Ordinary. She almost laughed at the bitter irony of it. How often had she heard that in the past? No one suspected the truth, not even her sister.

"Madeline, I don't mean—"

"It doesn't matter," she said, turning to face him. "I can't change what I am. Nor can I deny I'm afraid. But I just can't run off wildly without some proof."

He sighed. "I'm in no position to prove anything to anyone."

Mist drifted around him, darkening his hair where it touched. She wanted to reach out and touch him, to feel the heat of his body, to hold him close and caress away the lines of pain from his face. *Maybe I am insane. I want to touch this ghost in ways I never touched my husband.* Shaking her head, she stepped away from him.

Something flickered in his blue eyes, and a slight grimace twisted his generous mouth. It was almost as if he'd sensed the reason for her fear. *But that's ridiculous—he's a ghost, not a mind reader.* The sharp ring of the telephone interrupted the heavy silence. Maddie glanced at her watch and frowned. It was barely seven—who would be ringing her at this hour? She headed inside to answer it, then hesitated, meeting Jon's steady gaze.

"We won't meet again," he murmured. He reached out, as if to touch her cheek then let his hand fall. "For that, I'm sorry. Stay safe, Madeline."

"No..." Maddie watched him fade until there was nothing left but the warmth of his voice in her thoughts.

She closed her eyes and fought the rise of tears. Damn it, why should she cry for a ghost, when she hadn't cried for her husband? She bit her lip and watched the mist swirl around the spot where he'd stood. Maybe because Jon had shown her more warmth in the few hours she'd known him than Brian had ever shown in the six years they were married.

The insistent ringing broke through her thoughts. She took a deep breath then ran down the length of the verandah to the back door, fleeing her thoughts as much as running for the phone.

Slamming the back door open, she snatched the receiver from the hook and struggled to get her boots off. "Hello?"

"Maddie?"

She froze. It was Jayne...*Oh lord, let Evan be safe.* Yet the note in her sister's voice told her something was terribly wrong. "What is it?"

"It's Evan," Jayne sobbed. "He's disappeared, Maddie. Just gone... without a trace."

Two

"I need your help. You can see things...I need to know..." Jayne's voice faded into silence.

Maddie closed her eyes and leaned back against the wall. After all the years of denials, after all the years of fear, Jayne was not only acknowledging her abilities but also asking for help. It was a miracle Maddie had never thought she'd see, and one that left her oddly frightened.

If Jayne knew, maybe Steve did.

And maybe he knew about Brian, too. She took a deep breath. No, if Steve suspected anything, he would have reported it.

Her thoughts stuttered to a sudden halt. She'd asked Jon for some form of proof, and perhaps this was it. Evan had disappeared, just as he'd predicted.

Jon was real. And dying.

She clenched her fingers against the phone and tried to remain calm. "What do you expect me to do that Steve can't?"

"Steve's restricted by the law, though he's looking...but you're the only one who can...who can help Evan. Only you."

There was an odd certainty in Jayne's voice that made Maddie frown. Maybe she wasn't the only gifted member in the family, after all. "Jayne, my gifts are decidedly unreliable and...well, dangerous." Which had to be the biggest understatement she'd ever made. "I'm willing to try, but Steve's a detective. Surely he-"

"No! Maddie, you must look for him. Please, promise me."

The desperation in her sister's voice reminded Maddie of Jon. "Okay, okay. But I'll need to see his room, first." She hesitated, then added. "Does Steve know you're asking me to do this?"

Jayne's silence was answer enough. Maddie closed her eyes. She'd taken to visiting Jayne and Evan when Steve wasn't home. He'd never bothered to mask his opinion of her, and lately that opinion had been openly hostile.

"Maddie, please..."

She sighed. "I'll be there in an hour."

"Thank you," Jayne whispered, and hung up.

Maddie gulped down the remains of her coffee, then turned and ran towards her bedroom. Grabbing an old canvas carryall out from under a pile of sweaters, she threw in everything she thought she might need for the next week. Maybe Jayne was right. Maybe her hated abilities were the only way to find Evan quickly. Even so, she couldn't do it alone.

Once she'd seen Jayne, she was going on down to Taurin Bay to find the man who wasn't a ghost.

***

Maddie climbed out of the truck and studied Jayne's large, two-story home. It was barely eight-thirty in the morning, but the winter light was so bad it might as well have been early evening. Though the house was lit up like a Christmas tree, the silence that draped it was so heavy she could almost touch it. Maddie counted the windows along the top floor until she found Evan's room. From the outside at least, it showed no sign of forced entry.

She shoved her hands into her pockets and walked up the newly shovelled driveway, trying to ignore the insidious whisper in her mind telling her she should have stayed home— should have stayed safe.

Jayne opened the front door. Her eyes were puffy and red, her face suddenly old without its usual coating of makeup. Maddie stepped up onto the porch then stopped, unsure of what to do next. Jayne was usually the one in control, the one who believed any sign of emotion should be kept out of the public's curious gaze. Even as children, it had been always been Maddie who had lost her temper, Maddie who had cried, never Jayne.

"We should have taken your dream seriously," Jayne said, her gaze not quite meeting Maddie's. "But we didn't listen. Oh God, we just didn't believe..."

Maddie hesitated, then stepped forward and wrapped her arms around her sister. Jayne stiffened for just a moment, then collapsed against her, sobbing softly.

"I'll find him," Maddie promised. "Somehow, I'll find him."

Jayne sniffed and pulled away. "He hasn't left a note or anything. He's simply vanished."

Vanished. Just as Jon had warned. Maddie shivered. Something told her that if she was to have any hope of finding Evan, she first had to find Jon.

"I need to see the room, Jayne." If Evan had somehow drawn Jon to her, maybe there was something in the teenager's room that would link her back to Evan.

"Okay..." Jayne hesitated then stepped away from the door. "But hurry. Steve will be back at any moment."

He'd be furious to find her in the house—and would take his anger out on Jayne. Not physically, but emotionally. From what Maddie had observed, it was, in some ways, tougher to handle.

How had the two of them managed to marry men so like their father?

She clomped up the stairs, stripping off her coat as she approached Evan's room. The house was unusually warm— odd, given Steve's belief that it made better sense to put on a sweater than turn up the heat.

Nothing had changed in her nephew's room from the last time she'd seen it, three weeks before. Posters of rock bands and scantily clad woman still vied for space on the walls. His clothes were strewn all over the floor, and the football she'd given him for his last birthday still held pride of place on his overcrowded bookshelves.

And yet there was *one* difference—the smell. Maddie frowned as she tried to place it. It was burnt ash, mud, and a soft hint of citrus, all rolled into one. An odd and unpleasant scent that made her stomach roll.

She blinked back the sudden sting of tears. She had to find Evan. He couldn't die. He was all that stood between her and the utter loneliness of her life.

Biting her lip, she walked across to the windows. White dust covered much of the frame, highlighting the fingerprints. But as Jon had warned, there was no sign at all that the windows had been forced. Both were still key-locked.

She turned away. The odd smell grew stronger, became a cloud that encased her in sweetness and decay and darkness. She groped blindly for the nearby dresser. *Oh God,* she thought, *it's happening again.*

Her fingers brushed against something cool and metallic—the gold chain Evan had bought with the cash he'd received for his birthday. Maybe, just maybe, she could use it to try to control the direction of the dream. As the room spun around her, she squeezed the chain into her palm and hung on tight.

For several heartbeats, darkness encased her mind. Then pinpoints of light danced through the gloom, slivers that gradually lifted the darkness. Around her, she saw the rough wooden walls of a small cabin. Two small forms lay huddled on the dusty floor, wrapped in blankets that hid their faces from sight. One of them was Evan—she could just see the gleam of his red-gold hair.

The vision swirled slightly, and the shadows moved. A slender figure walked across the room, features hidden by a large coat and hood. It bent and lovingly touched the form lying beside Evan. A chill ran through Maddie. It was a woman's hand, and yet it had the claws of a panther.

"By the light of the new moon," the woman said, her sultry tones oddly tremulous. "Your youth will become my youth."

A hand touched Maddie's shoulder. With a small squeak of fright, she spun around. Jayne stared at her, glassy eyes widening in surprise.

"I didn't mean to scare you," she said softly.

Maddie licked her lips. "Sorry. Just a bit jumpy." She hesitated, noting the slightly pinched look around her sister's mouth. "What's wrong?"

"Steve just called. He's on his way home, and he wants to

talk to you."

Maddie swore under her breath. Trust her sister to mention she was here. "I can't, Jayne. He'll want to know how I knew Evan was in danger, and he won't believe me when I tell him."

Jayne nodded, though Maddie could see the uncertainty in her sister's eyes. Despite her earlier statements, Jayne still wasn't entirely sure whether to believe her or not, either.

"Okay, then. It usually takes him five minutes or so to get here from the station. If you hurry, you might avoid him."

She squeezed her sister's hands tightly. "I'll find Evan, Jayne. I'll bring him back." Somehow.

Jayne gave her a wan smile. Maddie stepped back, then stopped, her gaze caught by the brief flash of gold on the dresser. Evan's chain. She must have dropped it when Jayne touched her shoulder. Had holding it helped the vision's direction? Maddie suspected it had, if only because it was the first time she'd ever actually seen something she'd wanted to. Usually the dreams took their own course. Maybe if she took the chain with her, she might be able to use it to help find Evan.

Not giving herself time to doubt, she brushed the chain into her hand then followed her sister down the stairs.

The old truck rattled to life at the second turn of the key, which was something of a miracle. She reversed out of the driveway then turned north. It was time to go find herself a real live ghost.

***

Maddie put her foot on the brakes, then winced at the squeal of metal grating against metal. The brake pads had needed replacing for some time now, but it was a task she'd hoped to put off until she'd sold the next lot of roses.

But hours of driving—the last one up and down steep mountainsides—had quickly rearranged her priorities. If she made it down this road in one piece, she was going to get them fixed as soon as possible.

At least the bright lights of Taurin Bay were finally visible below. Though now that she was nearly there, she wasn't entirely sure what she should do next. For a start, she had to find the Sherbrook Inn, but she also had to find Jon—and quickly. Heavy snowfalls were predicted within the next twenty-four hours.

She remembered his face the last time she'd seen him—so pale and tired. If she didn't find him soon, it might be too late. At least Evan had the heavy layer of blankets to protect him from the cold.

A graceful bridge of latticed metal arched across the mouth of a wide river and swept her into Taurin Bay, where a familiar yellow sign caught her attention. She pulled into the drive-through, collecting a hamburger and the directions to the Sherbrook.

The inn was a large, square-fronted, Victorian-style house painted in pale pinks and grays. She stopped the truck and leaned against the steering wheel, studying the house.

Maybe staying here wasn't such a wise move. Jon had and had ended up down a well. Someone had obviously suspected he was here to find the missing teenagers and had tried to stop him. Would they suspect her as well?

The thought made her snort. Jon had called her ordinary and, outwardly at least, he was right. Why would anyone suspect she was anything more than a tourist? Besides, she had to stay somewhere, and most of the motels along the way had been full—not surprising with the early onset of the ski season.

She dragged her bag off the back seat and headed for the inn. The small foyer was empty when she entered, but a bell chimed softly in the distance. She shut the door and studied the room. The walls were covered in pale gold and silver wallpaper, and the window next to the front door draped with rich, burgundy curtains. An open fire blazed brightly in the sitting room to her left, lending a golden gleam to the empty plush velvet and mahogany chairs forming a semicircle around it.

The inn looked expensive. A weeklong stay would put a serious dent in her savings, but that was a small price to pay if she found Evan—and Jon—in one piece.

"Hello."

Maddie jerked her gaze back to the desk. A man stood in the doorway just behind it, his smile warm and friendly.

"Hank Stewart. I'm the night manager here," he continued, stepping forward. "How may I help you?"

She eyed him warily. Though his voice held nothing beyond politeness, something about him made her uneasy. "Do you have a room available for a couple of days?"

He opened the book in front on the desk, then nodded. "We have the Captain's quarters available at the moment."

It was his eyes, she decided when he looked up. Something unfavorable lurked in the mud-colored depths of his eyes.

She swallowed and pulled her gaze away. "How much is it?"

"It's our top room. One fifteen a night."

She winced but signed the register. Picking up her bag, she followed him along the hall and up the stairs. The Captain's quarters turned out to be a suite comprised of a bedroom, a lounge and a large bathroom—all ornately furnished.

"Feel free to call if you need anything," he said, smiling as he gave her the key.

His fingers brushed hers, hot and yet clammy. She shuddered and pulled her hand away.

"If you want to go out tonight, just let me know," he continued. "I usually lock the door after eleven, unless we've guests still out."

She hesitated and glanced at the clock. It was nearly seven now. Who knew how long it would take her to find Jon's well. "I do have plans to go out for a while."

He nodded. "Anything else?"

"Is there a map of the area I can use?"

"Over on the mantle," he said and walked away.

She firmly closed and locked the door behind him, then leaned her forehead against it for a moment. Her whole body was trembling, and she suddenly felt sick. Over what? A man with strange brown eyes who'd offered her no threat in anything he'd said or done. *I'm no good at this sort of thing. I should have stayed home.*

She took a deep breath, then walked over to the mantle.

Spreading the map out on the coffee table, she knelt to study it.

Jon had given her a fairly good description of the area where he'd fallen into the well. All she had to do was remember it—not an easy thing when she'd been so petrified by his appearance that first time.

She traced the lines of roads with her fingers until she found one that sounded familiar. She followed it along 'til it went through a state forest. That was it. That was the area.

After rolling up the map, she collected the room key and headed downstairs. The night air was cold, and the wind carried the hint of snow. Maddie glanced up. The stars had disappeared behind a wall of clouds. She hoped the snow held off—not just for Jon's sake, but Evan's as well. The teenagers might have blankets to keep them warm, but there'd been no sign of a fire in the old cabin. If bad weather moved in, they might freeze to death before anyone found them.

She just had to hope Jon's directions—or her memories of them—were accurate. The last thing she wanted was to drive around for hours. Every second was vital if she was to find Evan alive, of that much she was certain.

But if someone *had* shot Jon, there was no telling how accurate his directions were—though he'd seemed pretty lucid whenever he'd appeared before her.

Just how in the hell had he appeared, anyway? What was that? Some form of astral travel? Wasn't that the stuff of fairy tales? She snorted softly. *Yeah right, just like the ability to light fires with a thought was just a fairy tale.*

And in the end, did it matter? He could have horns and sprout wings, and she wouldn't give a damn. Not if he helped her find Evan.

She'd been the cause of far too much grief in her family in the past. Maybe now she had a chance to redeem herself.

She started the truck, then glanced at the street map one more time before driving off. Twenty minutes later she was back in the mountains. The road's incline grew steeper, and pines began to crowd the edges. It didn't seem the area in which to find a well, yet oddly enough, it *did* seem the type of area Jon would enjoy. Strange how she had gleaned so much from the few hours they'd been together.

She drove through the gates that designated the beginning of the state forest. The road became a dirt track several yards in. She slowed. If she'd read the map right, there was a small turnoff half a mile ahead. It would take her right past the shared fence line of the old farm Jon had mentioned.

The turn came up faster than she expected. She swung the steering wheel hard. Saplings slapped against the windows, and something hard scraped along the body of the truck. Heart pounding rapidly, she straightened the truck and slowed down even further. The headlights picked out the fine strands of wire running parallel to the road just ahead.

She stopped and got out. An owl hooted in the distance, a haunting sound in the silence. The chill breeze spun around her, stirring the pine branches above her head and whipping thick strands of hair away from her ponytail. She caught the flyaway ends, tucking them under the collar of her jacket, then studied the fields before her. Somehow, it felt right. She couldn't explain how or why, but she knew that Jon was here somewhere. Either that, or she was finally going mad.

She grimaced. That was still a very real possibility. After all, here she was in the middle of nowhere, trusting the words of a man who might yet prove to be a ghost.

She grabbed the flashlight and locked the truck. The fence was a mix of plain and barbed wire. After climbing through carefully, she studied the dark field. Where was the most logical position for a well? She swung the light from left to right but couldn't see any possibilities close. But in the distance she could see the dark outline of several buildings. The old farmhouse, maybe? It was as good a place as any to look for a well.

It took five minutes of tramping through the overgrown field to reach the outbuildings. To the right of what looked to have been a barn was an odd-shaped mound of stone. Her heart leapt, and she ran towards it. *Please, please, let this be it...*

She slid to a stop and leaned over the uneven wall. The knobby edges of the stone dug into her stomach as she directed the flashlight into the well. Deep down in the darkness, gold flickered.

"Jon?" She waited anxiously for an answer, but nothing came. Maybe he was unconscious. "Jon!"

This time something stirred. She leaned over the edge a little more, desperate to catch any noise.

"Jon!" Her voice echoed. After a moment, she heard a soft groan. He was down there all right, but he had to be awake if she was going to help him. She couldn't get him out of the well on her own. "Answer me, damn it!"

"Madeline?" His soft question was harsh with disbelief.

Tears sprang to her eyes, and she blinked them away quickly. Crying wouldn't help anyone. It certainly wouldn't help him out of the well. "I'm here. I've got some rope in the truck. I'll go get it, but you have to stay awake, okay?"

He grunted or groaned in reply—she wasn't sure which. She ran back across the field, the flashlight weaving uneasy patterns through the darkness ahead. She hesitated when she reached the fence. Was there a gate somewhere, or would she have to cut the wire? The light reflected oddly on something to her right—someone had looped the wire loosely around a pole. Once undone, the gap would be wide enough to drive the truck through.

She quickly undid the wire. The last strand snapped away from her grasp, tearing at her fingertips and palm. She swore and shook the blood away as she ran back to the truck.

Maybe it sensed her urgency, because the engine roared to life the second she turned the key. She reversed out of the clearing and drove down the road until she saw the gap in the fence. Changing gears, she headed into the field, the truck bumping and lurching over the rough ground.

She stopped near the well. Leaving the headlights on and the engine idling, she scrambled out and ran back to the well.

"Jon?" she called, leaning over the edge again. Stone shifted underneath her, and several rocks fell down into the darkness. Water splashed.

"Here," he called, his voice stronger than before. "Stop throwing things at me."

She smiled, and yet his comment made her uneasy. What sort of man made jokes in a situation like this? A man who was used to being in dangerous situations, that's who. Just how wise was it to get involved with this man? While she had no doubt she'd need his help, she knew nothing about him. Not even if she could trust him.

"Still with me, Madeline?"

There was a hint of tension in his voice, as if he'd sensed her sudden doubts. She nodded, then remembered he couldn't see her. "Yes. If I throw a rope down, will you be able to tie it around you?"

"Yes."

She ran back to the truck and hauled the rope out of the box in the back. She wasted several minutes trying to secure one end of the rope to the front of the truck, then ran back to the well.

"I'm lowering the rope." She fed the hemp into the well, but her gaze was drawn to the dark outline of the old homestead. Had something moved, or was it just a trick of the light?

"Got it," Jon said.

The sudden sound of his voice made her start. "Tell me when you're ready, and I'll reverse the truck to haul you up." She watched the rope dance around and wished he'd hurry. The feeling that someone was watching them was growing— or was it simply a case of bad nerves?

"Ready."

She climbed into the truck and shifted into reverse, grinding the gears in her haste. Wincing, she slowly backed up. The need to hurry, to get out of this area as fast as she could, was growing. She bit her lip, trying to ignore it. It didn't matter what was out there watching them. She had to get Jon out of this well. And if she backed up too quickly, she might just kill him.

When the top part of his body was visible, she pulled on the hand brake and climbed out.

"Not a trip I'd recommend," he gasped, looking up at her as she approached.

He was a mess. Sweat beaded his forehead, and his face was white with pain. His whole body was trembling, even though he was doing little more than simply hanging on to the edge of the well. She grabbed his right leg, helping him over. He fell, more than rolled, to the ground.

"We have to get out of here." She knelt beside him and undid the rope. He was so cold his fingers were almost blue. She undid her jacket and placed it around his shoulders.

He gave her a wan smile of thanks. "You have to...to do something first." He closed his eyes and leaned back against the well.

"What?" she asked, rubbing her arms as the wind whipped around her.

"Remove the shaft from my arm."

She'd seen the wound as she'd helped him over the edge of the well, and that was about as close as she wanted to get. His whole arm had swollen, and the handkerchief he'd wrapped around the wound was a bloody mess. She'd risk causing more damage if she tried to do anything other than getting him to a doctor. "No. I can't."

He grabbed her wrist when she tried to rise. "Madeline, you have to take it out. I can't last much longer."

There was something more than urgency in his voice. She fought the instinct to pull away from his touch and wrapped her fingers around his instead, offering him the warmth of her hand. Warily, she met his gaze. In the blue depths of his eyes she saw a hint of desperation—and a pain that went far deeper than anything she'd ever faced.

She tore her gaze away and shone the light towards the farmhouse again. Though she'd seen no movement nor heard any unusual sound, something was out there watching them. They had to get out of this area quickly. She glanced back at Jon and felt something tremble inside.

"I don't think we're safe." She hesitated, her gaze drawn back to the shadows. "I'll remove the damn thing if you want, but I won't do it here."

Jon bit back the urge to swear and nodded, reluctantly releasing her hand. What she said was true enough. While he couldn't hear anyone in the immediate area, he knew someone was bound to see the headlights sooner or later and investigate. Better they left before anyone got too curious.

He just had to hope moving around didn't drive the shaft and its deadly splinters too much deeper or he'd be in real trouble.

Maddie put her shoulder under his, lending him her strength as he tried to rise. His foot slipped out from underneath him, and he dropped heavily. She cursed, her breath warm against his ear as she went down with him. The shattered end of the arrow scraped against rock, and he bit back a groan. Heat flashed through his body. He gulped down air, fighting the rush of dizziness.

She had to take the arrow out. The white ash shaft was killing him.

"I'm sorry," she whispered, her voice full of concern and a slight edge of panic.

"Not your fault." He opened his eyes, desperate to find something, anything, to distract him from the pain.

Her face was close to his, and in the harshness of the headlights, her hair seemed afire. She wasn't what he'd expected. Smaller and slimmer than she'd first appeared, she surrounded him with the rich scent of roses. And fear. He couldn't tell if she was more afraid of the situation or of him.

"We have to get moving," she said softly. Her fingers twitched against his shoulder, her touch light yet warm.

He followed the direction of her gaze. Something stirred in the shadows, a whisper of movement accompanied by the slightest hint of a footfall. The smell of magic whispered across the wind, tainting the cold night air.

They had to get out of this field. He couldn't afford to find trouble now, when Maddie was in the firing line. She'd risked enough just getting him out of the well.

But he couldn't let her go before she'd removed the arrow.

They reached the truck. Maddie opened the door with her free hand. He grabbed the top of the door for support and pulled himself in, half falling across the seat as he tried to avoid catching the edge of the shaft again. He struggled upright and watched her wind up the rope at the front of the trunk.

There was another hint of movement in the shadows beyond her. He frowned, eyes narrowing. There was something awfully familiar in that momentary flicker, something that sent a chill racing through his body.

Again the shadows moved, and this time he saw it. The creature was big and black and moved on four legs.

And it was no animal.

Three

Jon twisted around in the seat, trying to find Maddie. They needed to move before the creature became too curious. It might be nothing more than a coincidence that it had appeared in the same field he'd been shot in, but there was no sense in chancing it.

Something slammed in the back of the truck, then Maddie opened the driver's side door and climbed in. He curbed the urge to tell her to hurry and looked out the window instead. The creature no longer sat in the shadows. Maybe it had lost interest in them and moved on. He smiled grimly. *The chances of that happening are about as high as me flying right now...*

Maddie ground the gears, and the truck jerked forward. He leaned back against the seat and closed his eyes, fighting his need to sleep. There was a lot he had to do. He couldn't afford to sleep yet.

Again, the faint hint of roses surrounded him. He smiled slightly. It was a scent that suited her. The rose was a beautiful flower, yet its stem was covered with such prickly thorns. He had a feeling much the same could be said about Madeline.

The truck slid to a sudden stop, and he was jerked forward, then back, abruptly. He clutched his arm and swore softly.

"Sorry." She barely glanced his way as she scrambled out. "Have to do up the fence."

"Leave it," he said through gritted teeth, but he was speaking to air. "Damn."

He rolled down the window and leaned out, looking for her. And saw the cat in the distance, its shape indistinct in the night as it sauntered towards them.

"Madeline, get back in the truck." He kept his voice low, not wanting to scare her or spur the cat into action.

She stopped looping the wire and turned towards him. Though he couldn't see her features clearly, he felt the leap of fear through her body. She was ready to run, but she didn't, and he thanked the gods for sending him a sensible woman.

"Why?" she asked quietly.

"Just get in the truck," he repeated, his gaze never leaving the creature.

"But-" She hesitated, then dropped the wire and walked back quickly.

The cat stopped, watching them for several seconds before it turned and sauntered back towards the dark outlines of the homestead. Had it lost interest, or had it found what it was looking for? He sensed it was the latter and hoped like hell he hadn't landed Maddie into trouble right alongside him.

He rolled up the window as the truck moved off. At least he had a starting point now——all he had to do was track down the cat once Maddie had removed the arrow. He grimaced. *Yeah. Real easy.*

The truck bumped quickly along the old road. He held on grimly as Maddie pulled around a sharp right-hand turn, then reached out and gently touched her leg. She jumped and gave him a wild-eyed look. Only then did he realize just how much he'd frightened her.

"It's all right. We're safe," he said, cursing himself for a fool. He was supposed to be an empath—why in the hell hadn't he sensed what she was going through? "Ease up a little. No one's after us."

She swallowed hard and nodded. The brakes ground harshly as she pulled over to the side of the road and stopped.

"What did you see back there?" she asked softly.

He half shrugged, not wanting to scare her any more than necessary. "Nothing. Just spooked by the darkness."

She studied him for a moment. He could sense her uncertainty—about him, and the situation she'd been forced into. He suddenly wished there was more light so he could see her eyes. He had a feeling they would tell him a great many secrets.

He frowned at the thought. He was in Taurin Bay for one reason only—to find the missing kids and to stop the people responsible for their disappearance. He didn't have time for any diversions, even one as interesting as Maddie.

"I need you to take the arrow from my arm," he said, more abruptly than he'd intended.

"And I think you should let a doctor do that…" her voice trailed off as she met his gaze. "Why are you so reluctant to see a doctor about this?"

Good question. "Walking into an emergency room with an arrow wound might attract the sort of attention I'm trying to avoid." Which was the truth but not the true answer to her question.

"It might have hit an artery or something." She hesitated, then added softly, "I might kill you."

It was a normal fear, given the look of the wound, yet instinct suggested her fear stemmed more from something else. The tremor in her voice spoke of a past acquaintance with death—and that it was an acquaintance she had no wish to renew.

"You won't kill me," he said quietly, sensing it wouldn't take much more to scare her into running. "If an artery was severed, I'd have bled to death by now."

"But-"

"I'll be all right. I just need the arrow removed. Every time I move, it digs a little deeper." Killed him just a little bit more.

She swallowed and nodded. "There's a first aid kit under your seat."

He leaned forward and retrieved the kit. She turned on the overhead light, then took the kit from him. Her fingers shook as she sorted through the bandages and antiseptics.

"There's not a pair of tweezers big enough."

"Just use your fingers." He reached across and caught her hand. Her fingers were soft and warm against his, silk compared to sandpaper. "I'll be fine."

"I damn well won't," she muttered, then took a deep breath

and gave him a shaky smile. "Try not to yell too loudly. Don't want to wake the neighbors."

Her smile lit her eyes and dimpled her cheeks. He closed his eyes, holding its image in his mind as the warmth of her fingers moved to his arm. White fire twisted through him, a living thing that could so easily kill if it was left too long. He held his breath, waiting, as she tentatively grabbed the shattered end of the arrow shaft. *One, two, three.*

As if she'd heard his unspoken words, Maddie wrenched the arrow from his arm. Pain ripped through his body, and he jerked sideways, falling against the door, gritting his teeth against the scream that tore past his throat.

"Oh hell…"

Her voice seemed a million miles away, the touch of her fingers suddenly so cold compared to the fire that raged down his arm and threatened to consume him.

He gulped down air, battling the urge to be ill—fighting the desire to just let go, to let the darkness in and take the pain away.

Moisture ran down his arm, then he felt the rough texture of a towel pressed against the wound. He bit back his curse and concentrated on the faint smell of roses, trying to build a wall around the pain and shut it away. She began to bandage his arm, and for an instant, the darkness loomed again. He took a deep breath and felt a wisp of magic run through his soul. He suddenly had to stop himself from grinning like an idiot. The white ash hadn't done as much damage as he'd feared.

But there was only one way he was ever going to find out. He had to get out of the truck and leave Madeline.

And he wasn't sure what was going to be the hardest to do.

"Jon?"

He opened his eyes and looked at her. There was fear in her warm amber eyes and blood on her hands. What could he say? Thank you for saving my soul, if not my life?

"Do you need this?" she continued, distaste in her voice as she dangled the bloody shaft between two fingers. "For evidence or something?"

If he touched the white ash again in his weakened condition, it would probably kill him. And whatever clues the shaft might have held had been lost during his plunge into the water.

"Get rid of it."

She opened the door and threw the arrow out into the night. Cold air rushed in, swirling around him. He struggled upright, fighting the lethargy taking hold of his body.

"Thank you," he said, as she slammed the door shut.

She smiled wryly. "I'd say you're welcome, but it's not something I'd ever like to do again."

"If I had more time, I'd take you out to dinner or something." It sounded cold, even to him. But the cat was out there somewhere. Even if he couldn't find it tonight, he still had to go back to the inn and get the stuff he'd left there. It might have been easier to stay in Maddie's company, but it wasn't right. Better she thought the worst of him and just left. He grabbed the door handle and pulled it back. "I guess we'll just have to take a rain check, sweetheart."

Maddie stared at him. For Christ's sake, she was still covered in his blood, and here he was giving her a casual brush off! "Don't you dare leave just yet-"

But she was speaking to the night.

Maddie blinked. How could an injured man move so fast? She scrambled out of the truck and ran to the passenger side. He was nowhere to be seen. She bit her lip and studied the darkness. He could barely walk ten minutes ago, so surely he couldn't be too far away. She grabbed the flashlight and swept the bright beam across the road. The undergrowth beneath the trees didn't look as if it had been disturbed recently. So where in the hell had Jon gone, if not through there?

"Damn you, Jon! Come back here."

The keen of the wind through the treetops was her only answer. She shivered and watched the shadows uneasily. Something didn't feel right. A twig snapped suddenly, and she swung the flashlight's beam across the thick stand of trees to her right. The undergrowth stirred, and out of the shadows stepped a dark-colored cat, its eyes green fire in the darkness. Not just any cat but a big, black panther.

Something in the creature's jewellike gaze made Maddie's soul tremble with fear.

She edged backwards, feeling for the truck door. The creature snarled silently, revealing teeth that were long and white. She jumped into the car and slammed the door shut. The engine started the first time she twisted the ignition, and she shifted into gear. Then she hesitated, eyeing the darkness beyond the headlights.

Jon was still out there, injured and alone, with a panther stalking the area. Would the cat smell his blood and hunt him down? Maybe she should find someone and report the panther's presence—only who would believe her? Panthers weren't exactly native to this area, and unless someone had reported one having escaped, they'd probably think she was nuts.

Or drunk.

If only. She took a deep breath and tried to calm the irrational rush of anger. She knew it stemmed more from her need to find Evan than Jon's casual gratitude and sudden disappearance.

But she wished he'd had the decency to stick around, even if it was just long enough to refuse to help her.

He never promised to help me, though. It's my fault I'm here, running from shadows and cats, not his.

And she couldn't leave until Evan was safe.

She drove the truck back onto the road and headed towards the inn.

Rain was pelting across the windshield by the time she reached it. She switched off the engine, then glanced across at the inn. The light peeking past the edges of the curtains indicated someone was still up, despite the fact it was after eleven. But the night manager had said he'd wait and let her in. So why was she suddenly wary?

Maybe the encounter with the cat had scared her more than she'd thought. Or maybe it was the way the shadows crowded the building and gave the appearance of skeletal hands creeping across the outer edges of light.

And maybe she was simply tired and needed to rest. She jumped out of the truck. Holding her coat over her head, she ran across the lawn to the front steps.

The bell chimed brightly as she closed the door. Maddie grimaced and shook out her coat. On nights like this, when her imagination seemed to be taking a walk on the wild side, she'd rather keep to herself. Especially if the person she had to talk to was a night manager with weird brown eyes.

Warmth surrounded her as she headed quietly towards the stairs. A woman talked softly in the parlor to her right, her voice mellow and deep, but beyond that, there was no other sound.

The sudden shattering of glass made her stop and glance upwards. Had a tree branch gone through one of the windows upstairs?

Footsteps sounded behind her. She looked around. The night manager stopped in the parlor doorway and leaned casually against the door frame.

"Hello again. Enjoy the drive?"

"Yes, thanks," she said.

Though his voice held nothing beyond polite interest, there was still something about him that made her uneasy. Maybe it was just the smug half-smile that touched his thin lips, or the way his gaze roamed down her body.

He raised his coffee cup. "Coffee's just brewed, if you'd like a cup."

The urge to run was almost overwhelming. What in hell was wrong with her tonight? He hadn't threatened her in any way, only offered her coffee.

"I'd love to but-" She hesitated, then shrugged. The best excuse was usually the truth. "It's been a long day. Thanks for the offer, though."

He pushed away from the door frame and took several steps toward her. "Thought I heard something break as you came in."

Again, though his voice was conversational, his dark eyes were intense, watchful.

Something odd was going on.

She licked suddenly dry lips. "Like what?"

"Sounded like glass breaking."

She raised an eyebrow, trying to sound calm. "I really didn't hear anything like that." And if he *had,* why didn't he mention it the moment he came out?

"Really?" He took a sip of his coffee, then glanced up the stairs. "Maybe I should check your room before you go up there. Make sure it's safe."

The last place she wanted this man was in her room. She shook her head and tried to smile. "I'll be all right. If anything's broken, I'll give you a call." *But not until morning, when there's more light and a lot more people around.*

"I'll be up in a moment to check the other rooms, so I'll be nearby if you need me." He hesitated, then raised his cup. "'Night."

She watched him disappear into the parlor, then turned and almost ran up the stairs. Her hands were shaking so much it took several tries before she could get the door open. She locked it behind her, then sagged against it and took a deep breath.

What was it about that man that made her so afraid? Or was Jayne right? Had she locked herself away for so long, she'd simply forgotten how to interact with people?

Maddie rubbed her eyes, then walked across the room towards the bedroom. She kicked off her shoes near the bed, then pulled off her socks. A cold breeze ran around her ankles and she glanced towards the bathroom.

Had a window broken? She hesitated, then cursed herself for doing so. What was she afraid of? Broken glass?

Opening the bathroom door, she switched on the light and looked in.

Jon lay sprawled on the floor, wet, bleeding and surrounded by glass.

Four

He was alive, she could tell that much from the rise and fall of his chest. But his color was appalling—he was so pale he could very easily have passed for a ghost. She quickly knelt down and felt his forehead. His skin burned, despite his color.

"Jon?" She ran her hand down his stubble-lined cheek and lightly pinched his chin, trying to get some sort of reaction from him.

He groaned and opened his eyes. The power of his vivid blue gaze pierced her heart.

"Madeline." His voice was little more than a harsh whisper, yet she heard surprise in it. "I'm sorry."

Sorry for what? Sorry for being such a bastard back in the forest, or for landing in a bloody mess on the floor of her bathroom? And just how had he managed to get back here so quickly?

"We need to get you out of these wet clothes," she said, in an effort to organize her scattered thoughts.

He nodded weakly and closed his eyes. "I've got dry clothes inside."

Inside? What was he talking about? She frowned and wondered if, in his delirium, he'd wandered into the wrong room. Yet that didn't explain the broken window or the fact he'd somehow got past her locked door.

"Let's get you off this floor," she said, deciding to tackle one problem at a time.

He nodded weakly, obviously hanging onto consciousness by a thread.

"Stay with me Jon," she said softly.

Again he nodded. Was he fully aware of what she was

saying or merely nodding every time she finished speaking?

"Okay, you've got to help me here." She shuffled around to his feet, then reached forward and took his hands. His fingers were long and strong and very cold. "One, two, three."

She rose, pulling back as hard as she could. He lurched forward, teeth gritted, eyes blue slits of pain as he struggled upright. At his nod, she let go of his hands. He caught the edge of the shower door, using it to balance himself.

"Remind me not to do that again," he muttered. His knuckles were almost white with the force of his grip on the shower.

Even so, he wasn't too steady. She quickly slipped her shoulder under his. The last thing she wanted was for him to fall back down. She'd never be able to lift him back up.

He stirred at her touch and opened his eyes, but his gaze was unfocused. She had the odd feeling he wasn't even seeing her, that something else held his attention.

"Don't let them find me." Anxiety edged his hoarse voice.

"Who?" Was he delirious?

"Downstairs," he whispered, then reached up, gently touching her cheek. "They'll hurt you."

His touch was cold, yet it sent fire racing across her skin. She licked her lips and wondered again at her sanity. Here she was, helping a man she didn't know and probably shouldn't trust. "I can take care of myself." *Only too well...*

"Not against them."

And maybe not against you, she thought, trying to ignore the tingle that raced through her limbs every time they brushed against each other. "Let's worry about the bad guys after you're out of these wet clothes."

He muttered something, his breath warm as it brushed over her cheek. Maddie shifted her grip on his arm. "Walk with me, okay?"

She glanced sideways at him. Even as pale as pastry, he was certainly handsome. He glanced up, a sudden gleam of amusement momentarily blurring the pain in his eyes. She quickly swallowed the thought. If she didn't know any better, she'd swear he'd read her thoughts. But that was impossible, wasn't it? At least, she hoped it was. She didn't want him to think she was after anything more than help to find Evan.

Anything else could be dangerous, for them both.

"Don't faint before you can get out of those clothes," she muttered, pulling her gaze away from his.

She found herself staring instead at his boots. They were snakeskin, for heaven's sake. And his jeans where so damn tight they looked painted on. As wet as they were, taking them off would be more than an effort and it was not a task she particularly wanted.

"Let's go," she continued, shifting her grip on his arm.

Supporting a good half of his weight, she staggered through the bathroom door and across the room. He dropped down to the bed with a sigh she echoed, and then he fell sideways towards the pillow. That was when she noticed the fresh blood on his bandages. The wound must have opened up when she'd hauled him upright.

A sharp knock at the door made her heart leap with fright.

"Miss Smith?"

Maddie jerked around. The voice belonged to the night manager.

"I can't be found here," Jon croaked softly.

She glanced back at him. In his pain-filled gaze she saw concern, not for himself but for her. Or was she reading more in those bright depths than there really was?

"Why not?"

"It was after I checked into this inn that someone shot me. I can't risk being seen here until I know if it's safe."

She raised a hand to her throat and looked back to the doorway. What if the night manager had a key? What if he let himself in and discovered Jon lying there?

"Miss Smith? You okay?" Hank asked again, voice louder this time.

"Answer him," Jon urged softly.

She cleared her throat. "Yes?"

"Need to check your windows, Miss Smith."

Damn. She couldn't very well tell him there was no damage and then report the broken window in the morning. She glanced quickly around the room. With Hank checking the windows, the bathroom was out. And the bedroom didn't offer much in the way of hiding places. "The only place to really hide is in the wardrobe."

"Help me up."

She pulled Jon upright, then put her shoulder under his good arm, wrapping her other arm around his back.

"Miss Smith?" Hank called again, his tone sharp.

"Coming!" she yelled back.

She slid the door open with her foot, then helped Jon inside. As he lowered himself down, she reached up to the shelf above and grabbed the spare blankets, shaking them out to drape over him.

Jon touched her hand lightly. "Be careful."

Maddie nodded and covered his face with the second blanket. She slid the wardrobe door closed then ran to open the suite door.

"Miss Smith, are you all right?" Hank asked, as she opened the door.

Maddie pushed the damp ringlets out of her eyes and forced a bright smile. "Yes, of course I am. What can I do for you, Mr. Stewart?"

His dark eyes met hers, and for an instant, delved deep into her soul. She clenched her fingers against the door handle and tore her gaze away. Her imagination was taking a trip again—there was no way on this Earth he could see into her soul. Too many late nights and horror movies for sure.

"As I said, I've been checking for broken windows." The warm tone of his voice belied the coldness in his eyes. "Have you had a chance to look around yet?"

He lied. How she knew she wasn't sure. Maybe it was the twitch near his thin mouth. But what did it matter? She had no choice but to let him in.

She nodded. "I was just getting ready to come down and tell you that the bathroom window's broken."

"I'll have a look at it if you don't mind, and see if I can repair it tonight or not."

Maddie minded very much but stepped back, allowing him to walk past her. She half-turned to follow, then stopped, noticing a smear of blood on the door handle. What the...? She raised her hand and saw her fingers were bleeding again...*Oh lord, there's blood on the bathroom floor.*

She spun and ran to the bedroom, almost slamming into Hank as he came back out.

"Oh, sorry," she muttered, slipping out of his reach when he tried to steady her.

"In a bit of a hurry, huh?" His eyebrow raised in query.

There was nothing in his tone or his eyes that hinted at suspicion, yet she felt it wrap around her. She squeezed her fingers together and remained silent. It was obvious he wouldn't believe her, no matter what she said.

"Bit of blood on the floor," he continued.

She nodded and held up her hand. "I slipped and fell on the glass. Guess that'll teach me to walk around in the dark."

He looked at her blood-covered fingers and frowned. He knew, as she did, that there was more blood on the bathroom floor than the cut on her fingers would allow.

"I'll get some plastic and cover the hole until morning," he muttered, walking past her.

She watched him leave then walked into the bedroom. Nothing appeared to have been touched. She moved across the room and opened the wardrobe. Jon pulled down an edge of the blanket and looked at her, but she held up her hand. At least he was still safe. Not that Hank could've disposed of Jon in the short space of time he'd been out of her sight. There was no way out of the room except through the front door where she'd been standing.

So how had Jon gotten in here in the first place? Even she, as slender as she was, couldn't get through the bathroom window.

She closed the door then turned and smiled as a cat sauntered through the bedroom doorway.

"Hi kitty," she said softly, walking over to it.

She bent down and held out her hand. Did the sleek black creature belong to the inn or to Hank? Somehow, she couldn't imagine the night manager with a pet, although the cat must have followed him into the room.

The cat stopped. The look in its jewellike green eyes was oddly contemptuous. Maddie frowned. The cat in the forest had had eyes just like that, eyes that could chill a person's soul.

The cat regarded her for a moment longer, then snarled and lashed out. Maddie snatched her fingers away and stood up. "Be unfriendly then. See if I care."

Hank came back into the room, carrying plastic and tape.

"Don't mind Lennie," he said, continuing on into the bathroom. "She just doesn't like women."

Or men, Maddie would have bet. As if reading her thoughts, the cat flicked its tail in disdain and sauntered past, heading straight for the wardrobe door.

"Oh no, you don't." She stepped in front of the cat and tried to scoot it away with her foot. The sleek creature hunkered down and hissed, its eyes green slits of anger.

"Glare all you like, sweetheart, you're not getting in my wardrobe."

"Maybe she just smells a mouse or two," Hank commented.

Her pulse jumped, and she glanced up quickly. Hank leaned against the bathroom door, arms crossed as he studied her. This time there was definitely suspicion in his bright gaze.

"Mice I can handle. It's cat hair all over my clothes that I can't stand. I'm allergic to it."

"Perhaps you'd better let her check it, all the same. Lennie's a pretty good little hunter."

Lennie looked mean enough to pull down a bull, but there was no way she could open the wardrobe door with Jon inside. Though Maddie wasn't sure if this odd pair was the threat Jon had referred to, she certainly didn't trust Hank one iota.

"If I hear any mice running around, I'll let you know."

And what sort of manager advertised the presence of mice, anyway?

Hank nodded, though she could see he was far from happy. "I've taped plastic over the window. I'll come back tomorrow and replace it for you."

By which time, Jon should be long gone. She hoped. Maddie nodded and watched Hank walk out the bedroom door, then glanced down at the unmoving cat. She'd throw the thing out if she had to, but she'd rather it just followed Hank of its own accord. The claws it kept flexing looked sharp enough to tear concrete to ribbons.

The cat continued to glare up at her. Maddie blinked, unnerved by the almost human intelligence in the animal's bright gaze. *You haven't seen the last of me, foolish child,* it seemed to say.

And I really have to learn to control my imagination. The cat finally rose and sauntered away. At the bedroom door, it hesitated and looked back. The warning was clear in its bright gaze.

It knew Jon was in the wardrobe. And it would be back.

Maddie clenched her fingers and followed the creature out of the room. She locked the suite door, closed her eyes and leaned against it for a moment. It was at times like this, when her imagination got the best of her, that she really needed a drink.

She licked her lips, pushed away from the door and walked back into the bedroom.

"Jon?" She opened the wardrobe.

His gaze met hers, and again she thought she saw concern in the rich depths of his eyes. "You okay?"

A chill ran over her. Sometimes he almost seemed able to read her mind. She held out her hand, and he took it, his skin rough against hers. At least his fingers were warmer than before. She helped him back to the bed, noting that his body was still icy through the damp shirt.

He practically collapsed back onto the bed. She studied him for a moment then walked around to get her carryall. Clothes had to be a first priority, then she'd re-bandage his arm.

She dug out her baggy old sweat pants and a T-shirt, and held them up. They'd go damn close to fitting him. He might not be too pleased at the jade coloring, but at least they would keep him warm until his own clothes dried.

She bent across the bed and lightly shook him. "Jon?" There was no response, so she shook him again.

"Don't," he muttered. "I need to rest."

So do I, buddy, and you're in my bed. "You have to change first. Put these on while I go see if I can find some fresh bandages."

He pushed upright. She dropped the clothes next to him and walked into the bathroom. The soft rustle of clothing told her he was at least attempting to change. She hunted around in the bathroom cupboards, but couldn't find any bandages. She'd have to go back out to the car and get the first aid kit. Maddie glanced at her watch and gave Jon a few more minutes before she walked back in.

The clothing was a whole lot tighter on him than it was on her. The T-shirt strained across the width of his shoulders, and the pants...well, they were tighter than his own jeans—if that was possible. She shook her head slightly. Where the hell was her mind? Jon was a stranger, a complete unknown. Yet she'd given him her bed and her clothes, and placed trust in the fact that he meant her no harm. Had she learned nothing from the past?

His head came up suddenly, his eyes meeting hers. There was no deceit in that slightly unfocused gaze, no lies. And none of the contempt that had been all too evident in her husband's gaze.

Jon reached out and gently caught her hand. His fingers were a warm, suntanned brown, and his palms slightly callused. Totally the opposite of Brian's...why did she keep thinking of him? What was it about Jon that dredged up a past she'd much rather forget?

"Trust me, Maddie. I mean you no harm."

Trust me, trust me. How often had she heard that? How frequently had it been the warning of trouble heading her way?

"I'll have to go out to the car to get some bandages," she said, jerking her hand out of his.

His gaze narrowed slightly. "Be careful."

She gave him a tight smile. "I always am." Too careful, too cautious. Because when she wasn't, people died. "You rest. I won't be long."

She turned and walked quickly from the room.

Five

Fear surrounded him, an acid cloud that stung his mind and forced him awake. Jon jerked upright and, for an instant, wondered where he was.

The morning sun peeped around the outer edges of the curtains, gilding the framed painting opposite the bed. He half smiled. He had to be at the inn—there couldn't be many paintings around that used such appalling colors to depict a farmyard setting. Or many places that would hang it on their walls.

So why was Maddie in his room? And why was she so afraid?

He shoved the blankets aside and swung his feet out of the bed, then stopped, staring down at his legs. Speaking of appalling colors, why in hell was he wearing these sweat pants? They were Maddie's—he could smell the lingering scent of roses. But what had happened to his clothes?

He couldn't recall much about the last half of last night, and what he did remember was a blurred nightmare he never wanted to repeat.

The fear swirled around him again. He rose too quickly and had to grab at the bedpost to remain upright. Although fast healing was a gift of his heritage, it would be a day or two yet before he would recover fully from the wound and the resulting blood loss. He took a deep breath, then padded quietly across the room.

"The room's a shambles—can't you come back later to fix the window, Mr. Stewart?"

Maddie's voice stopped him near the bedroom door. There was nothing in her soft tones to indicate the fear he could almost taste.

"Hank," the stranger replied. "And I'm afraid not. It's either now, or it won't get done for several days. Last night's storm caused a bit of damage, I'm afraid."

There was an underlying threat in the man's tone, one that told him the stranger wouldn't take no for an answer. But why was the man so determined to get into his room? And why didn't he seem surprised to find Maddie here?

Maddie's fear jumped a notch. Maybe she could sense the unspoken menace in the stranger's voice. She cleared her throat softly, then said, "Okay then."

Until he knew who was responsible for shooting him, he couldn't risk being seen with her. He'd put her into enough danger by simply asking her to rescue him. He walked across to the wardrobe and edged the door closed, only leaving a minute gap to see through.

Maddie walked in a second later. Her gaze went to the bed, then swept quickly to the wardrobe. She smiled tightly and continued on to the window. Her hair was a tangled mess of ringlets that bounced along with every movement. He'd been wrong about the color being chestnut. It was more a rich, red gold that hung down her back like a river of flame. The fluffy white sweater she wore hung to her thighs, and did nothing for the slender figure that had brushed against him last night and haunted his dreams. But at least her legs were clad in dark green leggings, not baggy old sweat pants—probably because he was wearing them.

She was, he thought with a slight smile, all color and energy and warmth, despite the fear that hung like a storm all around her.

The only outward sign of this was her hands, clenched by her side. Jon hoped she kept her gaze well away from the stranger. Her eyes were too expressive. One look into the amber flame of her gaze, and the stranger would know she was hiding something—or someone.

The man who followed her into the room was big. Not tall, just built like a man who'd spent half his life lifting weights.

And he wasn't the same Hank Stewart that Jon had seen pictures of several days before, although they looked enough alike to be brothers.

Maddie opened the blinds, and sunlight streamed in. The stranger winced and stepped back into the living room. A second man brushed past him, carrying a toolbox and a small pane of glass.

Jon studied the man now passing himself off as the night manager. Was he merely light sensitive, or did he have a more sinister reason for hiding from the sun? Was he dealing with something as simple as a vampire?

The big man shifted, moving back to the doorway. The sunlight touched him and, for an instant, revealed a gaunt, weathered face and muddy-brown eyes that were as dead as stone. Jon blinked, and the image was gone, replaced by the open, friendly face of Hank Stewart.

The man wasn't a vampire. Only the very ancient vampires could stand the touch of the sun, and the stranger certainly didn't have the presence of something old and powerful that was evident in ancient bloodsuckers.

Yet a faint wisp of dark magic told him that the stranger wasn't entirely human, either. He frowned. Scattered images ran through his mind, erratic memories of last night's events. This man had been in his room then, too, and with him had been a shapeshifter. Could it have been the same shifter he'd seen in the forest? Surely a town as small as Taurin Bay couldn't have more than one in the area?

The minutes ticked by slowly. Eventually, the repairman came out of the bathroom and gave Maddie a smile. "All mended and cleaned up."

She nodded and crossed her arms, staring at the night manager. The man posing as Hank Stewart was frowning at the wardrobe. There was no real indication he suspected Jon was hiding there, nothing more than a deepening of his frown before he turned away. Maddie followed the two men out of the room.

He stepped from the wardrobe and walked to the bed. Maddie came back into the room and stopped, her eyes showing the uncertainty he sensed in her.

"How are you feeling this morning?"

Her voice was soft and slightly husky, and as warm as a whiskey on a cold night. A sound any man could get used to. He wondered if it was natural, or caused by fear.

"Better," he said. "Though I would like to know how I got into these...pants."

Her gaze ran down his body then danced away, and he had to stop himself from smiling when he saw the blush creep across her cheeks.

"Your clothes were soaked, and I didn't want you running around naked."

After the flight here last night, he wouldn't have been able to run anywhere. And she still hadn't explained why she'd dressed him in her clothes instead of his own. "So why didn't you just get something out of my bags?"

The look she gave him was both wary and confused. "This is my room. Your clothes aren't here."

He glanced across at the painting. "This is the Captain's suite, isn't it?"

"Yes." She hesitated, and a flash of understanding ran through her eyes. "You were staying here, too—before someone took that potshot at you?"

Potshot. What a quaint way of putting the attempt on his life. "Yes. Looks as though someone didn't expect me back, either."

She shifted from one foot to the other then crossed her arms. He wondered if her uneasiness stemmed from the situation or his presence in her bedroom. "Someone obviously suspects you're still alive, though," she said softly.

The only thing obvious was that she was in serious danger. The night manager, or the man now masquerading as him, wouldn't have been acting so suspiciously if he didn't suspect her somehow. For her own safety, she had to leave.

But something told him that getting her to leave wasn't going to be an easy task.

His thoughts stilled...were the things he'd hidden behind the bathroom vent still there? Christ, he hoped so. He'd hate to have to tell his old man that he'd lost the ring. It was a family heirloom and had survived five generations of Barnett males. He wanted to pass it on to his own son one day. Not that *that* looked likely, given his present job.

He resisted the urge to get up and check. If it was gone, there was nothing he could do about it now. It was more important to sort out what was going on and find the missing kid before the next new moon.

"You're right. Someone does suspect I'm alive, which means you'll have to leave, Madeline."

"Please don't call me that. I prefer Maddie."

She wouldn't meet his gaze, but he caught her flash of pain anyway. Who had hurt her so badly that she now hated her given name? "Maddie, did you hear what I said?"

"Yes. But I'm not leaving."

"You have to-"

"I don't *have* to do anything!"

He raised his eyebrows at the vehemence in her voice. Pain ran through the swirl of emotions coloring her aura, a river of tears she would never shed. Her gaze was determined when it met his, and anger stained her cheeks a pretty pink.

"My nephew disappeared two nights ago. I want you to help me find him."

Damn. He ran a hand through his hair. Two teenagers this time, and only five days to the new moon. "I'll find him, but you have to go back home. I can't protect you twenty-four hours a day, and someone must suspect you're somehow connected with me." *Why else would the stranger be so interested in the room?*

She clenched her hands and glared at him. Even half-closed and full of anger, her almond-shaped eyes were lovely.

"I don't expect you to protect me. I can look after myself, thank you."

"Don't be ridiculous. These people have already tried to kill me. I don't want you hurt."

"I don't want me hurt, either, but I'm not going anywhere until I find Evan."

Her determined expression told him arguing was useless.

Still, he had to try. "Damn it Maddie, be reasonable. This is my job. Let me do it without having to worry about you getting hurt—or getting in the way."

He rose from the bed and stepped towards her. Terror flashed through her eyes, and she backed away quickly. He stopped in surprise. It was almost as if she were afraid he was going to hit her.

The thought shook him. There had been women in his past who'd called him uncaring and arrogant, but usually they had wanted more from the relationship than he'd ever been prepared to give. But never had he been accused of violence towards a woman, not by word or deed.

There was no way for her to know this, of course. They were virtual strangers, brought together by unusual circumstances. But what had he done to make her fear he was one of those morons who lashed out?

He raised his hands and sat back down. After a minute, the tension seemed to leave her body, and a slight flush invaded her cheeks. It wasn't him she was frightened of, he realized. Her reaction had been automatic.

"You saw the arrow. You saw the damage it did. I was lucky, but you might not be."

She raised her chin slightly, as if denying the fear he could almost taste.

"I can take care of myself," she repeated softly.

A flicker ran through her eyes—an emotion too fast for him to identify. He frowned. With her clenched hands almost lost in the sleeves of her oversized sweater, she looked absurdly young. Yet her reactions—and her fear—told him she was no stranger to pain and death. He had no doubt that she could take care of herself under normal circumstances. But this situation was far from normal.

"You're a fool if you believe that," he said harshly, wincing inside even as he did so. "And I won't be held responsible for your safety."

She'd no doubt saved his life, and while he had no wish to hurt her, if she wouldn't listen to reason, he had little other choice. His job, and his life, made him a dangerous person to be around. Hell, wasn't that one of the major reasons he'd cut himself off from his family?

"Just keep out of my way. The last thing I need right now is an amateur detective screwing up the clues."

"I'll get in your way if I feel it's damn well necessary," she snapped back, then blushed again and took a deep breath.

Someone knocked at the door, and she glanced at her watch. "That's probably the late breakfast I ordered. Your clothes are dry and hidden under the towels in the bathroom. Why don't you take a much-needed shower and meet me in the living room?"

So, not only would he *not* be obeyed, but he also stunk. He suppressed a grin, liking the sudden hint of fire. She studied him a moment longer, gaze narrowing, then she spun and walked away, her flame red hair and white fluff sweater flouncing along with every movement. He shook his head and headed for the shower. It wasn't going to be easy to get rid of her, especially if she kept making him smile.

***

Maddie kicked the door shut and carried the large tray over to the table. The smell of bacon and eggs turned her stomach slightly, but she'd figured Jon was more a traditional type when it came to breakfast. Just in case she was wrong, she'd ordered cereal, as well as a yogurt for herself.

Grabbing the yogurt and a spoon, she dragged out the nearest chair and sat down. How could she tell Jon about her visions of Evan and his captor without having him think her strange? Though *that* was something she should be well used to. So many times in the past she'd been called weird, or worse, when the trancelike state of the dreams hit her.

Her dad had even hauled her through dozens of psychiatrist's offices in the vague hope they'd cure her 'illness'.

She grimaced. Fat lot of good it had done him or her.

She scooped up some yogurt and stared at the small fire she'd lit in the hearth earlier. It was hard to judge how Jon would react, because it was hard to put him in one particular type of box. In the brief time she'd known him he'd been caring and gentle and funny, and yet he had switched so easily to being an ungrateful bastard.

Would he think her a freak, as Brian had? *Probably.* It was a thought that scared her more than it should have.

And yet, he'd somehow appeared in her home, asking for help and warning her about Evan. She wasn't sure if it was astral travel, some form of telepathy, or something else entirely—and in the end, it didn't really matter. If he could do that, then surely he would understand when she explained about the visions.

He walked into the room several minutes later, and she almost choked on her yogurt. How could any man manage to walk when his jeans were so tight? Not that she was complaining... there was nothing nicer than a set of well-defined thighs in tight jeans. Except, maybe, a well-defined rear, and, to her disappointment, his shirttails covered that.

He glanced at her, a hint of a smile dancing across his lips and touching the bright depths of his eyes. Heat invaded her cheeks again. *Good lord, I really do hope he can't read my thoughts.*

She quickly averted her gaze and took another spoonful of yogurt, only looking up after he sat down.

"I gather most of this is for me," he said in amusement.

"Wasn't sure what you'd want, so I ordered a mix."

He nodded, sending shimmers of gold running through his damp hair. Maddie watched him reach for the plate of bacon and eggs, and she smiled. *Right the first time.* The smell wafted across the table, and she wrinkled her nose.

"I gather from your expression you don't like bacon."

She glanced up. From the way he arched his eyebrow, she gathered she'd scored another point against herself. *Not that it matters. He doesn't have to like me to help me find Evan.* "No. I had a pet pig when I was a kid that became a family meal when it was big enough. Haven't been able to eat pork since."

"Ah, I see."

She wondered if he did. His easygoing manner told her he'd never wanted for friendship—that he'd never been forced to find companionship from a pet because he couldn't find it anywhere else.

"I noticed an incense burner on the mantle," he said. "Would you like me to light it?"

She nodded, surprised he'd even noticed the burner, let alone offer to light it, especially given his earlier hostility.

He walked to the mantle, and she resisted the temptation to watch him, only looking up when he sat back down. He placed the burner between them and flashed her a smile that made her heart do an odd flip-flop.

She obviously needed to sleep. She had to be exhausted if a simple smile sent her over the edge. She glanced away from the warmth of his gaze and found herself staring instead at his long, strong hands. For the first time since she'd first met him, she noticed he was wearing a ring. She was oddly relieved to see it was on his right hand, not his left.

Maybe she should get another room. Being confined with this man for any length of time was not a good idea. *Especially if he keeps wearing those damn jeans.*

She ran the spoon around the edge of the container, collecting the last of the yogurt. The small candle flickered and danced, and the smell of incense wafted towards her. She put the empty container on the table and sniffed the fragrance.

The pit of her stomach suddenly fell. Citrus smoke—the same sweet smell that had been in Evan's room.

Darkness swept around her. She gripped the edge of the table fiercely, fighting the desire to follow wherever the dream might lead. *Please, don't let this happen to me now.* Why couldn't it hit when she was alone? As much as she wanted to find Evan, she didn't want Jon to see her trapped in a vision.

"Maddie? Are you okay?"

No, I'm not! Can't you see that? I've never been all right. But she couldn't speak as the darkness encased her, sweeping her along for the ride...

Smoke coiled around the cabin, a dark plume that filled the twilight with the rich scent of citrus. In the far corner lay Evan and the other teenager, the mounds of their bodies almost lost amongst the heavy blankets covering them.

But her dream was not here for them this time. It swirled

away, centering on the opposite side of the cabin. Two figures were silhouetted against the dancing light of a bright fire. Though she could see no features or clothing, it was obvious from their size and shape that one was male, the other female.

"Maddie."

The soft voice broke through the dream. For an instant, the vision wavered, shimmering like a pond whose shiny surface is disturbed by a stone.

"Maddie, tell me what you see."

Jon's hand slid over hers, warm and strong. Maddie wished she could let go of the table and hold his hand, hold him, but the dream held her in its grip. She couldn't move.

"What do you see?" he repeated softly.

"Evan." She licked her lips. For the first time in her life she forced herself to concentrate on her vision. Despite the fire, the cabin was cold. The breath of the two figures condensed as they spoke, hanging in the air like smoke. Beyond the cabin confines, the wind howled, rattling windows she couldn't see.

"Tell me what else you see."

"It feels like snow." Chill fingers of air crept around her, and she shivered.

"Do you see any people?"

"Two. Male, female." The woman had long hair that she brushed away with a cat's paw. "She has claws. Cat's claws."

"Are they talking? Can you hear what they're saying?"

"Only the woman speaks." And though her voice was soft, its mellow sound stung Maddie's ears, as grating as fingernails across a blackboard.

"What is she saying?"

"I don't know."

"Listen harder. Concentrate on the sound of her voice."

Jon squeezed her hand, running warmth through her body. She licked her lips, trying to do as he asked. Like a radio suddenly tuned, the woman's voice leapt into focus, and she told Jon, "She plans an attack. Tonight."

"Who does she plan to attack?"

"I don't know-" She hesitated.

The woman turned. There was malice on her face, malice in the air, so thick Maddie suddenly struggled to breathe. Jon called her name urgently, but he sounded so very far away. She stared at the woman with the vibrant green eyes until they all but filled her vision, became a turbulent ocean awash with venom.

"You are mine," the woman spat. "Mine."

Maddie screamed, and the dream disintegrated into darkness.

***

"Maddie, come back to me."

She didn't respond, didn't move. She breathed rapid gasps that shuddered through her body, and sweat trickled down her cheeks. Jon thumbed the droplets away. Her skin was cold, despite the room's heat.

He frowned and glanced at the fireplace. Flames flickered, slowly catching the small logs she must have placed there earlier. But the temperature in the room seemed to have jumped ten degrees in the last few minutes, and the fire certainly couldn't account for it. Imagination, or something else?

She suddenly pushed his hand away, her eyes wide and unfocused like a dreamer fighting a dream. Her fear smothered him, making it difficult to breathe, to concentrate. He wondered why he was so open to her when he'd spent most of his life perfecting the art of blocking other people's emotions—and his own.

She pushed her fingers through her hair, her hands shaking. He sat back on his heels, watching her carefully. Something had frightened her enough to rip her from the vision, but she was not yet aware of him or their surroundings. Her mind was still caught in the backwash of the trance.

Which meant her gift was raw. Few trained clairvoyants were unable to pull out of a vision cleanly. He wondered how strong her gift was, how true. And how long she'd gone without seeking help. He suddenly wished he could call his mother. She was a strong clairvoyant and would know how to handle this situation.

"Maddie," he said softly.

The amber fire in her eyes began to burn more brightly as her awareness returned. She blinked rapidly, then took a deep, shuddering breath. The blanket of fear intensified.

"I'm sorry," she whispered. She pushed the chair backwards and scrambled to her feet, every movement frantic, as if desperate to escape.

He reached out to caress her hand, but she jerked her fingers away from his touch. He frowned and rubbed his fingertips together. Now her skin was burning hot. What the hell was going on?

She stopped in front of the fire, her back to him, her stance withdrawn. She looked isolated and very, very frightened. The firelight ran through her hair, making it burn a vibrant, molten gold. Such a pretty color, he thought, and so at odds with the darkness that seemed to haunt her.

He had no real experience in dealing with untrained talents, and no real time to help her. Not with only five days to find the missing kids. But any information, however small, might provide the breakthrough he needed. She'd definitely seen something in that dream, and that something just might make his task of rescuing the kids easier.

He sat astride the chair. Though she made no sound, her shoulders tensed. She was ready for a blow, whether verbally or physically. Anger uncoiled in his belly, and for an instant, he was very glad he'd only just met her. Otherwise, he might have been tempted to seek out the fool who'd hurt her so badly.

He leaned his forearms against the wooden backrest and fully opened the gate to his empathic abilities. He needed her to talk to him, and he had a feeling he'd require all his resources. One wrong word and she'd retreat further, mentally if not physically.

"Your gift is nothing unusual, Maddie," he said softly.

She laughed. It's harshness made him wince. "What do you know about it? Have you ever suffered these dreams, or the endless taunts of your friends?"

He held back a slightly bitter smile. In the ten years he'd worked for the Damask Circle, he'd seen and suffered more than she could ever imagine. "Clairvoyance is not so bad once you learn to control it."

Her fingers clenched by her side. "But I can't control it. I can't control any of it."

He had an odd feeling she wasn't talking about clairvoyance when she spoke of control. Did she have another gift she couldn't contain? "Didn't anyone try to teach you? Your mother, perhaps?"

Again she laughed bitterly. "No."

That one word spoke volumes. Obviously, she'd been left on her own to cope with her gift. Why? Abilities like this usually ran through generations, so surely there had been someone to guide her.

"Did your parents even know you were gifted?"

"They thought I was deranged." Though her voice was bitter, her confusion washed over him, along with a hint of guilt.

He wondered why. "Did they seek outside help, then?"

"Only in the form of psychiatrists." She snorted softly. "I lived a small town, Jon, with small town fears. I was an oddity, a freak. My parents tried very hard to make me appear normal, but people *knew.*"

The horror of her childhood was evident in the dark swirl through her aura. He silently cursed the fools who had brought her up to fear, even loathe, her gift.

"Then tell me about your gifts." It was evident from the way she stood that he wouldn't get much more about her past until she trusted him more.

"There's nothing to tell. I'm just a freak."

If she was a freak, then what was he? What would she say if she ever saw him change? *Not* that she ever would. That was one secret he shared with the very few people whom he trusted completely. "Maddie, you have a gift that can be valuable if you want to save your nephew. It doesn't make you a freak."

Only the attitude of uncaring people could do that. And someone in her past, someone other than her parents, had obviously torn her to shreds over her gift. He sensed that much.

He flexed the tension from his fingers and glanced at the

clock on the wall. Ten o'clock. Time was running out. If he didn't get moving soon, another day would be wasted. "Tell me about the people you saw."

Her shoulders tensed again. "I told you what I saw. It doesn't make sense."

To her, it wouldn't. She didn't know the woman was a shapeshifter, and he had no intention of telling her. It would only lead to questions he didn't want to answer. "The clairvoyant image isn't always clear, especially if you haven't been trained. Sometimes you have to interpret."

Finally, she turned around and looked at him. He was pleased to see the fear in her eyes had retreated slightly.

"How do you know so much about clairvoyants?"

He smiled. "My mother and three of my sisters are clairvoyants."

She raised a pale eyebrow, the ghost of a smile touching her lips. "Three of your sisters? Just how many do you have?"

"Five sisters and two brothers. You?"

The warm light in her eyes faded, to be replaced by ice. "A sister," she muttered, looking away. "My brother died when I was young."

And Maddie felt guilty about it. He wanted to ask why, but knew he'd pushed enough for one day. "Tell me about the cabin you saw."

She shivered and rubbed her arms. "It was an old log cabin. I could see the gaps between the logs, so it wasn't insulated or anything."

"There are probably dozens of cabins fitting that description, but at least it gives me somewhere to start."

She frowned at him. "Gives us, you mean."

He really did admire her determination, even if it also annoyed him. "I don't intend to argue about this-"

"Good, because I'm going."

Jon swore softly, but knew he couldn't afford to say any more—at least not here at the inn where his voice might be heard.

The heat in the room was quickly abating. Maddie pushed warm strands of hair from her eyes then crossed her arms. It was more a defensive action than an attempt to stave off the rising chill in the air. The fire, he noted, definitely wasn't the source of the earlier warmth.

"How are you going to get out of the inn without being seen?" she said

"Same way I got in—via a window."

He could manage a brief flight to the heavily treed park just down the road from the shops. He hoped. His first priority was to replace his missing clothes. He might not feel the cold that much, but walking around in short sleeves would only draw unwanted attention. That was something he certainly didn't need right now. Then he'd go retrieve his truck—which had, no doubt, been towed away from the three hour parking zone where he'd left it. With a bit of luck, the weapons he'd stashed in the specially built compartment would still be there.

She raised an eyebrow. "And where will I meet you?"

He scratched his head but knew there was no getting rid of her. Not this time. "There's a small cafe called Emerson's near the bridge." He'd heard it mentioned the night he disappeared. There was an odd chance he still might find a clue there. Besides, the breakfast she'd ordered had to be cold by now, and he was hungry. "Get us a table, and I'll meet you there in an hour."

She nodded and grabbed her old coat off the nearby sofa as she walked towards the door. Then she stopped and turned around, her amber eyes searching his. "You won't leave me sitting there, will you?"

"No," he said, and wondered who had.

She hesitated, her gaze still searching his. After a moment, she gave a small nod and continued on towards the door. He wondered what she'd seen in his eyes that made her trust him when she obviously trusted so very few.

He listened to the sound of her steps fading down the hall, then tugged his father's ring from his finger once again and walked into the bathroom. He wished he could take it with him, but it was made of silver and wouldn't change. He placed it back behind the vent then slid open the window. The wind whistled in, but he ignored its chill touch and leaned out. No one was near. Good.

He reached down, deep within his soul and called to the wildness. It came in a rush of power that filled his vision with gold and dulled his senses as it shaped and changed his body. Then the freedom of the sky was his, and he leapt towards it on golden-brown wings.

Six

Maddie frowned and glanced at her watch. Jon was nearly an hour late. Why she was surprised she wasn't entirely sure.

She picked up her milk shake and idly pushed the straw back and forth across the caramel froth. She'd been an idiot yet again. She'd stared into Jon's bright blue eyes and believed the truth she saw there.

Only the truth always hid deceit. She'd learned that lesson the hard way during the six long years of her marriage. What on Earth made her think Jon would keep his promise when it was so obvious he didn't want her around?

A waitress brushed past her, bumping against her arm. As the woman apologized, Maddie glanced up and felt her heart almost jump into her mouth. Hank stood in the cafe's entrance, looking around.

Had he followed her, or was it just coincidence that led them to the same place? She had no way of knowing and no way of finding out, short of asking him. Something told her *that* wouldn't be a wise move.

He stepped forward. She ducked her head, praying he didn't see her. After this morning, she wanted as little as possible to do with the night manager. The man was spooky.

His footsteps moved away from her. She sipped on her milk shake and glanced furtively sideways, trying to see where he went.

He stopped in front of a table on the far side of the small restaurant. She wished she could see whom he was meeting, but the width of his body blocked her view. It might be just a friend or a relation, but the way his shoulders were hunched and his head bowed told her this wasn't so.

She could remember standing that way herself over the years. He spoke to someone he loved, and yet feared.

Maddie frowned at the thought. Why did she keep thinking back to her marriage? The past was coming up too much lately; she was seeing reminders everywhere. Why couldn't she just forget it and get on with her life?

Because the past has shaped my present, and given me no life at all. She closed her eyes against the sudden insight. While her life might hold no excitement, it was safe. It was all she could ask for these days. And all she deserved.

Hank looked like he was arguing with the person in the booth. He made a short, sharp gesture with his hand that spoke of denial, and then he shifted slightly. For an instant, Maddie found herself staring into a woman's eyes—eye's that where as dark as the sky at midnight.

Relief surged through her. For some odd reason, she'd half-expected the woman to have the same chilling green gaze as the cat.

The woman rose, and Hank stepped back. Maddie was surprised to see that the woman was short. Somehow, Hank's manner had made her expect someone much taller, someone with more commanding presence. The woman walked toward the exit, and the provocative sway of her hips turned the head of every man in the café.

Would it have turned Jon's? Maddie smiled at the thought. He might be a loner emotionally, but she didn't see him as a loner *physically.* The man was too comfortable around women.

Hank followed the woman towards the door. Maddie ducked her head, hoping he would walk right on by.

But the sound of his footsteps hesitated, then headed in her direction. She took a deep, calming breath and glanced up.

Straight into Hank's suspicious brown gaze.

***

Jon shifted shape as he neared the ground, but his legs were trembling with exhaustion and wouldn't hold his weight. He stumbled forward, then collapsed, landing on his hands and knees. He stayed there, gulping in great gasps of air as sweat dripped from his forehead and pooled in the dirt near his fingers.

Maybe this was why he couldn't remember much about last night. He'd blocked out the fact that it damn well hurt to shapeshift.

It was a good ten minutes before he felt strong enough to move. He climbed slowly to his feet and wiped the sweat from his face. Despite the morning's late hour, the small park was quiet. From beyond the line of trees came the steady sound of traffic—it had to be the freeway that bypassed most of Taurin Bay. The traffic was too steady to be anything else. His destination lay to the left—Taurin Bay's quiet heart.

He brushed the dirt from his hands and jeans, then walked through the cedars. Shops came into view, and outside one, a phone booth. It reminded him that he'd yet to call his boss. He dug several coins out of his pocket and crossed the road, heading towards it.

The phone was answered on the second ring. "About time you checked in, cowboy."

The edge in her usually gentle voice told him she'd been worried. "Sorry Seline. Someone in this town knew why I was here—they tried to get rid of me."

"I did warn that they might," she replied, almost crossly.

So she had. He just hadn't expected the attack to come within the first two hours of his arrival. "I need you to do some checking for me."

"What?"

He heard the soft rustle of paper and could imagine her ferreting through the huge mound of documents on her desk, searching for a pencil to make notes—which she really didn't need. Despite her years, Seline had an incredible memory.

"The Hank Stewart we have on file is not the same man that's currently working at the inn. Might be worth checking whether any unidentified bodies have been found in the area recently. You might also check to see if he's purchased any other properties in the area."

"You think this Hank is responsible for the attack on you?"

"Bit of a coincidence, otherwise. I never actually met him

the day I checked in, so how he knew I was here for anything more than a vacation is beyond me. He's not the brains behind the operation, I know that much."

"Old magic is the key, cowboy. And old magic has ways and means of finding out information."

"Gee, doesn't that make everything so much clearer," he said sarcastically.

"If you're not careful, boy, I'll come down there and slap that smartness from your mouth."

He grinned. Seline was half his height, and twig-slender, but she could be a fearsome old bird when she wanted. And he had no doubt that she'd do as she threatened.

"Anything else?" she continued.

"Shapeshifters. I need to know if there are any known to be in this area. I've seen one, at least, but I need to know her human identity."

"Will do." She hesitated, then added, "You okay? I had this feeling you were in trouble."

"I was, but I found help." Help he didn't really want. He glanced at his watch. If he didn't hurry, he'd be late for his meeting with her.

"Well, be careful, cowboy. You could lose more than you bargained for on this one."

Alarms rang in his mind. He had an odd feeling Seline wasn't talking about the job, but something more personal. "I'm always careful, Seline."

Her laugh was a high-sounding cackle. "I know. That's what will make your fall all the more delicious. I'll be in touch."

She hung up before he could question her further. He swore and slammed the receiver back into place. Sometimes the old witch's tendency to speak in riddles was more than a little annoying.

It took him ten minutes to walk up to where he'd left his truck, only to discover it had indeed been towed away. He wasted nearly another hour finding the police station, filling in forms and paying the fine.

He glanced at his watch as he climbed into the driver's

seat and swore again. He still had to buy a jacket and some other clothes, and it was already well past the time he'd said he'd meet Maddie.

He just had to hope she didn't get sick of waiting and go off alone. There was a lot of strength in Maddie, despite her fears.

When he finally pulled into the café's small parking lot, he was relieved to see her truck was still parked there. But sitting right next to it, in an unfamiliar dark blue Ford, was a man he recognized. Terry Mackerel.

He'd known the FBI agent was involved with the investigation into the sixteen disappearances, but he was the last person Jon had expected or wanted to see in Taurin Bay.

He slowed, but at that instant the man looked up. Jon smiled grimly. Some days you just couldn't win. He parked the truck and climbed out, approaching the car cautiously. While Jon had worked on several of the same cases as the agent over the last ten years, their relationship was neither professional nor personal. Jon trusted the man with his life, but not his secrets.

The car door opened, and the big man levered himself out with an awkwardness Jon knew was highly deceptive. Mack might look overweight, but he was fast when it mattered.

"Well, well." The big man's hard gray eyes watched him carefully, as if ready to pounce given the slightest provocation. "Fancy meeting you here."

"About to say the same thing myself." Jon crossed his arms and leaned his shoulder against the outside wall of the restaurant. He knew there was nothing casual about this meeting. Never was with Mack.

Mack unhurriedly opened a pack of cigarettes and pulled one out. "Weren't you in Atlanta last week?"

He nodded. Another missing child had turned up. Another murder yet to be solved. "Met your partner there."

"So I heard." Mack lit his cigarette and puffed on it thoughtfully. "Find any clues yourself?"

"No." As usual, the only sign of injury had been the small wound on the kid's wrist—a cut so small it might have been missed. Only there wasn't a drop of blood left in the child's veins. But Mack knew that—he would have seen the same coroner's reports that Jon had.

"Then why are you here?"

Why was Mack here? There was no such thing as a coincidence where the FBI agent was concerned "Maybe I'm just taking a break."

Mack exhaled a long plume of smoke. "Yeah. And I just might sprout wings and fly."

His gaze narrowed. Had Mack been digging around? Though where he would look for such information, Jon couldn't even begin to guess. It wasn't the sort of thing kept in any official records *he* knew of.

"What can I do for you, Mack?"

"You know another kid went missing a week ago."

Jon nodded. He wasn't about to tell the big man about Maddie's nephew. He had a feeling she didn't want to get involved with cops—of any variety.

"Well, this time they've taken two." Mack reached inside his jacket and pulled out a photo. "Seen this woman around?"

It was Maddie standing beside a lanky kid who could have easily been her son. Evan, obviously. She looked different, he thought, staring at the photo. It was Maddie as she should be. Happy and laughing. He studied it a moment longer then handed the photo back to Mack. "Why do you expect me to know every pretty lady in the district?"

Mack smiled. A shark with a dental problem, Jon thought.

"The woman went missing several hours after her nephew disappeared. The kid's father is the local detective, and he's raising a hell of a stink. Seems to think she knows more than she was telling. It just might be the break we're looking for."

Maddie was only a few steps away from being in deep trouble. And though it would have been easy to let Mack grab her and haul her in for questioning, it wasn't fair. Not when she'd saved his life. He owed her more respect than that.

"What has all this got to do with me?" he asked casually.

Mack took a final puff on the cigarette, then threw it on the ground and crushed it under his heel. "I want to know what you know, Barnett." His cold gaze fixed onto Jon's. "We know you're working on this case for the parents of several missing kids. We know you work for the Damask Circle, a supposedly charitable, worldwide organization. Yet you, and others, curiously turn up to investigate the more bizarre police cases—and often get there before the police do. I want to know why you're in Taurin Bay, and what you know about the kids that have gone missing."

Jon smiled grimly. Mack had obviously been doing some research into the Circle. Professional or personal curiosity? "I don't know much." And wasn't that the damn truth.

"Ante up what you do have, then."

He had nothing to lose by doing so. Besides, it was always better to keep on the FBI agent's good side. Things got dangerous when you didn't.

"Whoever is taking these kids is using them for some sort of ritual that's performed on the night of the new moon. If we don't find them before then, we won't find them alive."

"Why Taurin Bay?"

Because an old witch told me the evil was centered on this area—for now. But Mack was not likely to believe that Seline, the president of the Damask Circle, was anything more than the harmless old lady she appeared.

"The bodies of four of the kids currently missing have turned up in nearby areas. The nick on the wrist, the lack of blood—it's all exactly the same as the five that have been found along the West Coast." He shrugged lightly. "Taurin Bay is the one thing all the recent disappearances have in common—they were all at school camps here sometime within the last year."

"Interesting," Mack drawled softly. "We've just found another body."

He stood up straight. "One of the missing kids?"

The big man nodded. "Found him up on Saddle Mountain."

The same area where he'd been shot down. "Which kid?"

"Samuels. The kid was only missing a month."

"They're getting careless," Jon commented softly.

"Or getting ready to leave the area and just don't care any more."

So Mack thought the people behind all this were in Taurin Bay, too. "Any suspects?"

The agent just gave him a toothy smile. "I want you to keep in contact with me. I want to know if you see this woman, or find any information. I want the people who did this alive and unharmed and in prison. Clear?"

Jon wondered if the man knew he was parked next to Maddie's truck. Probably, he thought, returning Mack's hard gaze. "Very. Anything else?"

Mack's gaze narrowed. "Don't mess with me, Barnett. Not on this."

Jon nodded, not moving until the agent had climbed into his car and driven away. Then he turned and made his way to the café's entrance.

A woman opened the door as he approached, and a familiar tingle ran across his skin. He stopped at the base of the steps and studied the woman's dark eyes. A brief flash of confusion, even fear, ran through her gaze. He didn't think its origin was something as simple as being confronted by another shapeshifter in her territory.

Then she smiled. He couldn't help responding.

"I do believe we've met before." She tossed back her mane of golden hair, her voice as smooth as a fine malt whiskey.

Designed for seduction, he thought. There was something about her that seemed oddly familiar, yet her eyes were dark, not the green of the cat he'd seen in the forest.

"Surely not," he replied lightly. "I'd never forget such a beautiful face."

Maddie, he thought with amusement, would probably have made a face at such an obvious line. Or gone into fits of laughter. This woman merely smiled, though he felt a wariness in her that matched his own. And it wasn't the usual wariness of two shapeshifters meeting for the first time.

"Eleanor Dumaresq," she said. "Perhaps you have time for a cup of coffee?"

He took her offered hand. Her fingers were warm and pliant

against his, yet he felt an inner core of strength in them. The woman was more than simply a shapeshifter. Old magic swirled about her, a sense so strong he could almost taste it.

He let his touch linger a little longer than was necessary and studied her eyes. Her gaze called to the wildness in him.

Old magic was the key—and the danger—Seline had warned of when she'd sent him to Taurin Bay. It was an image that seemed to fit Eleanor well. Yet there was nothing more than a gut feeling and the words of an old witch tying Eleanor to the disappearances.

But as much as he would have loved to accept Eleanor's invitation and pursue the mystery she presented, he couldn't. Not with Maddie waiting for him in the café. He didn't want to endanger her by introducing her to someone who might well be involved in the attempt on his life.

"I'm afraid I can't just now," he said, glancing past her to study the restaurant's interior. Why did he suddenly feel Maddie needed his help?

"A shame," Eleanor replied warmly. "But I'm sure we'll meet again. Taurin Bay is such a small town, after all."

He glanced at her sharply. There was definitely an edge of warning in her mellow tones. "I'm sure we will."

In fact, he'd make damn sure they did. Eleanor might not be the cat he'd seen in the forest, or even the one in the inn, but something told him she was involved in the disappearances. The brief flash of confusion in her eyes the moment they'd met told as much. As did the shimmer of hate that shone through her aura.

He watched her walk away, then quickly entered the restaurant.

***

"Mr. Stewart, what a surprise to see you here." Maddie forced a smile, and hoped she didn't look as nervous as she felt.

"I was about to say the same thing." He dragged out a chair and sat down opposite her. "This restaurant is not the usual tourist stop."

"My sister recommended it," she said quickly, then silently

cursed her own stupidity. Any mention of Jayne and Evan was plain suicidal if this man was involved with her nephew's disappearance.

"Really? Does she come here often?"

Though Hank's question was casual, she couldn't miss the edge of tension around his thin mouth. She nodded, lowering her gaze as she took a quick sip of her drink.

"What's her name? Maybe I know her."

"Jayne Smith," she replied, knowing her sister had only visited Taurin Bay under her married name of Gaskell.

The dangerous light in Hank's eyes faded. He sat back in the chair and lightly toyed with a knife. She suddenly felt like a mouse facing a large and hungry cat.

"The only Smith I know is the lovely young lady now sitting opposite me."

He meant to flatter her, but he only succeeded in making her feel ill. She pushed the rest of her milk shake away and gathered her bag. She'd be damned if she'd wait any longer for Jon—especially if Hank intended to keep her company.

"I'm sorry, Mr. Stewart, but I really must go."

"No time for another drink? It would give me a chance to apologize for my abrupt behavior this morning. You might even find yourself enjoying my company."

She forced another smile and shook her head as she stood. "I'm sorry, but I really have to leave."

"Why? Are you meeting someone?"

Her gaze jerked to his at the question. *He knows,* she thought, studying his eyes. *He knows I'm involved with Jon somehow. I should have stayed home, stayed safe.*

But being safe wouldn't find Evan.

"What business is it of yours?" she retorted tightly, her fingers clenched against the strap of her handbag. "Do you usually take this much interest in the inn's guests?"

He smiled lazily. "No. Just the exceptionally pretty ones."

The man was a sleaze, whether or not he was involved with Evan's disappearance. "I'm sure the inn's owners will be pleased to discover you take such an interest."

He laughed, white teeth flashing. Her stomach turned. Evil

haunted the depths of his laughter. Maddie swallowed and looked away. What on Earth made her think that? God, she needed a drink.

She licked her lips and tried to ignore the thought as she watched Hank warily.

"I'm only kidding, my dear," he said with a lazy smile. "No need to get nasty."

Despite his conciliatory manner, the amused light in his eyes told her he wasn't worried by her threat. Why? Did he have some kind of hold over the owner? Or was the owner somehow involved in Evan's disappearance?

"Madeline Smith? Maddie? Is that really you?"

She jerked around at the sound of Jon's voice. He was threading his way through the tables, wearing a black leather jacket that emphasized the lean strength of his shoulders and the brightness of his golden hair. His gaze met hers for a moment, and fear ran briefly through her heart. Despite his easy smile, there was a light in his eyes that made him look very dangerous. But she'd never been more relieved to see anyone in her life.

"Fancy meeting you here." He stopped beside her. His eyes held a warning as he lightly kissed her cheek.

She cleared her throat and tried to ignore the warm tingle his lips left on her skin.

"It's been a while," he continued. "What, six, seven years?"

She nodded, going along with his game. "You're lucky you caught me here at all. I was just leaving."

A hint of a smile tugged at his lips, but she sensed his attention was on Hank, not her.

"Surely you can stay for a cup of coffee?" He pulled out the chair she'd just vacated. "Don't believe we've met," he added, holding his hand out to Hank. "Jon Barnett."

"Hank Stewart."

"Really?" Jon said, the surprise in his voice at odds with the slight narrowing of his gaze. "You've changed. You look nothing like the photo that appeared in the *Gazette* ad a year ago."

"Ah," Hank's smile was easy despite the wariness in his

eyes. "That was my younger brother, Tim. He fills in for me quite often, and happened to be on duty the day the photographer came. Just as well, too. He's more photogenic than me."

The tension levels rose a notch. She touched Jon's arm, felt the tautness in his muscles. "Look, I really have to get going."

Jon took her hand from his arm and squeezed her fingers gently before letting them go. "Really?" he said to Hank. "Odd that we haven't seen him around much lately then, isn't it?"

Hank shrugged and rose to his feet. "It's been a delight, Miss Smith. Maybe we can do this again another day."

The predatory light in his gaze belied the blandness of his smile. She edged a little closer to Jon. "Sure." *When hell freezes over.*

"See you back at the inn, then," Jon said.

"That you can be assured of," Hank murmured. He nodded to Maddie and walked away.

She waited until he'd left the restaurant then grabbed Jon's arm, pulling him around to face her.

"What the hell was that all about?"

"You needed help, didn't you?" he replied mildly. He sat down at the table and reached across to her half-finished milk shake. "May I?"

She nodded. "What made you think I needed help? And why show yourself to Hank? He might be involved with the attempt on your life."

"He might. He might not." Jon shrugged and took a long drink.

She frowned. "Why on Earth were you going on about that *Gazette* photo?"

Again he shrugged. "Just stirring the pot, so to speak."

Jeez, he could be so damn infuriating sometimes... "Will you just answer my questions?"

"No." He pushed the empty shake container away and sat up straight. "Why didn't you tell me your brother-in-law was a cop?"

She blinked in surprise. "What has that got to do with

anything?"

"Plenty. He's reported you missing and claims that you may know more about Evan's disappearance than what you're admitting. The cops, as well as the FBI, are sniffing around Taurin Bay looking for you."

Trust Steve to do something like that. The man was a pain. And obviously, Jayne hadn't mentioned the fact that she'd asked Maddie to search for Evan. "Why is everyone in Taurin Bay? Why are you?"

"Because the bodies of several missing teenagers have been found nearby." He hesitated, his gaze searching her face. "And you didn't answer my question."

"I didn't think it was important enough to mention." Didn't think Steve's hate for her would blind his common sense. Damn it, it wasn't as if this was the first time she'd had a vision concerning Evan. Steve certainly knew about them, even if he didn't acknowledge them—or her. He'd even seen them hit her a couple of times.

But he also knew about her shady history with sudden disappearances. Maybe in his fear for Evan he was grabbing at straws. Maybe it was easier to believe she might have been involved in taking his son, simply because the chances of Evan coming back alive were greater.

She rubbed her eyes wearily. How was she going to avoid the police and still find Evan? Lord, another round of questioning was not what she needed right now. She'd had more than her fair share when Brian had disappeared. Nor had the questioning stopped when they found his remains among the smoking ruins of their house. She knew some of the investigators still suspected she'd killed him, even though his death had eventually been classed as accidental. And they weren't far wrong in their accusations, either.

"I'll go call him right now." Or at least, she'd call Jayne, and see if her sister could convince Steve to get his police buddies off her tail.

"I wouldn't." Jon caught her hand, his fingers warm and gentle against hers. "Your brother-in-law might know you're not directly involved in Evan's absence, but the fact of the matter is you did warn them of the disappearance before it happened. They'll want to know how and why, and they will question you until you tell them."

She closed her eyes. "And waste everyone's time in doing so."

"Exactly. We're all caught in a no win situation."

And Jon was going to use it to keep her out of the way of his investigations. A flicker of anger curled through her stomach. Doing what other people thought was best for her had never worked. She'd only married Brian because Jayne had convinced her he was the safe harbor she'd needed. How wrong they'd been. And Brian had died because of their foolishness.

Oh yeah? Didn't his ruthlessness have something to do with that as well?

She ignored the thought and pulled her hand from Jon's. "I'm not going back to the inn."

"Maddie-"

She held up her hand, cutting him off angrily. "No. I'm staying with you. I'm going to find Evan, even if I have to avoid every cop in the country to do so."

He raised an eyebrow, and leaned back in his chair, a grin twitching the corners of his generous mouth. "Can I finish now?"

She glared at him and didn't reply.

His smile broke loose, doing odd things to her stomach. Yet his bright eyes held a thoughtful note that calmed her rising anger. He *was* taking her seriously, despite his outward appearance.

"I can't let you go back to the inn. Not after I've just confronted Hank. And I don't want the cops to get hold of you, either, simply because interviewing you will take them away from tracking the real criminals. So like it or not, I'm stuck with you."

Stuck with you. What a great way to put it. She held out her hand. "A partnership, then? No more trying to get rid of me?"

"A partnership could be dangerous. The less you know,

the better off you'll be. I'm only trying to protect you."

"Protect me from what? Death?" She laughed bitterly. "Believe me, I've faced death, and it doesn't scare me. Not half as much as I..."

She broke off. Heat crept through her cheeks as she stared at him. She'd done it again. Confused his words with past pain, and in the process, had almost revealed entirely too much.

She had to get a grip on herself. She couldn't let her emotions run loose. People died when she did.

She took a deep breath and met his narrowed gaze.

His eyes were vivid, powerful. The same color and yet so different from her husband's. Brian's eyes had been cold and calculating, his gaze that of a man who liked to control. The blue of Jon's eyes was warm and inviting, even if the man himself appeared somewhat remote.

"You're right," he said, his voice lacking the hint of warmth it had held a moment earlier. "I have no right to try to protect you. A partnership, then. Together we'll track the bad guys and find the kids." He hesitated, then shrugged. "But that's all I'm offering, Maddie."

She saw the warning deep within the depths of his eyes. Don't expect anything more than tolerance, it said. Don't expect anything more than friendship.

As if *she* wanted anything more. "Fine," she replied stiffly, and tore her hand from his. "Are we going to start looking at cabins today?"

He nodded and patted his coat pocket. "I brought a detailed map of the area. We'll start looking at the old logging huts first and hope we get lucky."

The cabin in her dream had been old and made of wood. It took a long leap of faith to say it was a logger's hut, but they had to start somewhere.

"What about the police?"

"I'm hoping they're watching your truck, not mine." He tossed his keys in his hands, then gave her a somewhat grim smile. "Go out the back way. You'll find a small alley. Follow it. I'll meet you at the third cross street."

She raised her eyebrows in surprise. "Is that really

necessary?"

He shrugged. "I have no idea if they're watching your truck, but we can't afford to have them tailing us. If I'm followed, I'll dump my truck and get rid of them before I come back for you."

"Just make sure that you do come back." She shoved her hands into her jacket pockets and glared at him.

He returned her gaze evenly, giving nothing away. "A partnership won't work without trust."

Yeah, right. But he didn't really need her, did he? She nodded and spun away, heading for the back of the café. His gaze warmed the middle of her shoulder blades, but she didn't turn around.

The sun came out from behind a cloud as she pushed open the back door. She stopped and peered up at the mountains high above her.

Evan was up there somewhere. And so was the woman with the cat green eyes. She shivered and walked towards the street.

Her brave words to Jon only moments before were nothing more than a lie. She feared death, all right. She'd seen its specter twice, now, and somehow had escaped its touch. And she'd seen it again through her visions, in the woman's odd gaze.

Something told her if she met Death a third time, she would not be so lucky. But she had to save Evan, no matter what the cost. She owed that much to the ghosts of the past.

Seven

"Absolutely nothing." Maddie sighed and sat down on the top step of the old hut. "We've found ten damn cabins that match my description and haven't found a sign of the kids."

And wasted entirely too much time doing it, Jon thought, sitting down beside her. The sun had disappeared behind the tree line, and the night's shadows were beginning to close in around them. A chill wind had sprung up with the onset of dusk, bringing with it the smell of rain. If they didn't leave soon, they'd get drenched.

Maddie shivered and rubbed her arms. He'd asked her several times during the day if she was warm enough, and her answer had always been yes. He had a feeling she'd freeze to death before she admitted anything else.

"We can't do much more here tonight. We'd best head back to the inn." He took off his jacket and placed it around her shoulders.

He saw the brief flash of indecision in her eyes, and realized she didn't want to be seen as a burden. Didn't want to get in his way.

Maybe he was taking the bastard act too far if she thought the simple act of borrowing a coat would anger him in some way. "Keep it," he said softly. "I'm not cold."

She nodded her thanks and tore her gaze away from his. "I saw a couple of flashlights in the back of your truck," she said after a moment. "I don't mind going on."

Her stubborn expression made him smile. She was so tired she could barely lift her feet, yet she was willing to continue. "Well, I'm tired and hungry, even if you're not."

A touch of relief winged through her eyes before she pulled

her gaze from his again. "I guess it would be stupid to stumble around in the dark. We could so easily miss the kids."

A wildcat snarled in the distance, and magic whispered across his skin. That was no ordinary cat out hunting an evening meal. It was a shapeshifter hunting them.

He rose to his feet and offered Maddie his hand. She hesitated, then accepted his help, her fingers cold and stiff against his.

"What are you going to do about the inn?" she said, studying the dark tree line intently.

"What I do depends on how Hank reacts." And whether Hank believed that his meeting with Maddie was only an accidental meeting of old friends. "Someone at the inn obviously suspects I'm here to find the kids. It might be Hank; it might not. I'm hoping that my sudden reappearance might force them into action and give us a lead."

Her gaze flicked past his and settled on some point past his right shoulder. "What if that reaction is trying to kill you again?"

He frowned. She was looking at anything and everything but him, and it was beginning to annoy the hell out of him. He might have warned her not to get involved, but he'd never said anything about not looking at him. He liked looking into her eyes, damn it. Liked watching the flow of emotions through their amber depths.

"They won't attempt it with an inn full of guests." Or at least, he *hoped* they wouldn't.

A gold-red curl had broken loose from her ponytail and flipped across her face. He reached out and tucked it behind her ear, allowing his fingers to trail lightly against her cheek. It was like touching satin.

Her gaze jumped to his, and he saw a flash of fear in them. Not fear of him. Fear of herself. He wondered why.

"Don't," she said softly.

He took a deep breath, then stepped away. But distance didn't dampen his sudden desire to touch her. Hold her.

"We should get going," he said, more abruptly than he'd intended. "I can smell snow in the air."

She nodded and swung his jacket off her shoulders. He half expected her to hand it back, but she slipped it on instead. "Lead on, then."

When he didn't move straight away, her look asked why he was standing there. He smiled and led the way back to the truck.

***

The inn felt like a furnace after the chill of the night. Maddie quickly stripped off the two coats and handed Jon his with a smile of thanks.

"Ah, Miss Smith. So good to see you again."

She jerked around at the sound of Hank's voice. He was leaning casually against the banister, his smile warm and lazy. Yet there was nothing casual in the way he watched them.

Maddie swallowed uneasily. "Evening, Mr. Stewart."

"Please, call me Hank." He pushed away from the banister and moved across to the desk. "I'm afraid there's been a terrible mix-up in the room bookings. We presumed Mr. Barnett had left and gave you his room."

"Oh." She couldn't think of anything else to say without giving away the fact that she knew *why* there was a mix-up.

Jon's shoulder brushed against hers as he stepped slightly in front of her. It was an oddly protective gesture that warmed the pit of her stomach. His fingers touched hers, and she clasped his hand.

"How unfortunate," Jon said. He squeezed her fingers gently, his touch warm and reassuring.

Hank's gaze narrowed slightly. "I'm afraid the inn is fully booked, but we're willing to arrange other accommodations for you, Mr. Barnett. At the inn's cost, of course."

She wondered if the other accommodations would include another nice, damp well.

"Of course," Jon's tone was dry. "But I don't mind bunking down in Maddie's room for the night. We have a lot to catch up on."

His lazy grin left little doubt of what they'd be catching up on. Hank raised his eyebrows, his smile almost a leer.

Maddie tried to ignore the heat creeping into her face.

Hank had to believe she and Jon were old lovers catching up, or things could get dangerous. "We certainly do," she agreed softly.

Hank frowned, and a hint of confusion flickered through his eyes. "Well, then. If it's okay with Miss Smith, we certainly have no objections."

She met Hank's dark gaze. There was no way on Earth she'd take a room by herself with him around, anyway. There was something in his eyes that made her feel ill—a hint of depravity and menace and something else she just couldn't name.

"Good," she said levelly. Though she wasn't entirely sure spending several nights alone with Jon was a much better option. In some ways, it certainly wasn't any safer.

Hank gave them a smile she didn't trust. "It's something of a tradition at the inn to invite all our guests for Sunday dinner. Care to join us?"

She opened her mouth to say no, but stopped when Jon squeezed her fingers again. She frowned up at him. How did the man know what she was about to say before she said it?

"I think we can spare an hour or so," he said, then gave her a quick smile that was intimate and intense. Her heart skipped several beats, even though she knew it was all an act for Hank's sake.

"We've had quite a busy day," he continued, his tone suggesting they'd done more than merely walk around. "I, for one, am famished."

Hank raised an eyebrow. It was hard to see whether he believed their act or not. "Well then, please join us. The rest of our guests will be present, so it'll be a good opportunity for everyone to meet."

She could think of nothing worse than a room full of strangers. Especially if Hank was going to be one of them.

"Thanks." Jon raised her hand to his lips, mischief dancing in his eyes. "Shall we go get ready, my dear?" he said, and lightly kissed each of her fingers.

Heat shivered through her soul. She glared at him. This wasn't a game she wanted to play. It was far too dangerous to flirt with a man like Jon. Flirting could lead to caring, and that was something he'd already warned her against.

Still, for Hank to believe they'd once been lovers, she had to do more than simply stand there like a fool.

"Been ready for a while, lover," she said softly and arched forward, brushing a kiss across his lips.

Lips that were soft and warm and so inviting that she didn't want to leave.

But it was only a game, and Hank was watching.

She pulled away. Jon touched her cheek, the amusement in his eyes suddenly replaced by a warmth that made her breath catch in her throat. *Damn,* she thought. *I should have learned by now that it's dangerous to play with fire.*

She cleared her throat and quickly turned, heading for the stairs.

When they'd reached the safety of their room, she turned around to confront him. And made sure she kept a good deal of distance between them.

"Why on Earth did you accept his dinner invitation?"

Jon threw his jacket over the back of the sofa before sitting down. "We need answers. We're not going to find them hiding in our room."

She leaned back against the table and rubbed her arms. The room was cold, despite the embers still burning in the hearth. "How is going to dinner with strangers going to help us?"

He studied her for a moment, then rose and walked across to the fire. "I'm betting one of the guests will be the woman Hank met in the cafe."

He threw several small logs on the fire and stabbed the coals with the poker. In the firelight, flickers of gold appeared to run through his hair as it dropped across his eyes.

Maddie crossed her arms and stayed where she was. Cold or not, she didn't want Jon to think her brief flirtation was anything more than a game staged for Hank's benefit. Didn't want him to think she would be willing to continue once they were alone. Especially when she could still taste him on her lips.

"What will you do if she is there?"

He glanced up at her. "I will apply my many charms and see what happens."

She raised an eyebrow in surprise. "You're going to flirt with her? After the show we just put on?"

"Basically, yes." He studied her for a moment. "I'm not sure that Hank bought the act anyway, and Eleanor is the key to this whole situation. Besides, maybe he'll think I'm after nothing more than another conquest."

Another conquest. Somehow the words seemed to roll so easily off his tongue. Is that how he lived his life, seeing women as nothing more than prizes to be won? "And maybe he'll just try to kill you again."

He shrugged. "At least we'll know whether he's involved or not."

"But-"

"Maddie, the kids are what matter, nothing else. If we don't find them before the full moon, we won't find them alive. Now come over here and get warm."

She hesitated but realized she was being silly. He certainly wasn't showing any inclination to carry on their flirtation. He'd admitted it was nothing more than an act.

"We have to find them." Too many people had died because of her. She didn't want her nephew to join the list.

She knelt down next to him and held her hands out to the flames' warmth. "Did you ever find any of the other teenagers who were missing?"

He nodded. "Eleven, I think the count is up to."

She eyed him for a moment, then looked back at the fire. Something in his blue eyes told her she didn't want to know the rest of it. "And?" she asked.

"It looked as if they'd been used in some sort of sacrifice. They'd been drained of blood."

*Drained of blood...*She blanched. Christ, they weren't dealing with some sort of vampire cult were they? "You're not saying-"

He sat back on his heels, his face grim. "No, it's not a vampire, or anything as simple as that here. I think we're dealing with some sort of magic ritual."

Why would anyone in their right mind think a vampire was a simple solution? What sort of world did he live in? Obviously a delusional one. For a start, there were no such things as vampires. She shivered and crossed her arms. It was just another reminder of how little she really knew about the man kneeling next to her.

"What makes you think Hank and this Eleanor are involved with the disappearances?"

"The man's not what he appears to be. He's involved somehow, I just know it."

"And Eleanor?"

He hesitated. "The same can be said about her."

Despite his earlier promise, it was obvious he still wasn't telling her everything he knew. "Then how safe was it to reveal yourself at the café? Wouldn't it have been better to remain hidden?"

He sighed and ran a hand through his hair. Firelight caught the hairs on his arms, making them gleam softly. "I honestly don't know. I just have a feeling time is running out, and that nothing will be gained by hiding. I've learned to trust my instincts in cases like this."

Just as she'd learned *not* to trust hers. It had been the instinct to protect herself that had led to all the trouble in her life. She swallowed the lump in her throat and pulled her eyes away from his steady gaze. "Are you a cop or something?"

He hesitated. "I'm a private investigator, of sorts."

"Of sorts?"

He shrugged and didn't elaborate. Frustration ran through her. Why wouldn't he tell her anything about himself? Didn't he trust her?

"So, you charm the pants off this woman." Her voice held a slightly sarcastic edge that made her wince inside. "What happens then?"

He rose, moving away from her. "What happens next depends very much on her, doesn't it? Do you want to shower first?"

She glanced up at him. His bright gaze told her nothing,

but she sensed he was suddenly annoyed. Over what, she couldn't say. "No, I'll stay near the fire a bit longer."

He nodded. She watched him walk away and wondered what was going to be harder—being in the same room as Hank, or watching Jon flirt with another woman.

Eight

Jon accepted a glass of wine with a smile of thanks and leaned against the mantelpiece, watching Maddie. She was across the room, easily chatting with another guest. There was no way anyone would know by simply looking at her that she was terrified.

He sipped his wine and heard her laugh, a sound so warm and free it made him smile. Her hair fell down her back like a river of flame, gleaming brightly whenever she moved. Even with the long, loose, jade-colored shirt hiding her slender figure, she looked good.

As if she felt the weight of his stare, her gaze turned to his. In her expressive gaze he again saw wariness and fear—not of the situation, but of herself.

He frowned and wondered again what her other talent was. He had a feeling her fear was tied to it—as was the memory of death he occasionally saw in her eyes. His gaze flicked to her lips, and he remembered their taste, the warmth of her mouth against his own. He took a long gulp of wine. Such thoughts would only lead him into trouble.

Someone touched his shoulder lightly, and a sweet honeyed scent wafted around him.

He turned his back on Maddie. Even from across the room, he felt her annoyance, even hurt. He had no choice but to ignore it.

"Eleanor," he said, forcing more warmth into his voice than he felt. "What a surprise to see you here."

"Heard you were staying here and thought I'd drop by and say hello," she purred, brushing the thick strands of silken gold away from her face. "Unfortunately, I can't stay for long."

Her nail polish was the color of blood. Appropriate for a hunter like Eleanor. "Another appointment?"

"Business, darling. You know how it is." She screwed up her nose, then took a sip of wine and slowly licked the residual moisture from her ruby-red lips.

It looked like he wasn't the only one with seduction on his mind. He smiled and blatantly ran his gaze down her body. Eleanor had certainly come dressed for the part. Her black dress clung in all the right places and allowed plenty of long, honey-colored legs to be seen. Nice, real nice, but no Maddie.

He drowned the thought with another drink. He hadn't come here to seduce Maddie. It was time he started concentrating on the business at hand.

"We could meet for a drink later, if you like. Get to know each other a little better."

"Oh, I like," she purred, meeting his gaze with a look that was pure heat.

A dinner bell chimed faintly in the adjoining room. "Are you eating?" he asked, offering Eleanor his arm.

She linked her arm through his. "Only main course. Dessert will come later—if you're lucky."

His smile felt tight. As easy as this seduction was turning out to be, it was one he had no real desire for.

And yet, at any other time, it wouldn't have mattered. He too was a hunter, both in spirit and in profession. Sometimes he had no choice but to flirt with a woman to get information vital to his case, whether or not he was attracted to her. Many women seemed to relax their guard once flirtation had moved to kissing, making it that much easier to question them. His gaze flickered across the room until he saw the fiery gleam of her hair. Would Maddie ever drop her guard?

His gaze suddenly narrowed. Hank's dark head was close to Maddie's. Though he'd half expected this to happen, the sight of the man sleazing up next to her annoyed him more than he'd thought it would. There wasn't a thing he could do to get her away from Hank, though. He had a feeling that Eleanor was the key to everything, and with the lives of the teenagers at stake, she had to be his main concern, not Maddie.

He smiled and pulled a chair out for Eleanor. Some days at the office were definitely tougher than others.

***

Eleanor's laughter ran softly across the murmur of conversation, a smooth and seductive sound. Maddie gritted her teeth and tried to ignore it. A hard task since Eleanor appeared to be holding court at the far end of the room, with practically every male at the table hanging off each huskily delivered word. Only Hank seemed immune to the woman's all-too-obvious charms.

Maddie scowled down at her plate. Hank sat on her left, his chair too close for comfort. She didn't dare move around too much. Every time she did, their arms or knees brushed. It was an intimacy that left her feeling ill.

Eleanor laughed again. Maddie stabbed a piece of meat on her plate and quickly ate it. Maybe her best course of action was to get away from here as quickly as possible.

"I like a woman who enjoys her meat," Hank said, a suggestive leer touching his thin lips.

Her stomach turned. If she had to put up with another five minutes of this man, he'd quickly learn just how little she was enjoying his company.

"I don't eat it much," she said, glancing at the other end of the table when there was another burst of laughter.

Eleanor had one hand draped over Jon's shoulders, her golden head close to his. They were a good match, she thought, watching the light run through Jon's hair as he laughed softly at something Eleanor said.

Maddie scowled and looked back down at her plate. At least she had an answer for her earlier question. She'd rather sit next to a dozen Hanks than watch Jon with another woman.

She stabbed another piece of meat, then held it up on the fork and glared at it.

"I think it's dead," Hank said, dry amusement in his tone. "As I think the boyfriend might be, if you ever get him back this evening."

She glanced at him, startled that her thoughts were so obvious. "He's not my boyfriend..." she hesitated and felt heat creep through her cheeks when Hank raised an eyebrow. Their act earlier had certainly suggested they were lovers, and she couldn't very well deny it now. "I mean, we're old friends, but no longer an item, as such."

"Both free spirits, hey?"

Maddie shrugged. She'd never been a free spirit where men were concerned. Maybe that was why she'd married Brian. She pushed her plate away, suddenly not hungry any more.

"Odd coincidence that you both happened to be in Taurin Bay at the same time," Hank continued lightly. "Especially given that you checked into the same inn."

She licked dry lips. "Yes, it is, isn't it?"

"Not married by any chance, are you?"

She smiled grimly. "I was. My husband is dead."

"Oh," Hank murmured. "Sorry to hear that."

He sounds real sorry, too, she thought sarcastically. She listened to him tap his knife lightly against his plate and found herself gritting her teeth again.

"We've had a bit of trouble around these parts, you know," he said after a moment.

Her gaze jerked up to his. His dark eyes were watchful. He was baiting her, she realized, trying to make her give something away. "Really? What sort of trouble?"

"Kids have been disappearing lately. The only link between any of the disappearances was the fact that the families stayed here in Taurin Bay."

She swallowed nervously. How much had been written in the local papers about the missing teenagers? Was Hank telling her more than he could have found out from the local news?

"Bet that has played havoc with tourist numbers."

Hank smiled, though no humor touched the darkness in his eyes. "It hasn't yet, luckily. It will, if they don't get some results soon, though."

"I'm sure the police are working on it."

"Oh, I'm sure *many* people are working on it."

He smiled when she looked at him. She was reminded of a vulture hungrily watching its prey.

"Then someone will catch them."

Hank leaned back in his chair and continued to smile lazily at her. "Personally, I doubt it. So many kids disappear every day in this country that it's become an unfashionable crime to pursue."

She frowned. "This is different though."

"Oh? How?"

"I remember reading a bit about this in our local paper. Haven't sixteen kids disappeared?"

He smiled. Something in his eyes suggested she'd just made a major mistake, though she wasn't exactly sure what it was. "So they say. No one's really sure of the exact number."

She swallowed. The exact number was currently seventeen, if you included Evan. "Well, that's a rather large number to end up missing from the one area, isn't it? It'd have to raise the police's suspicions."

"But they haven't all disappeared from this area. I said the only known connection between the disappearances was Taurin Bay."

"Oh."

"So which newspaper did you read all this in?"

She shrugged uneasily. "Just a local paper. The *Mail*, I think. Or it could have been the *Courier.*"

"I'll have to hunt the articles up. Been keeping something of a scrapbook on the case."

Maddie forced a smile. It would only take one phone call to discover her lie. "Something to show the grandchildren later in life?"

"Something like that." His dead gaze ran past her for a moment. "That boyfriend of yours is getting mighty friendly with Miss Dumeresq."

"Let him. I don't care." She threw her napkin down on the table and pushed her chair back. Enough was enough.

"Going already?" Hank raised his eyebrows at her, a knowing smile touching the corners of his thin mouth.

"It's been a long day," she replied tightly. And it looked as if it was going to be an even longer night.

Jon could take his turn on the damn sofa tonight—if he

even bothered coming back to the room, that was.

"I don't suppose you'd like company?"

She glanced down sharply at Hank. He smiled blandly back.

"I meant to the door, of course."

"Of course," she muttered. "But I'll be fine, thanks."

He nodded. "See you tomorrow, Miss Smith." He gave her a smile that held more than a hint of malice, then added, "Maybe."

A chill ran down her spine. Maybe going up to the room alone wasn't such a good idea. She glanced back at Jon and found her gaze meeting his. But there was no comfort to be found in the blue of his eyes. He was doing his job, and she was only getting in the way. His gaze said as much.

She licked her lips and turned away. Hank's gaze burned a hole into her back as she walked quickly from the room.

***

"What about that nightcap, then?" Eleanor arched an eyebrow at him and walked her fingers down his chest.

Jon stopped her hand when it reached his stomach. "You choose. You know the town better than I do."

"There's a lovely little bar a couple of blocks away, on Fourth. Blue Moon, it's called. And the best thing is, it's only a five minute walk from my place."

He raised an eyebrow. "That sounds like an invitation."

"Play your cards right, and it just might be," she purred and lightly kissed his ear.

He resisted the temptation to move away from her touch and glanced down the table at Hank. The man was looking far too smug for Jon's liking. Eleanor's tongue whisked across his ear. This time he did pull away, smiling when she pouted.

"What about the boyfriend?"

Eleanor raised finely sculptured eyebrows. "What boyfriend?"

Jon nodded towards Hank. "Aren't you two an item?"

Eleanor's smile was pure seduction. "Sometimes we are. Sometimes we aren't."

Hank appeared to be ignoring them, yet Jon sensed the

man knew every move he and Eleanor made. There was some sort of link between the night manager and Eleanor, a tenuous thread of magic that tingled across his skin like electricity. It worried him, and yet at the same time, it told him he was right in suspecting these two.

"So he won't object to us going out?"

Her smile gained a hint of malice. "Oh, he may object, but I don't really care."

Her heart is as cold as her touch is warm, he thought. She looked briefly at Hank, her expression disdainful. At that moment, the electricity surged, a brief but potent charge that made the hair on Jon's arms stand on end.

Hank rose immediately, bumping into the woman on his left and spilling her wine. He muttered an apology then quickly walked from the room. The bell chimed as he left the inn.

Tension surged through Jon. He flexed his shoulders, trying to relax. Something had just happened between Eleanor and Hank, and until he found out what, he'd better be more careful.

She turned, facing him. His gaze was drawn to her ample cleavage. The woman was built, he had to give her that.

"So, what time should we meet?" she continued softly.

He glanced at his watch. It was nearly nine now. The sooner he got this over with, the better. But he wanted to check on Maddie first and make sure she was okay. She'd been a little upset when she'd left the table.

"I'm good any time. You're the one with the meeting, so why don't you decide?"

"This is going to be the shortest business meeting in history. I can't believe my lawyer chose such an ungodly hour." She ran a nail down his cheek. Though her touch was feather light, it would only take the slightest bit of pressure to slice his skin. Her nails were as sharp as a cat's. "How does ten sound?"

"Suits me." He caught her hand, raising it to his lips.

Amusement spun through her eyes. "Such a gentleman."

He smiled. "Only when the room is full of people."

"Good," she purred, and rose. "Because I like a man with

a bit of fight in him."

Most cats did. It seemed to be part of their makeup. He picked up his wine and watched her walk away. He'd better be damn careful tonight, or he'd find himself as dessert in more ways than one.

***

Maddie bolted the suite door but still didn't feel safer. Hank's warning seemed to echo through the silence and set her teeth on edge. After turning on every light, she checked the bedroom and bathroom for intruders. There was nothing unusual to be found, yet her stomach turned uneasily. Something felt wrong, and it wasn't just her nerves—or her imagination.

She bit her lip and rubbed her arms. The room was cold, despite the fire. She threw more logs on and stirred the coals. Flames leapt, fierce and bright.

Despite the light, the shadows in the far corners of the room seemed to loom threateningly. She shivered and held her hands out to the flames, trying to warm them. The encounter with Hank must have unnerved her more than she'd realized. She was getting jumpy over shadows, for Christ sake.

A floorboard creaked behind her. She whirled, her heart leaping into her throat. Something whisked through the light, a gossamer veil that held no shape.

She swallowed heavily. Fog. It had to be fog. The idiot repairman must have left the bathroom window open this morning, even though she hadn't noticed it when she checked earlier.

Another sheer form spun across the room. She closed her eyes. It was her imagination, nothing more. Ghosts *did not* exist.

She took a deep breath and opened her eyes. A phantom floated two feet away from her, staring at her with eyes that held no life.

Maddie tried to scream, but no sound came out. The creature laughed softly. It was a sound that chilled her soul.

"Flee," it whispered hoarsely. "Flee, or die."

She tried to back away from the wraith, but her feet were

like ice, refusing to move with any sort of speed. Something
lashed across her shoulders. She yelped in pain and spun
around. The mocking sound of laughter ran across the room.
She touched her shoulder; her fingers came away sticky. Real
or not, these creatures *could* harm her.

More wraiths skimmed through the room. Her back hit a
wall and sweat broke across her brow. She licked her lips and
closed her eyes again, praying for strength. The pressure was
beginning to build deep within her, pressure she feared and
could not control.

Oh God, it's happening again.

She clenched her hands, digging her nails into her palms.
The pain only intensified the burning deep within.

"Please, just leave me alone," she whispered. "I don't want
to kill anyone else."

The wraiths danced and mocked her, paying her words no
heed. Something flicked across her face, stinging. She jerked
her head away, and felt warmth seep down her cheek.

The heat in the room leapt. A log exploded in the hearth
and sparks flew through the room.

The wraiths laughed.

Maddie screamed as the burning broke loose.

Nine

A scream split the silence. Maddie. Jon knew it was her from the tone and the sudden leap of fear across his senses. He jumped to his feet and ran for the door.

The other guests had risen, getting in his way, slowing him down. He pushed past them roughly, ignoring their indignant mutterings as he took the stairs two at a time.

The suite was locked, and his key wouldn't open the door. Jon swore softly. She must have bolted it.

"Maddie!" he yelled, pounding his fist against the door. "Open up."

She didn't answer. Either she couldn't hear him or couldn't get to the door. He thumped the door again then realized the wood was hot to his touch. Burning hot.

Hell. "Maddie!" He stepped back and kicked the lock. The door shuddered under the force of the blow. He kicked it again. The wood near the lock cracked.

"Need help?" a voice said to his left.

Jon barely glanced the man's way. "Get everyone out of here," he said tightly. "There's a fire in the room."

The man nodded and began ushering the other guests back down the stairs.

Jon stepped to the side of the door, and grabbed a nearby plant box. He glanced towards the stairs to ensure no one was near, then heaved the heavy planter at the lock. The door exploded inwards, crashing back against the wall.

Heat rushed out at him, not flame. He threw up his arm to protect his face and stepped into the room.

The thick, acrid smell of magic swirled around him. A log

had rolled free from the hearth, and flames danced across the carpet, reaching fiery fingers towards the sofa.

He quickly kicked the log back into the fireplace, then stamped out the flames scorching the carpet. Why was the room so hot? Certainly the small blaze would not have caused such heat...

A small sound jerked him around. Maddie sat in one corner, hugging her knees and slowly rocking back and forth.

He could see her terror in the way she huddled, smell it in the confusing swirl of her aura. Yet oddly enough, he sensed it wasn't entirely fear of the dark magic that was thick and strong in the room. She was afraid of something else, something he couldn't name.

He frowned and knelt down beside her. "Are you all right?"

A cut marred her cheek. The wound was thin but deep— like the mark left by the lash of a whip. Something *had* attacked her. The lingering dark magic had to have been involved.

But were Hank and Eleanor? They had only been gone a few minutes before Maddie screamed. The spell, no matter what it was, would have taken longer than that to set up. Magic wasn't something you could rush into. It had strict rules that had to be followed, or it could lash back at the sender.

But the why and how weren't really important right now.

She gave no sign that she'd heard him, no indication she knew he was there. He touched her shoulder gently, but almost instantly jerked it away.

She burned as hot as the room. The fire wasn't the cause of the heat, he realized. *She* was. The other talent he'd sensed in her, the one she couldn't control, was pyrokinesis. The ability to light fire with just a thought.

"Maddie!" He grabbed her shoulder again. Heat burned into his palm as he shook her. He ignored it. He had to get her out of here. The foul taste of magic was still thick in the room and might be dangerous. "Are you listening to me? You have to get out of here."

"I know," she whispered without looking up.

He frowned when she didn't move. "Are you hurt?"

She hesitated, then shook her head. "No. But if I move, I

might lose control."

Just how strong were her abilities if the heat in this room was under control? "Well, you can't stay here, either."

He leaned forward and picked her up. It felt like he was holding a furnace close to his chest, not a woman.

She tensed in his arms, and her gaze jerked up to his. Her eyes were wild and unfocused, full of heat. "I don't want you to get burned.".

"I'll be fine," he said. "Just don't let the power go." If she did, they could all die.

She nodded and looked away. He turned and headed for the door. Heat washed around him, thick and cloying. Sweat began to run down his forehead. He ignored it, ignored the slick wetness running down his chest and arms as he held her close.

"Control it," he whispered, and made for the stairs.

From the little he knew of pyrokinesis, he had to get her somewhere cold and quiet until her power was under control. That meant outside, in the rain.

There was a small seat under the old pine out in the front yard. He gently placed her on it, then knelt on the wet grass in front of her. Though he wanted to keep her in his arms, he sensed that touching her any more than necessary was the worst thing he could do right now.

"Imagine the heat as a wall, Maddie." He sat back on his heels and watched her carefully.

Her gaze jerked up to his. Confusion ran through her eyes before her gaze skipped away.

"Why?" Her soft voice was hoarse, apprehensive.

"Because you have to contain it, or it will consume us all."

She blinked, and he saw the gleam of tears in her expressive eyes. So the fires had already claimed a life. Had it been someone close?

Her fingers clenched into a fist. "A wall," she said, and closed her eyes.

"Now, imagine yourself holding a rope of water around that wall." He was tempted to cross his fingers. His knowledge of fire-starters was limited, and he had no idea if this would actually work. The night air churned with heat, turning the lightly falling rain to steam long before it hit the ground. The smell of pine was growing stronger, as if the tree behind her were beginning to burn. If she didn't get the power under control soon, everything around them would ignite.

After a moment, she nodded minutely.

"Draw the rope back into your body. Let the water cool the fire as you draw it in."

He waited. After several long minutes, the heat began to abate. She took a deep breath, then opened her eyes and stared at him.

"It worked," she said softly. "I controlled it."

He forced a smile. "So you did."

This time. She desperately needed help, though, and more importantly, training. He didn't have the knowledge or time to do either.

"I thought-" She shuddered and looked down at her hands. "I thought I'd kill everyone."

"How long has it been like this?" He reached out and touched her hand. When she didn't pull away, he gently caressed her fingers. Her skin still burned with heat. The fire may have abated, but it was still close enough to spark to life if she wasn't careful—if *he* wasn't careful.

"Forever," she whispered. She shivered slightly and rubbed her arm with her free hand.

He took off his sweater and slipped it around her shoulders. Her shirt was torn near the top of her shoulder blade, the edges smeared dark with blood.

"What the hell happened?" he said abruptly.

She flinched and wouldn't meet his eyes. "Nothing."

Her tone told him she was suddenly afraid. Or was it once again fear of his reaction? He frowned slightly. Her spirit might be fire, but someone had given her self-confidence a hell of a battering. Anger ran through him, and he clamped down on it, hard. His anger wouldn't help her, and right now, she was all that mattered.

He gently thumbed away a slight trace of blood from her

cheek. "I need to know. It might help us find your nephew."

She was back to looking at anything and everything else but him. Even though he guessed it was a reaction tied-in with whoever had given her confidence such a shaking, he wished she'd stop it.

"I was attacked by ghosts," she said after a moment.

She had to mean a sylph of some kind. Ghosts, or at least those he'd come across, were generally harmless. Certainly they'd never had the capacity to physically harm anyone.

"Can you describe them to me?"

Her gaze leapt to his. "You believe me?"

There was an odd mix of yearning and loneliness in her gaze, and something twisted deep inside him. It was a look he understood only too well.

"Yes." He rose abruptly. "Stay here. I'll be back in a minute."

He loped back to the inn. He heard a babble of voices around the far side of the building and guessed the guests must have gathered there. In the distance came the wail of a siren. The inn's foyer was warm, and he glanced briefly over his shoulder. He really should get her out of the wet night air, but something told him she wasn't ready to face the inn just yet.

He grabbed the small first aid kit he'd seen behind the desk and went back outside. The guests were beginning to mill out the front of the building now, and the wail of the fire engine was drawing closer. He wondered where they were coming from—they seemed to be taking a while to get there.

He placed the kit on the seat beside Maddie and got out the antiseptic cream.

"Tell me about the fire starting." He leaned close to apply the cream and tried to ignore the faint scent of roses, the heat of her body where it brushed against his—and his own sudden response.

"It happens whenever I get really afraid." She hesitated and shrugged. "It builds up to a point where I just can't control it anymore."

Her fear churned around him, but it wasn't fear of what

had attacked her in their room. She was still terrified of his
reaction to her gifts, of what she had done in the past.

"I can remember lighting a fire when I was six," she
continued softly. Tears ran across her aura, so strong it
surrounded her with a faint shimmer of silver. "It got stronger
with puberty."

"As most talents do." He carefully pulled the edges of her
shirt away from the wound on her shoulder. Though the cut
looked red and vicious against the creaminess of her skin, it
wasn't deep. The sylphs had obviously been sent to scare more
than harm her. He gently applied some of the antiseptic cream,
his fingers skimming across her soft skin. Lord, she smelled
good...

He quickly withdrew his hand and sat back down on his
heels. His matter-of-fact tone seemed to be relaxing her, and
the last thing he needed to do was something that would
jeopardize that.

"Did someone get hurt?"

She nodded, still avoiding his gaze. "I don't really want
to talk about this."

"You must. You have to be able to understand your abilities
and what they can do before you can have any hope of truly
controlling them."

"I know only too well what my damn gifts can do." Her
gaze flashed to his. Anger burned deep in the amber depths,
as did old hurt. "That's why I-"

Retreated, he thought when she hesitated. But what
monster had made her lash out with her abilities? Who had
hurt her so badly that she'd had no option but to kill?

And if Eleanor and Hank, or whoever had sent the sylphs
after her attacked again, would she be able to control her gifts?
Or would she lose it and kill them all?

He clasped her hand and rubbed his fingers lightly across
her palm. Her skin was slightly callused, not smooth, as he'd
expected. "Maybe it would be better if you left the area."

She wrenched her hand from his and stood up abruptly.
He rose slowly, watching her warily. The street light caught
the gold in her wild red hair and illuminated the slenderness

of her figure under her thin shirt. She looked so young and frightened and alone that he wanted to take her in his arms and protect her.

He stepped away instead. He barely knew her, and he certainly couldn't afford to get more involved with her. His work was too important.

She clenched her hands and glared at him. "I won't run away. Not this time."

He thrust a hand through his hair. How could he make her understand it was better for them all if she simply left?

"Maddie, you're a loose cannon. You can't control any of your abilities, and someone obviously suspects you're helping me. What will you do if they attack you again?"

"I'll control it," she said tightly.

"And if you can't?"

"I'm not leaving."

"You need help with your gifts. I can't give you that help."

"I'm not asking you to."

No, she wasn't. She wasn't asking anyone for help, and that was the problem. "Don't you realize there are people who could help you, people who would understand what you're going through, because they've faced the same fears themselves?"

"And who will help Evan?" She clenched her fists again and glared at him. "I'm not abandoning him, Jon."

"No one is asking you to. But pyrokinesis is a dangerous gift, and it must be brought under control." He hesitated, and met her anguished gaze. "How many more people have to die before you admit you need help?"

She blinked back tears. "Damn you," she said through clenched lips. "You could never understand what it's like to be a freak of nature."

He sighed. "I understand more than you could ever guess."

It was time she faced up to the fact that she had a responsibility to understand and control her gifts. Neither of them could change what had happened in her past. The future was a different matter. If she didn't want the destruction to continue, she would have to learn to restrain and use her psychic abilities.

But to do that, maybe she had to learn she wasn't the only one in the world with unusual talents.

He ignored the pain in her eyes and glanced at his watch. He had a meeting with Eleanor to get to, and he couldn't afford to miss it. Not when the lives of two children were at stake. They were more important than Maddie's fragile emotions—or his own need to help her.

"I'm a shapeshifter," he said softly. "I can take on the shape of a hawk and fly. How's that for being a freak?"

Maddie stared him. "You can't be serious." Shapeshifters didn't exist. He was making fun her—just as Brian always had.

She bit her lip against a stab of pain. Up until a few moments ago she would have sworn that ghosts didn't exist, either—especially those who could use a wisp of smoke to lash your shoulders and draw blood.

He sighed. "There are stranger things in this world than you could ever imagine. As far as freaks go, you don't even make the list."

There was something in his voice that suggested he'd seen more than his fair share of those freaks. Had seen them, and maybe even killed them. She crossed her arms and shivered. "And that's supposed to comfort me, I suppose?"

"Yes." He glanced at his watch again. "I haven't the time to discuss this now. I have a meeting to get to."

Eleanor, she thought. "But you're soaking wet."

He shrugged. "I'd get wet walking there, anyway."

"Well, then, you'd better get going, hadn't you?" she said more tartly than she'd intended.

"Maddie-" He lightly touched her cheek. His fingers were like fire against her skin, his touch stirring something deep inside. "Eleanor means nothing to me. She's just a lead."

She snorted. How could he say that? She'd *seen* them together. If it was all an act, then he should win an Academy Award.

He dropped his hand, and a hard light replaced the warmth in his eyes. "I have to go. We'll continue this discussion later."

Memories rose to haunt her. *In a more appropriate manner,* Brian would have added. She shivered again. Jon frowned slightly, then thrust a hand through his hair and walked away toward the inn.

She watched him go. He was nothing like her husband. There was gentle strength in him, a confidence in every action that made him appear so much taller than he was. Brian *had* been tall—a mountain who had once made a frightened eighteen-year-old feel secure, and later terrified a twenty-year-old.

So why did she keep drawing comparisons between them? Why did the things Jon said or did remind her constantly of Brian? It wasn't as if they even looked the same—only the blue of their eyes was similar, and she'd seen more emotion in Jon's gaze in the last five minutes than she'd ever seen in Brian's during their six-year marriage.

Oh God, why couldn't she just take Jon's advice and leave this town and all the memories it raised?

She bit her lip. She might have done nothing to save Brian or her brother, but she'd be damned if she'd run this time.

A bitter laugh escaped her at the thought. She was already damned. No one could save her, not even Jon.

She touched her cheek. Her skin still tingled from the slight brush of his fingers. Moisture seeped from one edge of the cut. She wiped it away, then stared at the blood on her fingertips. The ghosts had been real. She had the wounds to prove it. So why couldn't shapeshifters be real as well?

She watched Jon disappear inside the inn. Anger surged through her. It wasn't fair. All her life, people had walked away from her. Or run, in some cases. And just when she thought she'd found someone who might at least understand, he too, had walked away—to be with another woman.

Would a few more minutes really have mattered? She needed to talk to him, needed someone to understand her pain and guilt. Needed him to hold her, touch her, and tell her everything would be all right. Even if she knew it was all just a lie.

She had a sudden vision of Evan lying cold and still on

the cabin floor, and took a deep breath.

She was being selfish. Her nephew was the important one here. He was all that mattered. What she wanted—needed—didn't count.

The fire engine pulled up next to the curb, and the other guests milled toward it. The red flashing lights washed across their faces, making them look almost bloody. Maddie shivered and rubbed her arms. She hoped it wasn't a premonition of more death headed her way.

"You were lucky in there tonight." The comment came from the night behind her.

She yelped and spun around. Hank stood near the seat, his hands in his pockets and a watchful gleam in his eyes.

She swallowed and put her hand to her throat. How long had he been standing there, listening to them? "I'm sorry. You scared me."

"Didn't mean to."

Not much, she thought, staring at the malicious gleam in his dead eyes. "How's the room?"

He shrugged. "The fire had been put out, but I called the fire department, just to be safe."

"Was there much damage?"

"I think the extinguisher caused more damage than the fire. You won't be able to use the room tonight, I'm afraid."

Maddie knew she wouldn't have been able to sleep in the room even if she *had* been able to use it. "Were my belongings touched?"

"Not by the fire."

It wasn't what she'd asked, and he knew it. A hint of a smile played around his thin lips.

She crossed her arms. "Would it be okay for me to go up and get them?"

He raised an eyebrow in query. It made him look more than ever like a vulture. A vulture waiting to pick the bones of his prey.

"Why? Intending to go somewhere?"

As far away from you as possible. She forced a smile. "I have to go home."

"A shame you have to cut your holiday short," he said and took a step closer.

She resisted the urge to back away. He wouldn't harm her, surely, with the other guests milling near the fire engine behind them.

But looking into the dead emptiness of his eyes, she suddenly wasn't so sure.

"But some strange things have sure been happening around here," he continued, and gave her a cold, almost cruel smile. "I'd leave immediately. Hell of a lot safer that way, if you catch my drift."

Up until now, she'd thought Brian was the most intimidating man she'd ever met. But he'd had nothing on Hank. Throat dry, she nodded.

Hank raised his hand and touched the wound on her cheek. Bile rose in her throat. She swallowed heavily and forced herself to remain still.

"I'd hate that pretty face of yours to get all messed up."

"So would I," Jon said behind her.

Ten

Jon stopped behind her, so close that his body brushed against hers. His scent spun around her, an odd mix of sea spray and old wood. Warmth that was all too comforting tingled across her senses. Maddie clenched her fists, as frightened by her response to his nearness as she was of Hank. But she didn't move. Even if she had wanted to, the two men had her penned, like a lamb caught between two wolves.

Hank smiled and lowered his hand. "Miss Smith was just telling me she's planning to leave."

"Then you'd better go get her bill ready, hadn't you?" Though there was no hint of menace in Jon's soft voice, a flicker of fear ran across Hank's thin features.

His dead gaze ran past them. For an instant, it almost looked as if he was consulting someone. Then he nodded and quickly scuttled away. Jon touched her arms and turned her around.

"You okay?"

His eyes were full of concern, and it was almost her undoing. For a minute it looked like he cared. She lowered her gaze and stepped away.

"I was doing just fine, thanks." Her voice sounded tart again, but she couldn't help it. She wanted this man to hold her, and that simply wasn't an option.

"Here, take this," he said, and held out her coat. "It's warmer than my sweater."

"Thanks." His gesture surprised her. Had he gone back into the inn just to get it? Why? As he'd pointed out, he had a meeting to get to. She slipped off his sweater, handing it to him before putting on her coat.

He slung the sweater over his shoulder. Maybe he liked

the rain. Or maybe he just didn't plan to stay in his wet clothes all that long. She bit her lip and looked down at her feet.

"Have you decided to leave after all?" he said.

"Just the inn. I don't think it's safe anymore."

"You may be right." He glanced thoughtfully at the inn then back at her. The warmth had fled his eyes again, leaving them carefully neutral. "I really do have to go."

"Then go. Have your fun with Eleanor. I can look after myself."

His eyes darkened with annoyance. Maddie grimaced. She wasn't being fair. He was doing his best to find Evan, and being catty about it certainly wouldn't help anyone. If he was treating Eleanor as nothing more than a lead, why couldn't she?

Because I saw the way she clung to him, and it annoyed the hell out of me.

She swallowed and looked away. "I saw a hotel on the other side of the bridge. Sea View, I think it was called. I'll grab a taxi to my car, then drive out and book us a room."

"All right, then." He hesitated, then reached up and touched her cheek with his fingertips. His caress was gentle and made something deep within her tremble in response. "Wash your wounds, then rest. I'll be there as soon as I can."

He walked away again. She watched him until he'd disappeared from sight, then sighed and headed into the inn. The firemen were still in the building, but they allowed her to collect her bag. She was glad of their presence, especially when she came out of the bedroom and found Hank waiting for her.

"So, you really are going?"

She studied him uneasily. "I said I was. How much do I owe you?"

"Considering what has happened, we'll make your stay complimentary."

"Thank you."

The nearest fireman headed for the door. She shouldered her bag and quickly followed him.

"I do hope we see you sometime again," Hank continued.

"Not likely," she muttered, giving him as wide a berth as possible.

His chuckle crawled over her skin. She shivered and involuntarily glanced back at him. *Don't come back,* his gaze warned her. *If you do, you'll die.*

She swallowed heavily, trying to ignore the premonition, then edged closer to a fireman's broad back and followed him down the stairs.

***

Jon leaned back on the sofa and watched Eleanor enter the room. She moved with feline grace, hair shining in the firelight. A golden cat, he thought, and guessed that was her alternate form. The cat he'd seen in the forest had been black.

She smiled when she caught his gaze, her midnight eyes filled with heat. He felt his body respond, even though he had no true desire for the woman. She was just another job.

And yet he knew this would not have been the case a week ago. Dangerous or not, he would have taken what Eleanor was offering and enjoyed it.

But every time he reached for Eleanor he saw Maddie's eyes—frightened and alone and yet oddly courageous. Somehow, she'd slipped past his guard and become a friend. And he didn't leave friends alone and frightened.

She had a hell of a lot to answer for, he thought grimly. Eleanor was the key to the kids, the figurative nut that had to be broken, through fair means or foul. How could he be expected to do his job when everywhere he turned he saw something that reminded him of Maddie?

He accepted his drink with a smile and patted the cushion beside him.

Eleanor folded down beside him, then caressed his thigh. He stared into her eyes and wished they were amber rather than dark.

"I'm so glad we decided to come back here," she purred quietly. "So much cosier."

He suspected it wasn't the coziness she was after, but rather the solitude. The Blue Moon had plenty of customers—and plenty of potential witnesses if something went wrong.

Though why he thought something *would* go wrong he couldn't say. He just had an itchy feeling he'd better watch what he did—and watch what *she* did.

"It's not often another shapeshifter drifts into my territory," she continued. "Taurin Bay is such a backwater."

Her hand was moving up his leg, creating heat wherever she touched. *The mind may not want her,* he thought wryly, *but the body sure as hell does.* "Which is why I was so surprised to find you here. You look more a city type of girl."

Eleanor gave him a lazy smile. "I am. Unfortunately, my other shape is not."

"Very few are." He reached forward, tracing the line of her cheek. "But Taurin Bay is such a small town. Small towns like to watch and gossip."

"Ah, but I like the danger of discovery." She leaned into his hand and lightly kissed his palm. "Besides, Taurin Bay has a city attitude. You can do what you want, and the neighbors have no wish to know about it."

Was that some sort of admission? Did she mean you *could* kill without the neighbors getting suspicious? Taurin Bay wasn't that insular. Someone, somewhere, had to know something.

"So what do you do for excitement in a place like this?"

Eleanor smiled. "You mean, besides trying to seduce passing shapeshifters?"

He ran his fingers down her neck, letting them linger momentarily over her pulse. "Yes, besides that."

"I hunt. I run the hills at night. I help Hank at the inn occasionally."

And she was hunting now, with him as the quarry. Excitement lit her eyes, raced through her pulse. The edge he was walking was getting decidedly thinner. If she changed form, he'd be in serious trouble. He doubted if his own form would have much hope against a panther.

"I didn't know Hank owned the inn."

"Oh, he doesn't. I do."

He raised his eyebrows in surprise. Maybe, just maybe, Eleanor had given them their first lead. "Really. I thought the inn was owned by a Randolph Barker."

"My former husband. Couldn't stand the demands of a shapeshifter, poor dear."

The demands, or the appetite, of a shapeshifter? Maybe they should check out just what had happened to poor dear Randolph, as well as find out if he owned any other properties in the area.

Eleanor's hand touched his thigh, then moved to the fly of his jeans. His groin tightened in response, aching with need.

He leaned forward and kissed her. Her mouth was hot and sweet, but it was a taste that suddenly went sour. Damn, he just couldn't do this.

He'd ignored Maddie's desperate need to be held and comforted, had ignored the flash of hurt when he'd walked away from her.

But he simply couldn't ignore the fact that he had no wish to make love to one woman when it was another he wanted.

He placed his hand on Eleanor's. "Eleanor, stop."

She raised an eyebrow and sat back. "Cold feet?" she questioned softly. "Or a case of not wanting to cheat on your girlfriend?"

"Neither," he replied calmly. "Just caution. What's your other form, Eleanor?"

"A cat." She sipped her drink, regarding him thoughtfully. "A black panther, to be precise."

So she *was* the cat he'd seen in the forest. Her hair had to be dyed—usually it was a clear indicator to the coloring of a shapeshifter's other self. "My spirit is the hawk, Eleanor. We aren't compatible." Not when she was likely to pounce at a vital moment.

She smiled, but it failed to reach her eyes. The light of battle was flaring deep in the midnight recesses of her gaze. "But think of the fun, Shapeshifter. We'd never know when one might change and devour the other. The thrill of fear will only add to the excitement."

It was the sort of fun he could well do without. "I wouldn't want to hurt you."

"Oh, you wouldn't, believe me," she murmured softly.

"So, where does that leave us?"

He took another sip of wine instead of answering, and saw a sudden gleam enter the dark depths of her eyes. A chill ran through him. The wine. Christ, he was a fool.

He put the glass on the table and caught her hand. "I guess I should do the gentlemanly thing and leave."

"Oh, don't. There is still so much we have to discuss."

Her glance flicked past him, no doubt studying the clock on the mantle. He wondered how much time he had left until the drug took effect.

He dropped a quick kiss on her fingers, then rose and did up his pants. "It's best if I go, Eleanor. We both know that."

She rose with him. The predatory gleam in her eyes was stronger—the huntress was rising fully to the surface. Magic whispered around him. Magic that was old and full of evil. It had the same foul taste that had been evident after the attack on Maddie.

She reached out, running her fingernails lightly down his cheek. Her touch burned, and moisture dribbled down his cheek, thick and warm. She withdrew her hand. Her fingers were smeared with red. She licked them slowly, her gaze hot.

The huntress was getting ready to pounce on her prey.

"I can't let you go." Her voice was sultry and yet somehow harsh—almost as if she were having trouble speaking.

Or having trouble remaining in human form.

"As I said, there is much we have to discuss. Like, who do you work for and how have you managed to stay so close on our heels."

He clenched his fists and barely curbed the sudden urge to answer her question. He'd obviously ingested some sort of truth drug. Lord, he should never have been arrogant enough to think he could come to her lair and escape unscathed.

"Sorry. Haven't got time for questions right now. Things to do, places to be." He gave her a casual smile and swung his fist at her chin.

Her head snapped back, and she crumpled. He caught her before she hit the carpet and laid her down on the sofa. The last thing he wanted was her head smashing against the coffee table or floor—not when she might be the only one who could lead them to the kids. He had no idea how deeply Hank was involved. It was still possible the man had no true idea what Eleanor was doing.

Possible, but not likely.

He quickly frisked her but found little beyond the fact she was wearing no underwear. He stood up and studied the room. There had to be something, somewhere, that would give them a more of a lead. He turned and walked towards the door. Maybe her bedroom was a good place to start...The light around him suddenly buzzed, and for an instant, the doorway blurred.

He shook his head, and the doorway steadied. He took another step, and the room whirled briefly. The buzzing was growing, shooting pain through his head. The drug—it may have been a truth drug, but it was also beginning to affect his ability to see and walk straight. He'd better leave while he still could.

He got out of the house then called to his alternate shape. He had to get back to Maddie before the drug took a firm hold.

***

Maddie glanced at her watch for the thousandth time. It was nearing midnight and still no word from Jon. Obviously, he was having such a good time he wasn't in a hurry to get back. *Let's just hope he remembers why he's seducing Eleanor...*

And that, she thought with a frown, was an extremely bitchy thought. She rose from the sofa and walked across to the window. The curtains were a sun-faded orange and smelled of faintly stale beer and smoke. Just like the room. The Sea View was not one of the more classy motels. But the old guy at the desk had been nice, even though she'd clearly woken him up. And it certainly felt a lot safer waiting here than it would have back at the inn.

She pushed the curtains aside, leaned against the windowpane and studied the waves lapping the beach across the road.

Trouble was, she was getting tired of waiting. Tired of

doing nothing but running.

It was way past time she started taking control of her life. Or at least one tiny part of it. Thanks to Jon, she now knew that it was possible to control her gifts. So why not extend that? Why not try to find Evan with them?

Fear leapt up and clenched her throat tight. She bit her lip and leaned her forehead against the cool glass pane. All her life she'd been taught to fear her gifts, to despise what they could do. And in truth, up until now they *had* caused her nothing but grief. But here, at last, was a chance to do some good, a chance to save a life rather than take it.

If she had the courage.

I can do this. For Evan, I can do this.

She took a deep breath then walked across to her bag, digging around until she found Evan's gold chain.

Maybe it would help. Maybe it wouldn't.

Sitting cross-legged on the sofa, she looped the chain around her hand and closed her eyes. She formed a picture of Evan in her mind and projected her need to find him.

Nothing happened.

She frowned slightly. Thought of him laughing as they played football together, remembered the look on his face the Halloween she'd dressed up as a witch and come visiting. Still nothing happened. No images came.

She sighed and opened her eyes. Maybe she needed another focus—what had set her abilities off recently? The smell of citrus—oranges!

She scrambled off the sofa and ran to the door. The light was still on in the office. She grabbed her key and ran across.

The old man looked up as she ran in. "Just caught me," he said with a smile. "What can I do for you, lass?"

"Is there anywhere near I can get some oranges?"

If he was surprised by her odd request, he certainly didn't show it. "There's very little open at this hour, I'm afraid." He frowned thoughtfully, gnarled fingers tapping the desk. "But I've a couple of old ones out back. If all you want is juice, they'd be fine."

Maddie grinned in relief. "That would be great. Thanks."

She collected the oranges and returned to her room. After locking the door, she found a small knife and sliced them open, putting the halves into a small bowl before returning to the sofa.

Her heart raced uncomfortably in her chest—a rhythm caused more by uncertainty than fear. She'd failed at everything else she'd tried to do in her life; she didn't want to fail at this.

She brought the bowl up to her nose and took a deep sniff. The faint scent of citrus ran around her, sweet and compelling. She picked up the chain and once again pictured Evan's smiling face in her mind. For a moment, nothing happened.

Then darkness rushed at her, pulling her down into its grip. She fought the tide, thinking of Evan, trying to compel the dream in that direction.

The darkness swirled then slowly cleared, revealing the familiar interior of the old cabin. In one corner she could see the bundle of blankets that was Evan and the second teenager. In the other, a bright fire. Sitting in a chair beside the fire was Hank. She frowned. What was he doing at the cabin when he was supposedly the night watch at the inn?

The dream shimmered, fading slightly. She forced herself to concentrate. She had to try to direct the dream to the cabin's exterior...the image blurred for a minute, then reformed. Suddenly, she was outside. Tall, snow-dusted pines surrounded the clearing like sentries on duty. A windbreak, she thought. The trees were too regimented to be anything else. The dream drifted forward; a rutted, slushy track led away from the front of the cabin and through the pines.

Her dream followed it. The track wound down the mountainside, past the bluish pines and into mountain wildness. Finally, it came to a main road. The letterbox on the side of the road said Malkin Cabin. The dream drifted on and came to a sign—"Jewell, 15 miles."

A huge crash wrenched her from the dream. With a squeak of fright, she leapt to her feet, her heart thumping rapidly somewhere in vicinity of her throat.

Someone or something was outside her room.

Eleven

Maddie took a deep breath, then gathered her courage and walked across to the window. Pushing the curtains to one side, she looked out.

Jon was sprawled across the front of her truck. That must have been the crash she'd heard—but how the heck had he gotten there? He looked as if he'd been thrown there, and he certainly wasn't moving.

Her breath caught in her throat...was he hurt?

She ran for the door. He jerked upright when she rushed out, a smile touching his full lips.

"Maddie. Glad to see you."

There was a cut on his cheek. Though it didn't look deep, blood was smeared over the right side of his face. His speech was slurred, and his blue eyes were slightly unfocused. *Great,* she thought sourly, *he's drunk. And he's dented my damn hood.* She frowned and glanced upwards. To cause such a big dent, he'd have to have done a swan dive from above the car, but there was no overhanging veranda, nothing he could have leapt off. So how had he managed to land face first in the middle of her hood? Fly?

Her gaze widened at the thought. Ohmigod, he *could* fly. He had told her he was a shapeshifter. That his other shape was a hawk. She licked her lips, studying him nervously. She hadn't *really* believed him before. Something deep within had refused to, even though she'd been attacked by ghosts, whose existence she would have relegated to the realms of fairy tales right along with shapeshifters.

Her gaze slipped to the dent underneath him. If he could fly, you'd think he'd at least be able to land a little better.

She saw the old guy in the office peering out his window and offered Jon a hand. "Here, let me help you inside before we attract too much attention."

The last thing they needed right now was the old guy calling the cops.

He grabbed her hand and slipped off the hood, but his movements were unsteady, almost awkward. She frowned. Sweat beaded his forehead and darkened his golden hair, his breathing was shallow and rapid. This had to be more than mere drunkenness—maybe he was ill. Worry snaked through her. Maybe she should just take him to the hospital instead.

She slipped his arm around his shoulders to hold him upright. His gaze met hers, his eyes filled with a warmth that cut through her soul. He touched her cheek, then ran a finger lightly down to her lips. She resisted the temptation to kiss his fingertips and jerked away instead. She had no intention of starting a fire she could not control.

His hand dropped back to his side. "We should get inside," he said shortly, looking away. "It's safer."

Safer from what? Eleanor? What had happened during their so-called date? Maddie frowned but helped him into the room. She sat him on the bed then went to lock the door.

His didn't say anything, but his gaze followed her as she walked across the room. Heat crept into her cheeks. She wet a cloth in the bathroom, then walked back to the bed. He hadn't moved. Was barely even blinking.

She frowned and carefully wiped the blood from his face. As she suspected, the cut wasn't deep. Had Eleanor attacked him with a knife? Or had something else happened...something in the heat of passion, perhaps? Maddie licked her lips. He was a shapeshifter, after all. Who knew what their mating habits were...

"Thank you," he said softly when she'd finished.

She nodded. Avoiding his gaze, she tossed the cloth into the bathroom and retreated to the middle of the room, as far away from the beds and any suggestion of intimacy as was practical.

"Did you find anything out about Evan? Or the cabin?"

She crossed her arms and leaned against the back of the sofa, watching him warily.

"No."

His answer seemed edged with an incredible amount of anger. She frowned. "Why not? What happened?"

He rubbed a hand across his stubble-lined chin. Lines of weariness etched his face, and his smile held a slightly bitter edge. "Nothing happened. Absolutely nothing."

Again the anger was heavy in his voice. She raised an eyebrow in surprise. It almost sounded as if he was somehow blaming her for whatever it was that didn't happen.

"What do you mean?"

His gaze clashed with hers. His blue eyes were bright and fired with some emotion she couldn't define. "I mean I couldn't go through with my efforts to seduce her, damn it."

Relief and surprise rippled through her. She clenched her fists and looked away. While she was intensely glad he hadn't been able to go through with his seduction, she knew it was wrong to feel that way. She barely knew this man—why should she care if he slept with another woman, especially if it provided information to find Evan?

Besides, he'd already warned her not to expect anything more than a partnership from him. He was a loner. He wanted a woman to keep him company at night, nothing more.

And as much as she wanted Jon to hold her and kiss her and make love to her, she knew one night with him would never be enough. He'd shown her a tenderness, a caring that she'd never thought to see from a man. Because of that, she was beginning to realize she didn't want to spend the rest of her life alone. She needed someone like Jon in her life. Only he'd already made it clear he wasn't available for anything more than friendship.

She returned her gaze to his. His arms were crossed, and his mouth was set into a grim line. She wondered why. "What went wrong?"

He grimaced. Annoyance ran across his face, thundercloud dark. "You."

"Me?" She raised her eyebrows in surprise. "How the hell

did I stop you? I wasn't even there."

He ran a hand roughly through the sweat-darkened tangle of his hair "You were everywhere."

His words whispered through her heart. She looked away from the sudden intensity of his gaze. If she wasn't very careful, she could find herself believing that he actually *cared* for her.

Then she frowned. Something weird was going on here. He wouldn't willingly say something like that, not after warning her so often not to get involved. So why had he? And why was he answering every one of her questions? "Why are you acting so strangely?"

He grimaced. "Eleanor slipped me some sort of drug."

"Is it dangerous?" She quickly pushed away from the sofa. "Do you need a doctor?"

"I don't think so." Again his answer seemed reluctant. "It's just screwing up my ability to see and walk properly and making me tell you things you have no right to know. And it's really pissing me off, Maddie."

She tried to ignore the accusation in his eyes. Evan was her nephew. She had every right, and every intention, of finding out all she could about the woman who'd taken him. And about the man who was helping her find him.

"So how did you escape if the drug is affecting you so badly?"

His smile was grim. "Hit her before the drug took hold."

He *hit* her? Images of Brian flickered through her mind, and she closed her eyes against them. Jon was no Brian. He didn't hit women for pleasure, that much she was certain of. Still..."Is she okay?"

"Of course she is. I just hit her once to knock her out." He frowned at her suddenly. "Why the hell should you care? The woman probably sent those sylphs to attack you, and she sure as hell tried to kill me with that white ash arrow. She probably would have finished the job tonight if I hadn't escaped."

"I know, it's just that I-" She hesitated and shook her head. What on Earth was she thinking? Jon had no need, and probably no desire, to learn about her violent history with

Brian. "Are you sure you don't need to see a doctor?"

"I'm sure. The effects aren't as strong as they were."

He was still watching her warily. She frowned, wondering why. Then it hit her. *He'd taken a drug that was making him answer questions truthfully.* A grin twitched her lips. That was a temptation almost too good to resist.

"Don't go there," he warned softly. "You may not like what you find."

She scowled at him. He sat in the middle of the bed, a golden man dressed in black, with a past just as dark. He was as much as an enigma to her now as when he'd first appeared in her bedroom. That wasn't likely to change unless she seized this moment and ran with it.

"Who do you work for, Jon?" she asked softly.

She saw the struggle in his eyes, could see his irritation in the sudden tension knotting the muscles in his arms. She knew it wasn't right, but what else could she do? Jon hadn't exactly been forthright with any sort of information—this might be her only chance to learn something about him.

"The Damask Circle." His answer was ground out between clenched teeth. He was fighting the drug in his system, fighting answering her questions.

I'm not being fair, she thought, but she had no intention of stopping now that she'd started. "And they are?"

He took a deep breath, then let it out slowly. His gaze condemned her. "It's an organization of psychics, witches and paranormal creatures such as vampires and shapeshifters. We hunt down the bad things, the creatures that hide in shadows and kill."

His voice was flat and cold. She stared into his eyes and saw the horror lying there. Vampires and shapechangers and God knows what else were an everyday part of this man's life, and it scared the hell out of her. As did the knowledge that there was actually an organization out there to fight these things. And to think she'd spent the last six years hiding from the world because she'd thought her firestarting abilities were a threat to everyone. What a joke that seemed now.

She rubbed her eyes wearily, then looked up again. Deep

down in the blue depths of his eyes, past the shadows and the death, she saw the hint of despair and wondered at its reason. "Things like the people who took Evan?"

"Yes."

"And Eleanor is one of those things?"

"Yes."

Sweat beaded his forehead. How much of the truth drug had he ingested? How much time did she have before he came out of its influence? What would he do or say to her when he did? "What is Eleanor?"

"A shapeshifter, and old magic. Evil incarnate."

And she had Evan, for God only knows what purpose. "Old magic? What do you mean by that?"

His fist slammed down on the bed. "Damn it, Maddie, just stop. You're putting yourself in greater danger by asking all this."

She crossed her arms and ignored his warning. "Just answer the question."

He made a sound that was almost a growl. "It means she can control magic. The older the magic, the older, more powerful the person."

"And Eleanor is both?"

"Yes."

A chill ran down her back. She clenched her fingers to stop their sudden shaking. Eleanor didn't look any older than *she* was, so how could she hold the sort of power he appeared to be talking about? "She doesn't look to be either."

"No, she doesn't. And that makes her all the more dangerous, in my estimation." *And damn you for continuing this,* his eyes seemed to add.

She licked dry lips. "But what would someone like that want with the blood of teenagers?"

Several seconds ticked by before he answered. "Blood rituals create powerful magic. It has many uses."

Blood rituals. *It's all too hard to believe...*and yet, staring into his eyes, she saw only the bleakness of truth. He couldn't lie to her, as much as he wanted to. She shivered and half wished she hadn't begun this line of questioning. He was right.

There were some things she was better off not knowing.

She rubbed her arms lightly. "What sort of uses?"

"It can be used to raise the dead, to extend life, to enhance the power of certain spells." His replies were becoming more abrupt, the time between her questions and his answers longer. Maybe the truth drug was starting to wear off.

She pulled her gaze away from his and studied the end of the bed. The tension level in the room seemed to leap several notches in the ensuing silence. She took a deep breath, then asked the one question that really mattered. "Why couldn't you seduce Eleanor?"

He didn't answer right away. The silence seemed to stretch, jarring against her nerves. A whisper of sound made her look up quickly—and far too late to back away.

He stopped inches away, blue eyes unreadable and yet somehow compelling. She swallowed heavily. The heat of his body rolled over her, mixed with the rich scent of his aftershave. Warmth spread through her. He was close, so close that her breasts brushed against his chest and sent flames of desire shooting through her soul.

It was time to retreat, to stop asking questions and just move away from him, but she couldn't. Something in his eyes made her breath catch in her throat and held her immobile.

"Tell me why," she repeated almost hoarsely.

And wondered if she'd just made the biggest mistake of her life.

"When I was doing this to Eleanor." He ran his knuckles down her cheek, his touch branding her skin even though it was butterfly light. "I wanted it to be you."

He cradled her chin with one hand and moved his head slowly towards hers. "And when I was doing this-" He brushed his lips over hers, then lifted his other hand to frame her face. "I wanted to be doing this to you."

His lips captured hers; his tongue parted them and gently explored her mouth.

Heat exploded deep in the pit of her stomach then burned through her veins, hot and swift. Dear God, it had been so long since she'd been held, been kissed, with any sort of warmth...and never in her life had she craved someone's touch as much as she now craved his. She moved into his kiss, deepening it, savoring the taste of his mouth as she molded her body against the heat of his.

His hand moved down her side and tugged up her shirt, then splayed against her lower back. He held her close, as if he never intended to let her go.

Heat and desire ran through her soul. She wanted this man to caress her, become one with her. Wanted him with such aching fierceness it was almost frightening. She wrapped her arms around his neck, tasting the salty sweetness of his neck, his ear.

"I need you," he whispered into her hair, his breath warm as it brushed along her neck.

His words jarred through her mind. Need, she thought with sudden clarity. Need was a long, long way from love. *Oh God, I think I'm falling for this man, and he just doesn't care.* It was a nightmare she'd sworn never again to relive.

She wedged her arms between them and pushed. His arms tightened around her, momentarily resisting, then he reluctantly let her go.

"I can't do this," she said softly. He was breathing just as hard she was, and he looked just as shocked by the sudden intensity of their kiss. "Though I won't deny I want to."

He took a deep breath, then ran a hand through his hair. He'd basically said the same thing to Eleanor less than an hour ago. And he didn't like having it flung back at him.

The red haze of desire still clung to her. Damn it, if she wanted him as much as he wanted her, what in hell was stopping them?

"This has not been my night," he muttered, then smiled wryly and stepped back. "But hey, you can't blame a guy for trying."

Anger and hurt spun through the swirl of her emotions and made him regret his words. But only for an instant. No matter how attracted he was to her, it could never amount to anything more than a fleeting moment or two of pleasure. It was too dangerous to want anything more.

She tore her gaze away and edged past him before retreating to the small table.

He sat back down on the bed. The farther away from her the better, he thought grimly. He was already aching with desire for her. The last thing he needed was to smell her perfume, the scent of her skin. To feel the close warmth of her body...

She cleared her throat, and he met her wary gaze. Her cheeks were still flushed, her mouth soft and inviting...

He smiled. One way or another, this was not going to be an easy night to get through. Particularly if the truth drug continued to linger in his system.

"You might not have had much luck finding Evan, but I did," she said quietly.

There was an endearing mix of wariness and pride in her expression. "Tell me how," he said. He knew she must have used her clairvoyant abilities, which was a big step for someone so afraid of her skills.

"I got tired of waiting," she said candidly, "and thought I'd try to find him."

He nodded. She met his gaze for a moment, then ran a trembling hand through the red gold tangle of her hair. Nerves, he thought, and wondered if it was her father who was responsible for making her so afraid of her gifts.

"He's in a place called Malkin Cabin. It's about fifteen miles from Jewell."

He didn't ask by which road, simply because she would have told him if she knew. It was a start, and certainly a whole lot more than he'd gotten. "Well done, Maddie."

A slight blush crept across her cheeks. She looked pleased and so very, very kissable. He cleared his throat and glanced at his watch. It was well after midnight. "Why don't we turn in for the night, and get an early start tomorrow? With any sort of luck, we'll find them quickly and get you all out of here."

Her gaze skittered across the beds and evaded his all together. "Would you like a coffee or something first?"

She was avoiding going to bed, avoiding any appearance of intimacy. "I won't pounce on you," he said with a wry smile.

He might want to, but he wouldn't. Self-control was one thing he'd learned all too well. "I'm a fast learner. No woman has to reject me twice."

Heat stained her cheeks again, and a hint of annoyance flashed through her eyes. Then she rose and walked across to her bag.

He watched her until she shut the bathroom door, then stripped and got into bed. He turned off the light, listening to the night and the wind whistle through the trees outside the window. A soothing sound, if it wasn't for the fact that he was a bare ten feet away from a woman he wanted and couldn't have.

After a long delay, she came out and climbed into bed. He didn't look at her, didn't need to. The smell of roses surrounded him, and her emotions filled his mind with color. He couldn't block her out, even if he had wanted to.

He crossed his arms behind his head and stared up at the ceiling. After a while, her breathing slowed, though something told him she wasn't asleep. He waited, wondering if she would ask the one question he feared.

"Jon?" she said softly into the silence.

"Hmmm?" This was it. And he had no choice but to answer her, whether or not he hurt her in the process.

"What do you really feel for me?"

I want you more than I've ever wanted a woman. I want you for more than just a night. But that was not the question she was asking.

"I don't know," he replied quietly. "I just don't know."

And that was what worried him the most.

Twelve

Jon waited until he heard the sound of the shower door closing then rose from the table and walked across to the phone.

The old witch answered straight away. "It's a bit early, cowboy. Don't you ever sleep?"

Not last night he hadn't. And he knew by the tone of Seline's voice that he hadn't woken her up. He smiled. In all the years he'd known her, she'd rarely seemed to sleep for more than a couple of hours a night. "I think we have a lead on the kids, Seline. If luck's with us, we'll have them out in a couple of hours."

"Don't depend on luck, Jon. It's a fickle friend."

"So I've discovered. Have we any records of shapeshifters living in this area?"

"None recorded, but that don't mean a damn. Most of your lot are a migratory bunch."

Most, but not all. Wolves and hawks tended to be more settled than most—probably because, like the animals whose shape they took, wolf and hawk shifters tended to mate for life. He glanced at the bathroom, then scrubbed a hand across his eyes.

"What did you find out about Hank Stewart?"

"Nothing much more than what's on file. He was born in St. Helens nearly sixty years ago—"

"And he barely looks thirty."

"—and he was an only child. Moved to Taurin Bay ten years ago. Lives by himself and rents a small house on Maxwell Street. Never married as far as I can find, and has no living relatives."

And obviously a loner or someone would have picked up

on the fact that the man was missing and someone else was using his name. "No unidentified bodies have been found in the area?"

"None yet. We're still sifting through police reports from various states."

Which could take days. They didn't have that much time—and in the end, it wouldn't make that much difference. "I've found our killer, Seline. I think she's using blood magic to extend her life and the life of her bodyguard—the man now masquerading as Hank Stewart."

"Anyone we know?"

"No. Her name is Eleanor Dumaresq, and I've a feeling she's seen more than a couple of centuries go by."

"Then wear the damn amulet I gave you. It will protect you from the worst of her spells." She hesitated, and an edge of concern crept into her voice. "Do you need help?"

His gaze went to the bathroom door again. Maddie kept insisting he couldn't cope with Eleanor and Hank alone, and maybe she was right. But he also knew there was no one in the Circle close enough to help him at the moment. "Mack's turned up in Taurin Bay. I'll use him if I have to."

"I have a feeling you *will* need him, cowboy. I suggest you call him now. And keep in touch."

"Will do." The tone of her voice told him her suggestion was more an order.

He hung up and glanced at his watch. Six o'clock. Mack should be awake by now. He punched the agent's number.

"Yes?" The gruff tone told him he'd been correct in his guess, but only just.

"Mack, Jon Barnett here."

"Really? What's wrong?"

The sarcastic edge to Mack's voice made him smile. "You asked me to call if I got any information. I'm doing so."

"Wonders never cease," Mack mused dryly. "What have you got?"

"I think you'd better check the background of a woman called Eleanor Dumaresq. She slipped a drug into my drink last night and tried to pump me for information. Might be worth finding out what happened to her late husband, as well as what properties he owned in the area besides the Sherbrook Inn."

"You think she's involved with the missing kids?"

"I think it's likely, but I've no evidence to prove it at this point."

"We'll keep an eye on her." Mack hesitated, and Jon could almost hear the mental gears shifting up a notch. "Heard there was a fire at the inn last night."

The big man's voice was neutral. *He knows,* Jon thought. "Really?"

"A young woman fitting the description of Madeline Smith was rescued by a man remarkably similar to yourself."

"I wasn't staying at the inn last night."

"Maybe not. But I checked the register, and a Madeline Smith was."

Jon swore under his breath. He'd forgotten about the register.

Mack continued on. "And two nights ago, you were also registered at the inn—and staying in the same room."

Jon ran a hand through his hair. He'd better give Mack some information, or he'd haul the two of them in to the station for questioning. Another delay was not what they needed right now.

"She's not involved with the kid's disappearance. She's trying to find him."

"Then why disappear?"

"She's a psychic. And from what I can gather, she has a somewhat strained relationship with the kid's father."

"And a somewhat strained relationship with the police, too. The kid's father isn't the only one convinced that she's responsible for her husband's death."

Husband? Maddie had been *married?* Jon swore softly. "What was the official reason given for his death?"

"Died in a fire."

Jon closed his eyes. It explained so much—her fear, her need to retreat. He wondered if she'd loved the man she'd married and killed. Wondered if the fire had been a mistake, or intentional.

"Mack, I need her help. Can you keep everyone off our backs for a couple of days?"

"I could—if you agree to let me know when you discover any new information."

"Agreed." *When* he'd let the agent know was an entirely different matter. Despite Seline's warning, he didn't want to bring Mack in just yet. The FBI agent wanted the justice system to take care of Eleanor and Hank, and that simply wasn't an option. Justice wouldn't understand the likes of Eleanor, and it certainly wouldn't be able to hold her.

Only death could do that.

"Good," Mack growled. "I'll be in touch."

Jon hung up. At least now they could move around without having to worry about the police spotting Maddie. He frowned and leaned a shoulder against the wall, staring at the bathroom door. Now all he had to do was convince her that the intensity of their kiss had been nothing more than a result of the drug. That it had meant nothing to him, as she meant nothing to him.

After the attack on her last night, it was obvious both Eleanor and Hank suspected she was working with him. The longer she stayed in Taurin Bay, the greater the danger to her life.

Acting cold hadn't succeeded in driving her away so far, but he had a suspicion it would eventually. Something in her eyes told him it brought back memories of a past she'd much rather forget. Maybe those memories were of a husband she'd feared enough to kill.

He pushed away from the wall and moved back to the table. Before he did anything else today, he had get back to his truck and the weapons stashed there. After last night, Eleanor would be waiting for his next move. He had no intention of walking into a fight without the means of protecting Maddie.

***

Maddie tilted her face up to the showerhead and let the spray massage her skin. She was a fool—a fool to kiss Jon, and a fool to ask that damn question.

And what had she really expected him to say? If she wasn't certain of her own emotions, why should she expect him to be any different? They were strangers thrown into a dangerous situation by chance. When it was over, and Evan was safe, they would go their separate ways. Why would she ever expect anything more?

Because when I'm with him it almost seems as if I've found the other half of myself. She closed her eyes and turned her back to the spray. Maybe she felt so attracted to the man simply because he seemed to understand. For the first time in her life, she'd found someone who didn't mock or belittle her abilities. Only death had stopped Brian's viciousness.

Memories rose unbidden. She clenched her fists and tried to stop them—to no avail. Once again she felt the pain of Brian's fists smashing into her body, her face. Felt fire burn uncontrolled through her body. Heard his laughter turn to screams as the flames engulfed him.

She shuddered and leaned her forehead against the shower wall. In the worst of her dreams, she could still see him burn, could see his flesh blacken and peel away, smell his death in every pore of her skin. In reality, though, she'd run the minute he'd let her go. She'd never seen him die, hadn't wanted to, despite everything he'd done to her. But neither had she called for help, not until she knew he was well and truly dead.

I've killed, and I'm still a risk, because I can't control my abilities. That she'd managed to control those same abilities long enough to see the location of the cabin in which Evan was a prisoner meant nothing. They might help save Evan, but it would never really ease the weight of guilt.

It was all very well for Jon to suggest she find help, but what if it was too late to make any true difference now? What if her firestarting had grown so wild it could never be truly contained?

It wasn't a risk she was willing to take. It was safer to stay alone—and lonely. At least then she could kill no one but herself.

If only Jon's kiss hadn't stolen her breath and her heart

and made her want him more than she'd ever wanted anything
in her life.

If only she didn't have to face him this morning and
pretend that nothing out of the ordinary had happened.

She sighed and stepped out of the shower. Maybe they'd
get lucky and find Evan and the other teenager this morning.
Then she could leave before she did something foolish.

Like admit her feelings to a man who just didn't care.

She dressed quickly and ran a comb through the thick
tangle of her hair. Then she took a deep breath and eyed her
reflection in the mirror. The woman looking back had dark
rings under her eyes and a figure well hidden by a loose, vibrant
green sweater. Not her most attractive outfit, which was
probably just as well. If he gave her one of his heated looks of
last night, she might just melt.

Only he didn't even bother looking up from the newspaper
he was reading when she walked out of the bathroom.

So much for worrying about any lingering tension, she
thought with a scowl. She sat down at the table. Maybe all the
heat had been little more than a fallout from the drug—at least
on his part. Maybe he couldn't even remember it.

"Eat up," he said, picking up the coffeepot and pouring
her a cup. "It'll be light soon, and we don't want to waste too
much time, in case they move the kids."

She picked up the coffee to warm her hands and looked at
the toast and cereal. She suddenly didn't feel hungry any more.
But she picked up some cold toast and ate it anyway.

He only looked up when she'd finished, and there was
nothing but polite interest in his face. "Ready to go?" he asked,
pulling his gaze away from hers.

But not before she'd seen the shadows under his eyes.
Maybe he hadn't slept as soundly as she'd first thought.

She rose and collected her purse and keys. "Can we take
your truck? That way I can study the map and look for the
place I saw last night."

He hesitated. "It's still parked near the inn. I walked to
the restaurant to meet Eleanor, remember?"

"Oh." She frowned, not wanting to think about him and

Eleanor. Even if he hadn't succeeded in seducing her, the thought of them together still churned her stomach. "It's just that I'm worried about my brakes—they're not really safe at the moment, especially if it rains, as they're predicting."

"The inn's not that far away, Maddie. We can walk there, or catch a cab."

"What about Hank? And Eleanor?"

"With an inn full of guests to guest to worry about, and the clean up after the fire, I doubt they'll be spending too much time staring out windows. Besides, it's parked on a side street."

There was more than a hint of sarcasm in his voice. She crossed her arms and glared at him. "I was only asking a simple question."

"And I was answering. What do you want to do?"

"Walk. The sun is out." And she didn't have enough spare cash for another cab ride.

"Are you going to be warm enough in that old coat of yours?" he asked, following her out the door.

She glanced up. The sun might be out, but it didn't look as if it would hold for long. Dark clouds were racing across the sky, and the wind was ice-cold. She shivered and quickly zipped her coat. It barely kept out the wind's chill. Against heavy rain, it would be useless. But she'd be damned if she'd admit it. Not when she wanted to be seen as a useful member of this partnership rather than a burden.

"I'll be fine."

He made a sound suspiciously like a snort of disbelief and slammed the door closed.

She ignored him and marched up the street. He was beside her almost instantly, his stride long and loose, arm casually brushing against hers when he shoved his hands into his coat pockets. They walked in silence for several long minutes, but she was very aware of him watching her.

"I think we need to talk about last night," he said softly.

Last night was a nightmare she'd rather forget, as he was no doubt about to tell her to do. "Don't worry," she said, her voice holding an edge of annoyance she just couldn't help. "I know you were drugged. I took advantage of it, and I'm sorry."

He lightly touched her elbow, guiding her across the street.

"That's not what I was talking about."

Heat flushed her cheeks. She knew exactly what he was talking about. Pulling away from his hand, she strode on, keeping her gaze well away from him.

"I realize what happened between us was just a result of the drug, nothing more."

He didn't answer straight away. Almost against her will, she found her gaze drawn to his. There was a hint of wry amusement in his smile that just didn't make sense.

"Took the words right out of my mouth," he murmured, then grabbed her arm, lightly pulling her sideways. "Dog shit," he explained when she glanced at him. "Not a smell I recommend in the confines of a truck cabin."

"Thanks," she muttered, and once again pulled her arm from his grasp. It felt too good, too comforting.

Too *intimate*.

They walked on in silence. Ten minutes later they reached his truck. Jon opened the door for her. She climbed in, carefully avoiding his touch and his gaze, then reached for the road map shoved down the side of the seat.

"Head up the freeway. According to this, the turn off to Jewell is about twenty miles out of Taurin Bay."

He nodded as he drove off. "When we find this cabin, I want you to stay in the truck—with the doors locked."

"No." She crossed her arms and stared out the window. She felt his annoyed gaze flicker over her.

"Maddie, we have no idea who will be in the cabin with the kids. It's safer if you stay here."

His voice held a barely controlled edge of impatience. She ignored it and shook her head. "You can't handle both Hank and Eleanor alone."

"You only saw Hank last night."

Last night seemed little more than a bad dream. Suddenly weary, she pushed her hair back from her face. "Eleanor has had plenty of time to get there, you know."

"I know."

His answer seemed ground out between clenched teeth, as if he didn't like to be reminded of it. She glanced across at him. Dark stubble lined his cheek, and tiny crows' feet edged the corners of his eyes. He looked tired. And worried.

"They've had plenty of time to arrange a trap."

"They don't know we're coming," he replied reasonably.

Too reasonably. Tension surrounded him, edged with anger.

"After last night, they'd suspect the worst. They'd plan ahead." She watched his fingers flex against the steering wheel and knew she was sitting next to a volcano ready to explode.

How often did he come this close to losing control of his emotions? Last night she'd thought he'd been just as surprised by the passion of their kiss as she, but now that she'd had a chance to think about it, maybe he was more surprised over the fact that he *had* lost control.

I need you, he said. The words made her heart tremble, even now. She had a feeling that he rarely admitted to needing anything—or anyone—even for something as basic as sex.

They passed a road sign, and she glanced down at the map to check their position. Her stomach tightened. They were close.

"We're almost there." She glanced at him. There was no mistaking the worry she saw in his blue eyes this time. Her heart did an uneven little jig.

"I can't let you go in alone," she continued, and glanced out the side window. "And I won't run, no matter what you do or say."

"And I can't let you endanger yourself needlessly."

She met his gaze and steeled her heart against the brief flash of emotion she saw deep in the bright depths of his eyes.

"What are you going to do—hit me? Knock me unconscious, too?"

"Don't be damn ridiculous. You know I could never do anything like that to you."

"I know nothing of the sort. We're partners, nothing more. Remember?" She paused and watched the chill steal through his eyes. "You have no right to stop me from doing this." *No right to act as if you care, when we both know you don't.*

He didn't reply. She returned her gaze to the side window and watched the scenery grow ever familiar. Her fingers clenched, crushing the map. This was it. This was the area. Her dream had been true.

"Slow down," she whispered, her throat dry with fear.

He did, pulling off the road slightly. After a few minutes a letterbox came into view. *Malkin cabin* was painted on the side in big bold letters. Jon stopped the truck.

"How far up the road is the cabin?" he said, leaning his forearms against the wheel.

She studied the muddy track. It showed no sign of recent disturbance. Hank was still up there, then. She swallowed. "A fair way up. It was a bit hard to tell."

He nodded. "Any place to hide the truck before we get there?"

She sifted through the images in her mind. "There's a pine grove about halfway up."

"Good. That's where we'll park."

He switched to four-wheel drive, then drove forward. The truck pitched and jerked, almost tossing them into the line of trees crowding the edges of the track. She held onto her seat and hoped they didn't meet Hank or Eleanor coming back down the mountain. There was no room to maneuver, no room to turn and run on such a narrow road.

They reached the beginnings of the pine grove. Jon drove the truck in deep, until there was nothing to see but the greyish-brown trunks of the pines, then stopped.

She undid her seat belt and reached for the door handle. He touched her thigh. Warmth leapt through her leg, through her soul. She licked her lips nervously but didn't move.

"Maddie, stay here. Please."

Her gaze met his. Something shivered deep inside her. "I can't," she whispered. *I don't want anyone else to die because of me.* "Evan's my nephew, and my responsibility." She hesitated, then added, "I can look after myself."

"If that's what you want, fine," he muttered and let her go.

She climbed out of the truck. The wind shivered through the trees, its touch like ice as it whispered around her. She hastily zipped up her coat and shoved her hands into the pockets. Should have bought gloves, she thought. Jon spent several minutes at the back of the truck, then walked up behind her.

"Stay behind me," he said shortly. "And if I say run, you run. Right?"

Running was the one thing she was very good at—and something she'd sworn to stop doing. She stared at the bleakness in his eyes, then nodded wearily.

"Good. Follow me quickly, but quietly."

The ground was a thick carpet of needles, and the silence through the trees absolute. She kept close to his heels, not wanting to lose him in the dusky green light that filtered through the pines.

The ground became steeper, rockier. Moisture dripped slowly from the branches above, splattering around them. She glanced at the green twilight above them and hoped it wasn't raining. Her foot slipped out from underneath her, and she came down hard on one knee. She hissed in pain and blinked back tears.

"You okay?"

She glanced up. He was standing on top of a small ridge, no emotion in his expression. Though his hands, shoved deep into his jacket pockets, looked clenched.

"Yes," she muttered, and knew the answer would have been the same even if she'd broken her leg.

"Then get up. We haven't much time to play with."

He was back to being a bastard. She pushed upright. Her knee protested vehemently, and she bit her lip. *I don't need your help* she'd said in the truck only moments before. And she'd be damned before she'd ask for it so soon.

Limping slightly, she followed him up the hill. He stopped when they reached a ridge and silently pointed downwards. A small valley was visible through the pines below them. The cabin lay nestled in the middle of the clearing, smoke drifting lazily from the chimney.

Her stomach clenched. They were so close to rescuing Evan. "Wonder if Hank's still there?" she said softly.

"Hard to tell. I can't see any cars, but they might be parked around the back."

"What's the plan, then?"

He gave her a hard-edged look. "You stay here while I look around and see if it's safe."

"I thought we'd already argued about this? I won't be left behind."

"Maddie, be sensible." He touched her cheek, his hand warm against her cold skin. "I'm a shapeshifter—and I have the senses of a hawk. I'll call you down once I know it's safe. Just trust me, and wait."

As much as she hated to admit it, what he said made sense. Hank was down there. She was positive of that much. And despite her brave words, it was an inescapable fact that she'd rather face an army of Eleanors than one Hank. Which was odd, considering Jon thought Eleanor to be the more dangerous of the two. She swallowed heavily and nodded.

His hand lingered a moment longer, his gaze dark with some indefinable emotion. "Here, take this for me." He tugged the ring off his finger and pressed it into her palm. "It's my father's, and I don't want to risk losing it."

A shiver of alarm ran through her. She frowned and glanced down at the ring. "Why would you lose it?"

"It's made of silver and won't shift shape with me." He stepped away, and his eyes became hard again.

"I'll be back in a moment," he continued, and turned, making his way down through the trees.

She slipped the ring onto her middle finger and watched him until he'd become one with the shadows. The silence slowly became stifling and seemed to hold an edge of expectancy. She shifted uneasily, her gaze darting through the trees. Though she'd heard no sound, she suddenly felt as if someone was watching her. She glanced back at the cabin and saw Jon move through the shadows crowding the porch. He hesitated at the far corner, then slowly edged around out of her line of sight.

A twig snapped softly behind her.

She spun. Dust danced through the odd, soft-green light, stirred to life in the wake of something passing. Had that something been human or animal—or something in between?

She glanced over her shoulder. There was still no sign of Jon—maybe he'd entered the cabin. She shifted her weight from one foot to the other, then crossed her arms. If he didn't hurry up, he'd find her down there with him, whether he liked it or not.

Another twig snapped. She jumped, staring at the silent line of pine trees. A shadow stirred. Her stomach flip-flopped, and she licked suddenly dry lips.

Something was moving—and she had no intention of hanging around to see what it was.

She headed down the hill. Brush rustled to her left, then something small and brown darted out near her feet. She bit back a yelp and jumped away, her heart thumping loud enough to wake the dead.

The furry form scurried off through the trees. A rabbit, she thought in relief. She wiped the sweat from her forehead and grinned at her own foolishness. Thank heavens Jon wasn't around to see her so jumpy.

She studied the cabin for a moment, then continued on down the hill. Surely he wouldn't object to her moving down to the edge of the pines?

Something snapped to her left, and her heart rate leapt again. She hesitated, then saw the rabbit stand up straight and stare at her.

"Pest," she muttered, and ran her hand through her hair. At this rate, she'd be gray by the time she got down to the cabin.

"I do hope you're talking about the rabbit, my dear."

She spun, her heart in her mouth and a scream caught somewhere in her throat.

Hank stepped out the shadows, brown eyes gleaming with triumphant malice. "I rather object to being called a pest. I try to be so much more."

Maddie backed away. She tried to scream again, tried to

warn Jon, but no sound came out of her fear-frozen throat. She spun, but Hank jumped forward and caught her arm. His fingers dug down deep into her flesh and jerked her backwards.

"Don't run. I have so much fun planned for us this afternoon," he said, then leaned forward, brushing a kiss across her right ear.

She shuddered and swung her fist. He caught it with his free hand and laughed. It was a hollow, cruel sound.

Images of Brian flooded her mind. She had a feeling Hank's idea of fun was very similar to her ex-husband's. Force was something that seemed to excite some men. Panic stirred the embers in her soul to life, burning through her veins. She kicked out, struggling against his grip. No matter how evil Hank was, she didn't really want to be responsible for his death. If she didn't get away, she just might be.

Something cold and hard touched her throat. "Stop fighting," he warned. "Or I'll cut your pretty throat."

He smelled of sweat and dirt and death, and bile rose in her throat. She swallowed heavily. Being sick would not help her cause right now—though the thought of vomiting over Hank was certainly appealing.

"Let me go," she pleaded softly. The fires burned brighter, heating her skin. She clenched her fist, desperate to keep them under control. She couldn't kill Hank. He might hold the clue to Evan's whereabouts if the teenager wasn't in the cabin.

Hank laughed, a soft sound that sent chills running up her spine, then clamped a callused hand over her mouth.

"Can't do that, sweetheart. But hey, why don't we go down and surprise the boyfriend?"

***

The only sound to be heard was the wind whispering through the trees, yet something felt out of place. There was an edge of expectancy to the silence that worried Jon.

He frowned and edged around the corner of the cabin. Hank's old car was parked a few yards away. He ducked past the window and touched the hood. It was cold; the car hadn't been driven in the last few hours. He quickly scanned the trees. Hank wasn't inside the cabin, so he had to be out in the forest somewhere. Worry snaked through his gut. Maddie might think she could take care of herself, but against the likes of Hank, she wouldn't stand a chance.

He took a step towards the trees then stopped and clenched his fists. This might be the only chance he got to rescue the teenagers—if they were in the cabin as Maddie predicted.

He swore softly, then moved back to the window and looked inside. The cabin was small and sparsely furnished. On the side closest to the fire were two chairs and a sofa. A box full of canned food sat underneath the table in the center of the room, and on the far side of this, an uneven clump of blankets.

He reached into his boot and dug out a knife. Slipping it into the small gap between the window and the frame, he forced the catch open.

After a quick look at the trees to ensure he was still alone, he climbed inside. Heat assaulted him. It was hot, stifling hot, in the cabin. Did Hank prefer it like this, or was the heat some weird requirement for the lead up to their ceremony?

There's too much we don't know, he thought with a grimace. He shoved the knife back in his boot, then walked across to the blankets. Kneeling down, he flipped away one edge. Red hair gleamed at him. Evan. The other teenager, a girl with brown hair, lay quietly beside him.

He felt for a pulse. Both were alive, though obviously drugged. All he had to do was get them out of here.

He studied the room for a moment. He couldn't risk using the door. It was the only entrance and likely to be alarmed, especially given that Hank was wandering around outside somewhere. Which left the window he'd forced open.

He wrapped Evan in several blankets and carefully lifted him. The kid was light, considering how long he was. Built slender like his aunt, Jon thought, and felt a pang of anxiety run through his soul. He had to get back to Maddie—something told him she needed him.

He slid the teenager through the window, lowering him carefully to the ground before climbing out after him. The wind moaned lightly through the pines. Tension ran through him. Something was definitely very wrong.

He scanned the hillside. Every sense told him Hank was near and closing in, that he didn't have the time to make one trip up the hill to Maddie, let alone two. The teenagers' safety had to be his first priority. And if Hank was closing in on *him,* he certainly had no desire to lead the fiend back up to Maddie.

Jon studied the pines a moment longer, noticing a ridge of rocks to his left. Maybe there was a cave or something nearby. He picked up Evan and ran across the clearing, following the ridge deep into the pine forest. Several minutes later he found what he was looking for—a shallow cave, half hidden by bushes. Certainly not good enough to conceal the teenager from Eleanor, especially if she was hunting in her cat form, but secure enough from the likes of Hank.

He hid the teenager, then used a tree branch to erase any sign of footprints before quickly returning to the cabin. There was still no sign of movement as he climbed back through the window. Maybe, just maybe, luck was with him.

He bent next to the second teenager and wrapped the blankets around her.

"Shapeshifter!" Hank's harsh voice grated across the silence.

Jon cursed softly under his breath but didn't answer. Maybe Hank would believe he wasn't there.

"I know you're here, Shapeshifter. Come out."

He swore again. Five minutes more, that was all he'd needed. Five lousy minutes.

"If you don't want to see your girlfriend's pretty neck sliced open, I suggest you come out real soon."

For a moment, Jon froze. Maybe Hank was bluffing...

"She's bleeding as you wait, Shapeshifter."

Rage rose, so deep and powerful it shook him to the core. Maybe he wasn't as uncertain of his feelings for Maddie as he'd first thought.

He took a deep breath, then quickly rearranged the blankets to make it look like there were still two bodies carefully wrapped inside. Maddie's chances of survival now depended on making Hank believe he hadn't had the chance to rescue the teenagers. He moved back to the window and climbed out, then slid it shut and walked around the far end of the building.

"What do you want?" he said, turning the corner.

Hank stood in the middle of the clearing, a knife held to Maddie's neck. Even from where he stood Jon could see the slight trickle of blood down her throat.

His gaze met hers. Deep in the amber depths of her frightened gaze he saw the fires burning. She was close to losing control, and if she did, she'd kill not only Hank, but also herself.

Jon sensed she wouldn't mind that death, and the thought made his gut clench.

Hank's smile was slick and victorious, but the relief in the fiend's eyes was unmistakable. Maybe, just maybe, his bluff had worked.

"What I want, Shapeshifter, is you dead."

Jon flexed his fingers. "Then why don't you release Maddie and attempt to make your wish come true?"

Hank grinned. "I'm not that foolish, Shifter. I've seen your type fight before. Until I get a better weapon, I'll settle for you leaving this area and not coming back."

Jon kept his gaze on Maddie, watching her struggle for control. If she lost, he'd have to move quickly to stop the fires from consuming her too. If he *could* stop them.

"And what about Maddie?"

Hank grinned, a lizard enjoying its brief time in the sun. "She's my insurance against your return."

Hank obviously didn't suspect Evan was gone, or he wouldn't have been so keen to get rid of him before he'd gotten the teenager back. If Jon left now, he could still ensure the teenager's safety. And that, he thought, studying Maddie's frightened eyes, was all she'd care about.

"Then you'd better take real good care of her, hadn't you?" he suggested softly. "Because your insurance will only work for as long as she lives."

Hank's smile faded, and his knuckles went white against the knife. Maddie gasped slightly, and another trickle of blood ran down her neck. *Leave,* her eyes seemed to plead, *leave and be safe.*

He had no other choice. He couldn't risk any sort of attack with the knife held so closely to her neck—and he had to get Evan to safety. She'd never forgive him if something happened to her nephew now that he was so close to freedom.

He caught her gaze again. "Don't do anything foolish," he warned softly. *Just hold on until I can get some help.*

Hank merely smiled. "I hold your queen, Shapeshifter, so don't dare threaten me."

"That wasn't a threat, my friend," he said softly and leapt skywards on gold-brown wings.

Thirteen

Maddie watched the hawk until it disappeared from sight. Maybe because of all the old werewolf movies she'd watched over the years, she'd half expected his shapeshifting to be an event of both power and pain. It was powerful, yes, but also very beautiful.

"First time you've seen him change, huh?" Hank whispered into her ear. "Exciting, isn't it?"

She was all too aware of the exact state of Hank's excitement—and of the growing tremble in the hand that held the knife so close to her throat. The fires flared brighter within her soul. She bit her lip, desperate to keep them under control.

Don't do anything foolish, Jon had warned her. Don't lose control is what he'd meant.

"Why don't we move on inside?" Hank continued. "I have a pain that needs to be eased. Maybe you can help me."

A chill ran through her. If Hank tried to touch her, she'd surely lose control and kill them both.

He nudged her forward. The knife was a thin line of heat against her neck. If she so much as stumbled, she would die.

And despite everything, she knew she really didn't want to die. There was so much of life she'd yet to experience.

Like love.

She clenched her fists and felt Jon's ring bite into her palm. He'd given her something of his to hold on to, something he seemed to value more than life. Something he'd come back for. All she had to do was hang on and wait.

After all, Hank couldn't do much to her that her husband hadn't already done.

She edged up the steps, hissing slightly when the knife bit into her neck. Blood trickled down her throat. Hank chuckled, his breath hot and unsteady near her ear.

They reached the door. Hank kicked it open. A bell chimed harshly above them, jarring against her already taunt nerves. He pushed her through, then quickly drew her back against him while he closed the door. The knife nicked into her throat again. She bit her lip and fought the sting of tears. The last thing she wanted was to give Hank the satisfaction of seeing her cry. He was probably the type who'd enjoy it—just as Brian had.

But at least Brian was dead, and no longer able to hurt her.

Shoving the thought from her mind, she squinted, hoping to see Evan and the other teenager in the fire-lit darkness.

Two long bundles of blankets lay in the far corner of the room. She hoped it was the two of them—and that they were still alive.

Hank moved the knife away from her neck, but she didn't relax. He still held the knife close enough to use it should she move the wrong way.

"Why don't you go sit down while I tend to the fire." He gave her a hard shove in the direction of the sofa. "It's gotten a might cool in here."

She stumbled forward, then caught sight of the window near the back of the cabin. If he turned away long enough...she edged sideways.

"Don't event think about it, sweetheart."

She froze. Hank's dark gaze gleamed viciously as he grabbed her arm and forced her down onto the sofa.

"You know, up until today I wasn't entirely sure if you were involved with the shapeshifter." He sat down beside her. "And I still don't entirely understand why you are."

She watched his fingers lightly tap the cushions that separated them. If that hand moved any closer to her thigh, she was running, knife or no knife. "As you said yourself, he's a charmer."

His smile gleamed briefly. "We both know he's not your type, sweetheart."

"He's not Eleanor's type either, but she didn't seem to

mind."

Anger darkened his eyes, and Maddie bit her lip. She sure could pick the perfect moment to start answering back.

"No, she doesn't," he growled softly. He grabbed her wrist, squeezing it tight. "Hell then, what's good enough for the goose is good enough for the gander."

He yanked her toward him. She thrust her hand into his face, desperate to keep his lips from hers. Fire leapt up through her body, running heat through her veins. But the heat of it told her if she did release her fire, she'd kill not only Hank, but herself and the teenagers as well.

And if he didn't stop soon, the choice might be taken from her.

"What the hell do you think you're doing, Hank?"

Eleanor's voice sliced through the room. Hank flung Maddie away and scrambled to his feet. She edged as far away from him as was practical on the sofa.

"Just having myself a little fun." Though his tone was defiant, there was no escaping the hint of fear in his stance. Just as Jon had guessed, Eleanor was the power behind everything.

Maddie studied her. She stood in the doorway, a shadow outlined by sunlight. You didn't need to see her face or her eyes to taste the evil in her soul. It wrapped around her as closely as the coat she wore.

She licked her lips and hoped that Eleanor, like Hank, saw her as a form of insurance against Jon. Otherwise, she was dead. Eleanor would have no qualms about killing her. She was certain of that much, if nothing else.

The heat in the room leapt several notches. She clenched her fists and felt the cool silver of Jon's ring bite into her skin. Its touch seemed to calm the fires somehow. Not much, but enough.

Eleanor stepped into the room and slammed the door shut. The look she gave Maddie was that of a cat about to devour a mouse. Appropriate, she thought with a shiver, considering Eleanor's other shape.

"What is *she* doing here?" Eleanor all but snarled.

"The shapeshifter was sniffing around here. I used her to ensure he left."

Eleanor shrugged eloquently, her gaze running past them. "So why keep her? Get rid of her."

Maddie edged forward, getting ready to fight. Even if it meant letting the fires loose and killing them all.

Hank's gaze met hers, and she stilled. Something in his eyes warned her not to move. Her gaze dropped to the knife he still held in one hand. Her blood was a small dark stain across its blade. "It could so easily be more," his eyes seemed to warn, "if you try anything."

"She's insurance against his return, Lennie," he said. "Through her, we can control him. At least until the ceremony."

Maddie stared at him. Lennie. That's what he'd called the cat at the inn. Did Eleanor have more than one shape?

"He can't touch us, anyway. He's nothing but a weak fool-" Eleanor hesitated, then stiffened. "Where the hell is the second kid?"

Hank jerked around, staring at the bundles in the corner. "What do you mean?"

Eleanor strode across the room and flipped the blanket away from the teenager's face. It wasn't Evan, Maddie thought with a sudden sense of joy. Jon must have gotten him out of the cabin somehow.

"Where's the other kid, Hank? What in hell have you done?"

Hank swung his fist, connecting with Maddie's chin before she had time to react. The force of the punch threw her backwards, over the arm of the sofa and onto the floor. Her head smacked against something hard, and a kaleidoscope of color rushed past her eyes.

Hank leapt forward and grabbed her coat. He drew her upwards, so she was close to his face and his stinking breath. "You will tell me what you've done with the kid," he said menacingly.

He looks old, she thought weakly. Old and frightened. His mouth moved again, but his voice seemed to be coming from a great distance, almost drowned out by the roaring in her ears.

He shook her so hard it felt as if her teeth were rattling. His eyes were dark pools that promised death. "Tell me," he repeated, his voice suddenly a roar that reverberated through her brain.

I can't, she wanted to say, *because I just don't know.* And she smiled as the darkness rushed through her mind and took the words away.

***

Jon glanced at his watch for what seemed like the thousandth time. Nearly two hours had passed since he'd left Maddie in Hank's clutches. It seemed like an eternity.

He thumped his hand against the wall, then stared out the window, watching the rain dance across the pavement. There was nothing more he could do just yet but wait. He had to ensure Evan's safety before he did anything else.

He glanced toward the bed. The teenager was still in a drugged sleep, but in the last ten minutes he had at least shown some sign of stirring. But the process of waking was taking entirely too long.

Jon shifted his stance impatiently, then studied the white mark around his ring finger. He still had no idea why he'd given Maddie his father's ring. Granted, he didn't want to lose it, but he'd made the change with the ring on his finger before and had just scooped it up in his talons and taken it with him. So why give it to her when he'd sworn never to give it to any woman, except the one he loved?

Because it's something of me she can hold on to. It's all I can give her, all that I'm free to give.

The thought shook him. But what shook him more was the sudden, desperate need to have her close, to hold on tight and never let her go.

His father had once told him a hunter only gave his heart once, to one special lady. Well, he'd long ago dedicated his heart and his soul to his work. There was no room for anything else. No room to worry about anyone else. He just couldn't afford any sort of entanglements in his work.

Wasn't that why he'd cut himself off from his family so

long ago, why he continued to rebuff their efforts to talk to
him, to understand why he'd become such a stranger? It was
safer that way—if he had no one to love, he had no one to
become a target for his many enemies.

At least now that Evan was safe, Maddie could leave the
area, go home and be safe, as she'd wanted all along. And he
could get on with the job of apprehending Eleanor and Hank
without having to worry about her.

There was a slight rustle of blankets from the bed. Jon
turned and met the teenager's wide eyes—eyes that were same
warm amber as Maddie's.

Finally, he thought, and forced a smile. "You're safe, Evan.
There's no need to worry."

The kid blinked, still wide-eyed, and yet curiously not
afraid. "I know you," he said in a voice that was little more
than a cracked whisper.

Jon raised his eyebrows. "I doubt it-"

"No," Evan cut in. "You were in my dreams. I saw you. I
sent you to Aunt Maddie."

He remembered the force that had drawn him to Maddie.
He'd known it was somehow connected to her, but up until
now, hadn't even thought about it being Evan himself. Psychic
abilities obviously ran in the family—did Maddie know? Was
that why she was so close to Evan?

He smiled to relieve the suddenly anxious look on the
kid's face. "Yes, you did, and we got you out."

"But where's Aunt Maddie now?" Evan sat straight up in
bed, his face white with fear.

Jon wondered if it was the normal anxiety of a kidnapped
kid wanting to be safe in the arms of his family, or the fear of
a psychic who knows a loved one is in terrible danger.

What in hell is happening to her? He swallowed a sudden
rush of tension and walked across the room. Kneeling next
the bed, he placed a calming hand on the kid's shoulder—
even though calm was the last thing he felt himself. "She isn't
here. I have to go get her, as soon as we have some protection
for you."

Evan stared at him, his amber eyes dark with fear. So like

Maddie's, Jon thought, and knew he'd have to move soon, before the wait drove him mad.

"They have her," Evan whispered. "They'll hurt her."

If they did, they'd pay. He forced a smile, even though Evan was smart enough to see past it.

"I'll bring her back. I promise."

Evan stared at him, then solemnly nodded. A sharp knock at the door rattled the silence, making the kid jump. Jon squeezed his shoulder and went quickly to the window. Mack and a bear of a man in a police uniform stood out front.

The teenager had huddled back down in the blankets when he glanced back. "It's okay. Just the police," he said, unlocking the door.

"This better be good, Barnett," Mack stated, dripping water onto the old carpet as he stomped past. "I *was* enjoying a mighty fine lunch."

Jon closed the door once the second man had come through. He knew they wouldn't have been here if Mack had the slightest suspicion of being led on some wild goose chase.

"Mack, meet Evan. Evan, Mack's trying to help the police. Why don't you tell him what you know about the people who took you."

Evan licked his lips, glancing quickly at the big man before looking back at Jon. "He's okay?"

Jon smiled at Mack's raised eyebrow, then nodded. It was odd that Evan seemed to trust him, even though they barely knew each other. But then, the kid had not only reached him when he was stuck down the well, but had guided his astral travels towards Maddie, as well. Maybe there was some form of psychic connection between him and the teenager. He'd learned long ago that anything was possible.

He crossed his arms and leaned back against the wall, listening to the harsh rasp of the kid's voice. As anxious as he was to rescue Maddie, there was nothing to be done until Evan had told his story. The last thing he wanted was to rescue Maddie from Hank's grip only to have her fall into Mack's. At least this way she'd be free to go.

Mack glanced at him once the kid had finished. "Then

you were right about Eleanor Dumaresq."

Jon nodded. "Did you find out if she or her ex-husband owns any other properties in the area?" If Hank moved Maddie and the remaining kid, the information might just give them a chance of finding them quickly.

"Besides the inn and the house on sixth, nothing. But I'm checking for aliases, just in case she has a history with us." He stopped and glared at Jon for several minutes. "You realize, of course, I should haul your ass down to the station and charge you for impeding an investigation."

Jon grimaced. "Maddie's psychic talents are somewhat raw. I wasn't going to waste your time until I knew for certain we'd found the right place." He hesitated, then added softly, "There's one other problem, Mack. They took Maddie hostage when I was getting Evan out."

"Isn't that just great." Mack's gray eyes were hard with anger. "You haul a civilian into a crime investigation and end up losing her. Real smart move, Barnett."

He ran a hand across his mouth. What Mack said was true. If he'd made her stay here, as gut instinct had told him to do, she'd now be safe. But he'd given in to the plea in her eyes, and now she was paying for his weakness.

"Where's the damn cabin?" Mack continued roughly.

"The place is called Malkin cabin. It's off 202, about fifteen miles out of Jewell."

"Is there a chance that they're still there?"

He shrugged. Hank wasn't a fool, but there was always the chance he couldn't move quickly. It would depend on the type of ceremony Eleanor was preparing. "Maybe."

Mack shook his head and looked across at the police officer. "Better get those descriptions out right away." As the man rose and moved to the door, the agent's gaze came back to Jon. "You and I *will* sit down and have a serious talk after all this is over."

He nodded. Mack had to catch him first. "If we move now, we might still find them."

He watched the FBI agent stalk to the door, then pushed away from the wall and walked across to the bed.

Evan stared up at him, eyes wide and full of a fearful desperation. "You have to go now. Aunt Maddie needs you."

He squeezed the kid's shoulder again. "I made you a promise. I'll bring her back."

Or die trying, he thought bleakly, and turned away.

Fourteen

Mack glanced up as Jon walked out the door. "Jerry's staying with the kid, and I've organized local help. I'll meet them up near the cabin."

Jon pulled up his coat collar to stop the rain from dribbling down his neck. "I'm coming with you."

Mack studied him for a moment, gray eyes hard. "Give me one good reason why you should."

"Eleanor's a sorcerer." He gave Mack a bland smile. "I know magic. You don't."

It was hard to tell whether Mack believed him or not, simply because there was no reaction from the man. But after a second of silence, he nodded. "Get in."

Mack climbed in and started the engine. Jon got into the passenger side and glanced at his watch. Two and a half hours gone. Maddie and Hank could be anywhere by now.

"Anyone would think from your behavior that you cared for this woman," Mack commented. The rear tires squealed as the car sped off.

Jon smiled grimly. "I barely know her." Which was both the truth and a lie. He probably understood Maddie better than he understood himself. And he sure as hell liked her more than he liked himself.

Mack lit a cigarette and took a long puff. "That's not what I meant," he said, exhaling.

Jon glanced across at him. "Just drive, Mack. I'm not in the mood to have my life analyzed right now."

The big man gave him a sharklike smile and planted his foot to the floor.

***

They'd missed them. Jon knew it the minute Mack pulled the car to a halt. Though why he was so sure he couldn't honestly have said. Ignoring the stares of the local police, he walked across to the road leading up to the cabin. The heavy rain had quickly turned the mud to slush, but it was still thick enough to capture the imprint of a tire as it had slid in the turn onto the road. He ran a finger around the outline of the track. They'd missed them by about ten minutes, if not more. The rain was beginning to wash the deep prints away.

Mack squatted down beside him. "Recognize them?"

He shook his head. "No. But they're recent."

"So our quarry has probably flown." Mack stood up and studied the muddy driveway. "We'll go check, anyway."

"They might have left something for us." He rose to his feet, hoping like hell that that something was a ransom note and not a body. Either way, he had to know before he gave chase to Hank's car. "We'll have to walk, though. I doubt if the cars will make it up the hill in this rain."

Mack nodded in agreement and motioned for the local officers to follow them. Jon led the way, listening to the wind whistling through the dripping pines. There was no sign that Eleanor was still in the area.

The cabin came into sight. Mack pulled him to a halt, and Jon bit back his impatience. The man was only doing his job. He stood in the shadows of a pine and watched the cabin. There was no noise or movement to be heard. The place had to be empty—or at least empty of life.

His gut clenched painfully. Maddie had to be alive—surely Eleanor wasn't stupid enough to get rid of a potential hostage?

"Stay here," Mack ordered, checking his gun.

Jon nodded. Until he knew if Maddie was okay, he would obey. He watched the four men run across the clearing to the front of the cabin. Watched as they smashed the door open and tumbled inside. When no gunshots or snarls met their appearance, he walked down to join them.

Mack glanced up as he entered the cabin. "Our birds have flown, but they left us a note." He offered the sealed plastic bag to Jon.

He scanned it quickly and frowned They wanted an exchange—Maddie for Evan. But that didn't make sense. Why not just go find another kid if they needed two? Why did they need Evan back?

At least it meant there was a chance that Maddie was still alive. At least she wasn't lying dead on the old worn floorboards. The relief he felt was frightening.

He handed back the note and tried to remind himself it didn't mean she *was* still alive. "Let's go find the bastards," he muttered and spun around.

Mack caught up with him as he strode down the steps. "Leave this to the experts, Barnett."

He wrenched his arm from Mack's grip. "In this case, that's me. Eleanor is something you've never seen before, something you have no experience in handling."

"I wouldn't bet on it," Mack stated grimly. "I've seen a lot of strange things in my twenty years of service."

Jon smiled impatiently. He'd bet his life Mack had never seen the likes of Eleanor. Or him. He glanced at the sky.

In many ways, what he was about to do meant his life now rested in the FBI agent's enormous hands. At the very least, Mack could make his life hell with the knowledge he was about to give him.

"Maybe." He studied Mack a moment longer. Maddie and Seline were right. He couldn't handle Eleanor and Hank alone—at least when Maddie was around to get caught in the middle. "Have you got a spare cell phone handy?"

Mack frowned, but dug a small phone out of his pocket. "You know my number."

Jon nodded. He'd called Mack less than a handful of times in the ten years they'd known each other, but he knew the number by heart. Once it had even saved his life.

Maybe this time it would save Maddie's.

He shoved the phone into his pocket, knowing it would change when he did—though the how and why of it escaped him. It was just a part of the magic that enabled him to shift shape. "I'll call when I find them," he said, and stepped away from him.

"Damn it, Barnett—"

The rest of Mack's comment was cut off as Jon made the change. With a flick of his wings, he flew skywards, ignoring the rain, the wind and Mack's startled curse as he began his search for Maddie.

***

There was a madman inside her head, beating a thousand drums. Maddie groaned softly and wished he'd leave her alone. Though it wasn't only her head that felt ready to explode— her whole body ached, as if the madman had thrown her around like some rag-doll.

She opened her eyes. The light, though murky, made her eyes water. She blinked the tears away, and dark gray vinyl met her gaze. She frowned in confusion and blinked again. The stretch of gray vinyl became a seat—the back of a car seat.

She was in a car. Hank's car, she thought, suddenly smelling old sweat and dirt. And they were still moving.

She shifted slightly, struggling to look around without letting Hank know she was awake. She couldn't see the second teenager, but Eleanor and Hank were both in the front seat.

She tried to shift again, but a sharp twist of pain ran down her arms and stopped her. She bit back a yelp and tried to ease her arms forward. They wouldn't move. She pulled again, then realized they were tied—and so tightly that she was beginning to lose feeling in her fingers.

Cursing silently, she glanced up at the back window. Rain beat against it, a torrent that made it impossible to see anything. There was no hope of seeing where she was, or where they were going.

"Damn you, Hank."

The sudden sound of Eleanor's voice made Maddie jump. She squeezed her eyes shut and prayed they hadn't noticed she was awake.

"How was I to know he'd already been inside? I told you, he came around the side, and the windows were shut." Hank's voice was an odd mixture of contempt and fear.

Eleanor gave an unladylike snort. "Shut, but not locked,

you fool."

Opening her eyes a little, Maddie saw Hank hunker down in the seat. "We still got one kid—can't we just go kidnap another?" This time there was definitely an edge of fear to his voice.

"I told you, we need the Maxwell kid for the ceremony—there's not enough time to go through another cleansing."

"Barnett's probably handed him over to the police by now."

"No doubt." Contempt ran through her sharp voice. "But the police station is the least of our problems."

Hank grunted. For several long minutes, the growl of the engine was the only noise to be heard above the heavy pounding of rain against the windows.

"Stop here." Eleanor leaned forward in the seat as the car jerked to a halt. "Get the kid out of the trunk."

Maddie shut her eyes again. The car doors opened, then there was a sharp rap of boots against loose gravel. *I should run while I have the chance.* But what hope would she have against Eleanor, who had the shape and speed of a panther?

The trunk opened, and Maddie risked a quick peek again. The dark branches of an old Christmas-tree type pine hung low over the car, protecting it from the worst of the weather.. They were somewhere in the mountains, obviously, but beyond that there was very little to be seen.

Eleanor and Hank dragged something out of the trunk before slamming it shut. *The second kid.* The certainty made her stomach turn. She'd been so worried about Evan that the safety of second teenager had slipped her mind entirely. She bit her lip, then slowly levered up on her elbows.

Hank and Eleanor where about twenty feet away, carrying a bundle wrapped in blankets down a steep incline. Now was the time to run. She sat fully upright and studied the area. The dark outline of trees met her gaze. A small dirt road disappeared past the pines on her left, and on her right, past the huge old Christmas tree, the land rose sharply. If there was anything else to be seen, it had disappeared into the rain.

It would be stupid to run when she had no idea where she was—or if there was even help nearby. Running might not achieve anything but making Eleanor angrier—and Maddie had a feeling that was something she might not live through.

She lay back down on the seat and, after several minutes, heard Eleanor and Hank returning. But only one door opened. The front seat squeaked as Hank climbed in, then the engine started.

"Now remember," Eleanor's usually mellow voice was sharp and cold, "dump our hostage and find where they've got the kid. I doubt if Barnett will agree to an exchange, no matter what his feelings for the woman."

"I've seen the two of them together. He'll come for her."

"Maybe." Eleanor's tone made it obvious she didn't agree. "Just find the kid, Hank. Remember, if you want your life extended again, you need that kid."

The door slammed shut. Maddie kept her eyes squeezed closed. The wheels spun as Hank took off, and for several second the car did nothing but drift sideways. Hank cursed fluently, and as if suddenly fearful, the car surged forward. She didn't know whether to feel relieved or not. Granted, she was free from Eleanor's sharp gaze, at least for a while, but she still had Hank to contend with.

She frowned slightly and wondered what Eleanor had meant in her last statement. Life extended again? Did that mean this was not the first time she'd extended their lives through magic? Sure, sixteen kids had disappeared, but would Eleanor need a blood sacrifice every month to extend her life? And Hank's?

She didn't know, but she had a feeling Jon would. She rubbed her thumb against the cold metal ring on her finger. Its presence was oddly comforting, if only because she knew he'd come back for it. She wasn't alone—someone was out there, looking for her.

The car bumped along, the rhythm oddly hypnotic. After what seemed like ages, it slowed and turned. The rain eased as suddenly as someone turning off a tap. Out the back window she saw a garage door closing behind them.

Her stomach rolled. She closed her eyes and listened to Hank getting out. After a few minutes the back door opened.

Hands grabbed her shoulders and hauled her out. She kept her eyes shut and forced herself to relax. Her only chance of escape might lie in convincing Hank she was still out of it.

"Christ, how can a little thing like you be so damn heavy."

His mutter was almost a curse as he hauled her up and over his shoulder. She watched his feet move across the concrete, then heard a door open. The rain and the cold hit them. Moisture ran down her back and around her throat as he hurried across the wet grass.

Where in the hell were they? She risked shifting slightly and saw the vague shadows of a house and trees. And below them, the dark outlines of other houses.

They were back in Taurin Bay—or at least on the outskirts of it, anyway. Hank's house maybe, or Eleanor's.

The scream of a hawk suddenly cut across the rainswept silence. Hank yelled, letting go of her legs as he dove out of the way. Air swooped past her. Maddie had a brief glimpse of brown-gold wings as she tumbled from Hank's shoulder. She hit the ground hard and grunted in pain, struggling to breathe and briefly seeing stars. Hank cursed and reached for her. She kicked out at him and heard the hawk scream again. As Hank's gaze jerked skyward, she rolled away from him, heading down the hill towards the house, and as far away from him as she could possibly get.

The hawk swooped, and Hank's scream of terror filled the air. Maddie thumped into a tree and struggled to a sitting position. Dizziness hit her and, for an instant, her vision blurred. She shook her head and took a deep breath. Rain dripped hotly from her nose. She ignored it and watched the hawk sweep around for another attack.

Hank ran for the trees. The hawk circled around, then with a flick of its wings, came back to her. As it neared, a gold haze crawled over its form, and the hawk became Jon.

"I didn't think you'd find me so quickly," she said, blinking back tears of relief and pain.

He knelt down beside her and quickly undid the rope binding her hands. "Neither did I." He touched her face, momentarily brushing his fingers over her bruised and swollen cheek. "Are your hurt anywhere else?"

Everywhere, she wanted to say, but bit the words back. *I'm not going to be a burden, remember?* Life rushed back into her fingers, fast and furious. She swore and blinked back the tears still threatening to embarrass her. Jon took her hands in his, rubbing them gently.

"Maddie, look at me."

She took a deep breath and glanced up. His eyes were a deep blue ocean in which she could so easily drown.

"Are you hurt anywhere else?" he repeated slowly.

She shook her head. Her head ached almost as fiercely as her arms, but not enough to mention. And that wasn't the question he was really asking, anyway. She swallowed and gave him a shaky smile. "He didn't touch me."

She saw the flash of relief in his eyes before he smothered it. She shivered—and knew it was more of a reaction to the warmth of his hands against hers than the cold rain dribbling down her back.

He took off his jacket and wrapped it around her shoulders. "Can you stand? We have to get out of this weather."

"If you help me."

He rose to his feet and gently guided her upright. Then he pulled her against him, holding her tightly. She leaned her cheek against his chest and listened to the thunder of his heart. It felt so good, so right—as if she belonged right there in his arms, and nowhere else.

"Next time I tell you to stay behind, will you kindly listen?" he whispered into her hair. "I think I've aged ten years in the last few hours."

His breath brushed past her cheek, and something deep inside shivered in reaction. She swallowed and forced a smile as she pulled away slightly. "I'll consider it."

At his quick frown, she reached up and brushed a kiss across his rain-wet lips. Only to be caught totally unprepared by the sudden flaring of heat and her own intense need.

He groaned slightly and splayed his hand across her back, holding her close as she deepened the kiss. Their bodies molded together, and heat trembled through her veins. When the tremulous ache began in her heart, she knew, really knew, that she was more than just attracted to this man. God help her, she was falling in love with someone she barely knew.

His hand moved from her back to her hair—then stilled. "You're bleeding," he said, pulling away.

She glanced at his hand. It was smeared red. She frowned and touched the back of her head. It felt tender and sore. She looked at her fingertips. They were bloody.

"So I am." She felt absurdly calm and wondered why. "Maybe I opened the cut when I fell off Hank's shoulder."

Jon swore softly, then swung her up into his arms. "Let's get you out of the rain."

She nodded and rested her head against his chest as he ran towards the garage. The warmth of his arms and the strength and gentleness with which he held her were both comforting and arousing. Or maybe it was just the hit on the head affecting her senses.

He kicked the door open, then gently sat her down on a large crate. "Now, tell me about the cut." He squatted down in front of her and took her hands again, rubbing them briskly.

She shivered, more from the force of his touch than from the chill beginning to creep through her body. "I hit my head when he hit me."

He paused, his fingers tightening around hers momentarily. "He hit you?" he repeated, his voice oddly devoid of any emotion.

She nodded. The little man with the drums was starting up in her head again, and it hurt.

"The bastard has to pay," he muttered. He glanced past her, listening intently. She could hear a distant wail of sirens, growing closer with every breath.

"Don't move." He rose and opened the garage door, then rummaged around in several boxes. After a few minutes he came back and wrapped a blanket around her shoulders.

"Maddie?" He shook her shoulders slightly, forcing her to look him in the eyes again.

Such nice eyes, she thought with a smile. Eyes that she'd love to wake up to in the morning—all the mornings—for the rest of her life.

"Maddie, are you listening to me?'

She smiled again. "No."

He frowned and suddenly looked more worried. "I said, I called the police before I attacked Hank. A man called Mack is in charge. His men have Evan. You'll be safe with them until I get back."

Evan—lord, she'd forgotten all about him. Guilt washed through her, thick and strong, and momentarily cleared the fuzziness from her mind. "Is he hurt?"

"He's in better condition than you are." His gaze ran past her again. "Mack, get some medical help, will you?"

His gaze came back to hers. Anger and worry burned deep in the wild blue depths of his eyes. Her heart did an odd flip-flop. She reached out, touching his full lips with her fingertips.

"Let the police handle it," she said, suddenly realizing he was going after Hank. That he would make Hank pay for the hurt he'd inflicted on her.

"I can't." He reached up and took her hand, gently kissing her fingertips. "Hank and Eleanor are my field of expertise. I'll handle them."

"You can't go alone. Let me come."

"Ah Maddie, you continue to amaze me," he whispered. Leaning forward, he kissed her lips, his mouth hot and yet so gentle against her own.

Heat whispered through her soul and made her heart ache. She closed her eyes and leaned her forehead against his. It was scary to realize just how far she'd fallen.

"Don't go," she whispered after a moment.

"I have no choice." He kissed her forehead then pulled back and glanced towards the doorway. "Mack, this is Madeline Smith. Maddie, Mack's from the FBI." He rose and squeezed her hand. His eyes became cold, so cold. "He'll look after you until I get back."

"Damn it Barnett, just wait—" The big man cut his sentence short and frowned darkly as Jon disappeared through the doorway.

"Not one for taking assistance or orders, is he?" he

commented. With surprising grace, he knelt down beside her.

She shivered. "No, he's been alone too long to depend on anyone but himself," she said softly. And wondered where the hell that left her.

***

Hank had a good ten minutes' start on him, but that was nothing when you could fly. He barely even felt the wind and the rain buffeting him. All he could think of was the pain in Maddie's amber eyes, the touch of her blood against his fingers.

The bastard would pay.

After a while he saw a flash of movement through the trees and quickly dove. When he neared the ground he changed, landing with little noise and on the run.

"Hank!"

There was a brief flash of white face as Hank glanced over his shoulder. Jon smiled grimly. Hank leapt forward in a frantic burst of energy. His quarry smelled of sweat and fear.

"You're a dead man, Hank!"

Taunting your prey was not usually a wise move, but it gave Jon an odd sense of satisfaction. The man was afraid— but not as afraid as Maddie had been.

And not as afraid now as he would be when Jon caught him.

He leapt across a fallen tree stump, took two quick steps then launched himself at Hank. He hit him hard, and, locked together, they tumbled to the ground with bone-crunching force. Hank kicked and screamed as they rolled off the faint path. Jon ignored him, hanging on grimly as they crashed down a rocky incline and slammed against the trunk of a pine tree.

"Bastard," Hank spat. He swung his fists, punching wildly.

Jon grinned flatly and caught Hank's left wrist in one hand, crushing it until bones cracked and Hank screamed. "I haven't even began to be a bastard yet, my friend."

Hank swore and kicked. Jon jumped away, evading the full force of the blow, but lost his grip on Hank's wrist. Quicker than lightning, Hank was up and running.

Jon loped after him. He'd flown over this area when he'd first arrived in Taurin Bay and knew that Hank was headed straight for a cliff. There was no escape.

The trees gave way to barren, rocky ground. The full force of the wind hit them, driving the rain with needlelike force. Hank staggered several steps sideways, then stopped and swung around. Jon saw the anger in his eyes, the desperation. But it was the sudden lack of fear that made him wary.

"I tasted the sweet delights of your woman, Shapeshifter," Hank snarled, his voice full of venom. "I made her squeal, made her beg for more."

Jon barely resisted the urge to leap forward and rip the life from the lying fiend's heart. *That* pleasure could come after he'd found out where Eleanor was. "Where is your master, Hank? Has she gone and left you to face the murder charges alone?"

The flicker of fear through Hank's dark eyes told Jon the thought was not a new one.

"She needs me, Shapeshifter." But the tone of his voice was uncertain.

"Needs you to be the fall guy, nothing more." The wild wind twisted suddenly and blew Hank's long coat around from the back of his legs. Silver gleamed in Hank's right hand. Jon grinned flatly. "Wrong animal, Hank. Silver affects werewolves, not shapeshifters."

Hank snarled and lunged forward, the knife gleaming brightly in his hand. Jon dodged but Hank's weight hit him and knocked him sideways. The knife, aimed at his heart, slammed into his thigh instead. Pain ripped through his body. He ignored the burning ache and smashed his fist into Hank's face. Hank staggered a few feet backwards then stopped. His mouth was bloody, and there was surprise in his eyes. Jon didn't move. Couldn't move.

But he wasn't about to let Hank know that.

"Didn't I tell you silver wasn't effective against shapeshifters?" Jon gritted his teeth and slowly pulled the knife from his leg. He held it out, letting the rain wash his blood from the gleaming blade. "Now tell me where Eleanor is, Hank."

"I'll see you in hell first," Hank snarled, then turned and

ran for the trees.

He threw the knife. Hank made a gargled sound and fell to the ground, the knife buried hilt-deep in his back.

Jon watched him silently, ignoring the buffeting wind and the rain that ran down his face as fast as the blood down ran his leg.

Hank didn't move. Either he was very good at lying still or he was dead. Jon grimaced. He hadn't intended to kill him—not until he'd found out where Eleanor was, at least. But then, nothing in this damn case was going the way he wanted, so why should things change now?

Suddenly weary, he took off his shirt and wrapped it tightly around his leg. Blood soaked quickly through the wet material. He swore softly. He'd have to get medical attention, but he couldn't leave just yet. He still had to find Eleanor.

He limped over to Hank and bent down awkwardly, pulling the fiend onto his back. Death had ripped Hank's mask of humanity away, revealing a face that was all bone and little structure. The look of surprise on what was left of his features made Jon frown. Hank obviously hadn't expected to die—why?

Had Eleanor promised a victory over all forms of death, not just the natural ravages of time? Just how old was Hank, if he looked like this in death? How old was Eleanor? If Hank's quickly disintegrating body was anything to go by, they were both more than several centuries old. Which made Eleanor older, and more powerful, than he'd ever imagined.

He quickly patted down what was left of Hank's body. No wallet, no keys. Nothing to give any clue as to where Eleanor might be.

"Just not my day," he muttered, standing up. And noticed a blood red ring gleaming softly on a skeletal right finger.

He slid it off and held it up to the light. It was a ruby, and etched onto the gleaming surface of the stone was a snarling cat. The ring was ancient and rare. He'd only seen its like once—on the hand of the man bound to serve a vampire for all eternity. Eleanor certainly wasn't a vampire, but she was a powerful enough sorcerer to work a ring of binding.

He flipped it lightly in his hand, watching the red glitter in the cat's stone eyes. He could almost feel Eleanor's presence as he held it, could almost taste the darkness that was her soul.

He wouldn't have to find Eleanor. With the ring in his possession, she'd find him.

All he had to do was get Maddie out of harm's way.

Fifteen

Maddie leaned against the wall and closed her eyes. The soft murmur of conversation rolled across the room, a soothing sound in the stark, cold surroundings of the police station. At least it would have been, if she hadn't known they were discussing her. It was obvious from his questions that the FBI agent didn't entirely believe her—at least when it came to the point of how she knew Evan was in danger hours before he'd actually disappeared.

Or maybe he was just a cop doing his job, and she was being entirely too suspicious. Maybe she'd let Steve's antagonism color her judgement a little too much when it came to the police.

She rubbed her hand across her eyes. The madman in her brain was still pounding away tirelessly, and the cut on the back of her head ached, despite the pain killers the doctor had given her. All she wanted was to go home and sleep. But that wasn't likely to happen any time soon, if the attitude of the FBI agent and the police was anything to go by.

Why couldn't they just believe her and let her go? The only two people she really wanted to speak to were Evan and Jon, and the fact that she hadn't seen either in over five hours worried her.

But what worried her more was, now that Evan was safe, Jon had no real reason—and maybe no real wish—to see her again. That maybe he'd use this time to go after Eleanor then simply leave.

She wanted—needed—to see him again, if only to hold him one more time before he said good-bye.

"Miss Smith?"

She opened her eyes. Mack stood about three feet away, holding out a mug of what looked liked dirty dishwater.

"Coffee?"

She nodded and accepted the mug. At the very least, it would warm her fingers. "How's my nephew? When can I see him?"

"Soon." Mack sat back down at the table and motioned her to do the same. "Your statement." He pushed several pieces of paper across to her. "Read it and sign it, if everything is correct."

She quickly scanned the papers, then signed the bottom and pushed them back.

Mack shuffled them together without looking at them. "You realize, of course, that you are a prime witness in this case. You'll be expected to appear in court."

Something in his gaze told her that he was well aware of her past, or more precisely, her lack of cooperation when it came to the investigation of her husband's death.

"I realize that," she said, her voice sharper than she'd intended.

He smiled slightly. "Your...abilities will come out during the trial."

"My abilities are nothing when compared to Eleanor's, believe me."

Though she privately doubted if the case would ever make it to trial. There wasn't a prison built that could hold a woman like Eleanor—a shapeshifter well versed in the art of black magic.

She remembered the coldness—no, deadness—in Jon's blue eyes as he'd left to go after Hank, and she suddenly realized he had never intended handing Eleanor and Hank over to the police. Jon was judge, jury and executioner.

He'd come to Taurin Bay to kill, not capture.

Ice crawled over her skin, splintering into her heart. She shivered and rubbed her arms.

Mack frowned at her. "Better drink that coffee up. Your brother-in-law will be here soon to collect both you and Evan."

Oh joy. That was one fun trip home she planned to miss.

"I'd like to speak to Evan before then, if possible."

Mack regarded her for a long moment. She had a feeling there was little he missed. Even her dislike of Steve.

"Okay. I'll go see if the doctor has finished with him." He rose and walked quietly from the room.

Left with nothing else to do while she waited, Maddie sipped the coffee. It tasted as bad as it looked. The minutes crawled by, and the coffee slowly cooled.

"Aunt Maddie?"

She glanced up. Evan stood in the doorway, staring at her with an odd mixture of relief and uncertainty on his face. It made him look older, and yet somehow more vulnerable. She smiled and opened her arms. He ran across the room like a child and fell into her hug.

"I knew you'd come for me," he whispered. "I watched you in my dreams."

She closed her eyes. So it was true. Evan had inherited abilities just like hers. And like her, he had a mother and father who didn't want to know.

But at least she was here, and she'd do whatever it took to ensure his abilities didn't take him down the same path as hers. One murderer in the family was more than enough. "Are your mom and dad here yet?"

"No." He hesitated and pulled away slightly. "Why isn't Jon with you?"

She raised an eyebrow at the unexpected question. "He went after Hank."

Evan grabbed her hand, sudden desperation filling his eyes. "You have to save Teresa. You just have to."

Teresa was obviously the name of the other kid. Maddie wondered how he knew her, then saw that Evan's gaze was distant and shadowed, as if he were viewing the scenes of a movie no one else could see.

Maddie rubbed a hand across her eyes. She really wasn't up to this. It was only thanks to Jon's intervention that she had escaped Hank's clutches. And if she stayed any longer in Taurin Bay, she had a horrible feeling she'd have some sort of run-in with Eleanor. And escaping *that* woman's claws a second time would not be so easy. Better to avoid her all together.

"Jon will find her, Evan."

"No!" The sudden urgency in his voice made her shiver. He sounded so much like his stern, uncompromising father it was frightening. "Jon will go after *her*. You have to rescue Teresa—promise me you will. Promise me you won't leave."

She took a deep breath. It would be nothing short of madness to make such a vow. She'd been lucky up until now, but that luck surely wouldn't hold. It never had. She opened her mouth to refuse, but the sheer desperation in Evan's amber-brown eyes made her hesitate. He was seeing the future, and it obviously wasn't good for the second teenager. Could she handle the weight of another death?

She sighed and closed her eyes. "I promise."

Evan blinked, and his eyes became clear again. "Good. So tell me, why is Dad mad at you?"

It was almost as if a switch had been flicked somewhere in his head. He obviously suffered none of the confusion she had. She sipped at the cold coffee, searching for a tactful answer. "You've talked to him?"

"Yes. And he's angry."

She smiled grimly. How did she explain to a thirteen-year-old that his father's anger stemmed from the fear that she would destroy his family, as she had destroyed her own?

"He's not really mad, Evan. I think he's a little scared." She hesitated and brushed the stray red-gold strands of hair out of teenager's eyes.

Had it only been three weeks since she'd last seen him? The way he stood, the way he studied her—suddenly he wasn't a child any more, but a man. And while the kidnapping might have had something to do with that, she thought the explanation was more likely to be found in the arrival of his gifts. Her own had forced her to grow up fast, and she'd barely been six.

"I think he knows that you have similar gifts to mine. I think that's why he's scared."

Evan tilted his head and studied her for a moment. "But if I wasn't gifted, you would never have found me."

She smiled. There spoke the logic of a child. "True, Evan. Perhaps you should remind your dad of that when he gets here."

"I will." He hesitated, and fear touched his gaze. "She'll come after me, you know. I'm not safe, Aunt Maddie. Not here, not at home."

She remembered the venom in Eleanor's voice—and the fact that they still needed Evan to complete the ceremony. Remembered the shapeshifter's contempt of the protection the police station offered. Evan was right. He *wasn't* safe—not until Eleanor was caught, or dead.

She squeezed his shoulder lightly. "I'll talk to your mom and dad. I'll get them to go somewhere else for a couple of days."

He nodded. Footsteps rattled down the hall, and she glanced at the door. Mack walked into the room, followed quickly by Steve. Meeting her brother-in-law's steely gaze, she saw only contempt. Evan ran to his father, and Steve's big arms all but engulfed him.

"They tell me you helped rescue Evan," he said, his lips thin as he glared at her. "I guess I owe you thanks, and...I'm sorry for giving you so much grief."

Any apology, however reluctant, was the last thing she'd expected. "No matter what you think of me, Steve, I couldn't just sit around and let something happen to Evan."

Evan glanced across at her. He knew, as she did, that the police would never have found him. Not in time to save his life.

Steve's sun-browned face held a hint of malice. "As you did your husband, you mean?"

She sighed. Trust him to bring the subject up with the police and the FBI in the room. "He physically and mentally abused me, Steve, and I have the scars to prove it." She hesitated, then shrugged away the rise of guilt.

She'd paid for the mistake she'd made that day—through isolation, loneliness and fear—and it never seemed to be enough. And yet, if she had the chance to undo the past, she wouldn't.

"That's no justification for killing him."

She lowered her gaze from his. "I didn't. The fire did."

"The fire that you lit."

Yes, the fire was hers, but she'd just wanted him to stop, to leave her alone. She briefly closed her eyes, then repeated the same old lie. "It was an accident, Steve." She shrugged. The scorn in his face told her he would never believe her, no matter what she said. "And it's not important now. You should be worried about Evan, not about my past."

He frowned, sudden worry replacing the contempt in his eyes. "What do you mean?"

"The woman has already taken Evan once from your home. What makes you think she can't do it again?"

He snorted. "If she has any brains, she'll be on the run. She has to know the net is closing in on her."

"Are you willing to bet you son's life on that?" She could tell by his suddenly defensive stance that he wasn't. "Take Evan and Jayne and go on a vacation. Don't tell anyone where. Just get the hell out of here, and keep Evan safe."

She pushed the coffee mug away and rose. "Am I able to leave yet?" she asked, glancing across at Mack.

He nodded, then frowned when Steve snorted softly. "For the moment. But if you happen to see Barnett, tell him I need to ask him some questions."

She nodded and dragged her sodden coat off the back of the chair. "I don't suppose you can give me a lift back to the motel?"

"I can take you," Steve growled.

Getting into the car with her brother-in-law was the last thing her headache needed. The light in his eyes told her he hadn't yet said everything he'd come here to say. Even the ten-minute trip to the motel would be too much time spent in his company. She shook her head. "No. I meant it when I suggested running, Steve. The sooner you get away from this place, the better." She glanced down at Evan. "I'll talk to you when I get home."

If I get home, she thought, and followed the FBI agent from the room.

***

Dusk was beginning to creep across the sky by the time she got back to the motel room. Maddie kept a careful eye on the shadows as she made her way across the parking lot. Though she knew Eleanor wasn't likely to leap out at her, there was an uneasiness to the bitter wind that made her nerves tingle.

Something felt wrong. She just wasn't entirely sure what.

The room was dark when she entered, but it wasn't empty. She could feel Jon's presence, a warmth that surrounded her as securely as a cloak.

"Don't turn on the light," he said softly.

His voice came from the direction of the beds and was edged with tiredness. She frowned and locked the door before she walked across to the bed.

As her eyes became adjusted to the dim light, she realized that he wasn't wearing much beyond boxer shorts—and a huge bandage on the upper part of his well-muscled left thigh.

"Are you okay? What happened?" she asked, sudden concern making her stomach churn.

"I'm fine. Hank just stuck a knife into me."

His tone was touched with reluctance, as if he didn't want to discuss the matter. Her frown deepened. The uneasiness she'd felt walking across the parking lot was nothing compared to the tension suddenly filling the room. "And what happened to Hank?"

He didn't reply immediately, though the tension rose by several degrees.

"He died. No great loss, really."

So Hank was dead and no longer a threat. She shivered and rubbed her arms. It should have been a relief that he was no longer able to hurt her or Evan, or anyone else, but it wasn't. She had a bad feeling that Eleanor would make them all pay for his death.

But what scared her more than anything else was the callousness in Jon's voice. It was almost as if he had killed so often that it just didn't matter to him.

And yet, deep down, he seemed to be in pain.

"Want to talk about it?" she asked softly. "Sometimes it helps if you do."

He snorted. The quickly fading light that washed through the windows highlighted the derision on his face. "He got a knife in the back. He died. There's nothing much more to say, Maddie."

There was when you thought yourself a coward. And while she understood Jon had every intention of killing Hank, he wouldn't have intentionally knifed him in the back. It wasn't his way.

She touched his leg. His skin twitched slightly beneath her fingers, and a sudden shock of awareness ran warmth through her body. It was a sensation hard to ignore, and yet she would have to if she wanted to get any answers from him. She had a feeling he'd reject a physical approach a whole lot faster than he was rejecting emotional ones.

She softly cleared her throat. "Except that you're lying here filled with anger and self-loathing."

He glared at her. "If I'm angry, it's because you won't leave the damn subject alone."

She stared back at him steadily. His anger was nothing compared to the anger she'd faced during her marriage. She might have known him only a few days, but it was long enough to understand he would never hit her. He might break her heart, but he would never physically hurt her, as Brian so often had. "Did Hank say anything before he died?"

Something flickered in his eyes before the shutters came back down. It wasn't hard to guess that Hank's departing words had been aimed in her direction.

"Did he say anything else besides sullying my reputation?"

Just for an instant, the hint of a smile tugged at his full lips. Then he ran a hand through his disheveled hair and frowned at her. "If he did, it's none of your damn business."

His voice held an edge that cut her to the quick. She bit her lip and glanced at the window. The wind was beginning to pick up outside, rattling the old windows in their frames. Maybe it was something of an omen, a sign that trouble was brewing. But if she was to have any hope of fulfilling her promise to Evan, she had to keep pushing for information. Whether Jon liked it or not, she had every intention of staying until she found Teresa.

But maybe it was time to try a change of tactics. "How bad is the leg?"

He shrugged, a gesture that could have meant anything. "It's fairly deep and required several stitches. The doc reckons I'll have to stay off it for several days."

She raised her eyebrow and wondered how he'd gotten around the problem of the doctor reporting the wound to the police. Or maybe he hadn't—maybe he'd literally flown the coop before the police arrived to question him. "And will you?"

He smiled, though no amusement touched the coldness in his eyes. "No. Quick healing is a gift of my heritage. I'll be able to move around in the morning." He hesitated and studied her for a long moment. "When are you leaving?"

That was the reason for his behavior. He wanted her out of his way—it was evident not only in what he said, but in the *way* he said it. Even in the way he looked at her. Ignoring the deep thrust of hurt, she shook her head. "I'm not going anywhere."

He quirked an eyebrow. "Up until now, I didn't think you were a fool."

She smiled grimly. "Then you really don't know me, do you?"

"No, I don't." Just for a moment his voice was edged with a hint of regret that warmed her heart. "But you can't stay here. Eleanor will come after me, and I don't want you in the firing line."

So Evan was right. Jon was going after Eleanor, not Teresa. "You can't handle Eleanor alone when you're injured."

"I can, and I will. I don't want you here, Maddie. Just face that fact and leave."

Heat crept into her cheeks. "I really don't care what you want. I made a promise to try to find Teresa, and that's exactly what I intend to do."

"Who the hell told you her name was Teresa?"

"Evan did."

"And how will you achieve this miracle?" His voice was knife-edged, thrusting deep into her soul. "I'll find her. I just don't want you blundering around any more, putting everyone's life in jeopardy."

"It was my so-called blundering that found Evan in the first place!" She jumped to her feet and glared at him. "Why are you pushing me away like this?"

"You've done what you came here to do. It's time to leave."

"I made a promise. I can't go back on that."

"Just as you made a promise never to use your gifts again?" He gave her a cold smile. "Some vows are made to be broken, I'm afraid. You could no more find the teenager than you could stop using your abilities. Face those facts and just get the hell out of my life."

She stared at him. While she understood that he was deliberately being nasty in an attempt to get rid of her, his words hurt nevertheless. "You can be such a bastard."

"I have the soul of a hunter, a hawk. I am a killer by nature." He hesitated and gave her an almost savage smile. "And I love my work."

Yes, he loved his work—but not the killing. It might be an essential part of his job, but it was one she sensed he abhorred. She could see the self-loathing in the back of his eyes, hear it in the edge in his voice. And because of his work, because of what he was forced to do day in and day out, he was keeping everyone at arm's length. If you didn't care, you didn't get hurt.

It was a hell of a way to live. And yet, in many ways, wasn't she doing exactly the same thing? Maybe her reasons were different, but the result was still the same. A life locked in unending, unbearable loneliness.

He'd once told her life was made to be lived, that she couldn't hide forever. Maybe it was time they both took his advice.

"But that would make you no better than the monsters you chase," she said softly. "And you're not a monster, Jon. Just a man who needs to open up and let someone in."

"Like you?" His short laugh was derisive. "We're little

more than strangers. I've killed. I will keep on killing. I have no desire for anyone I-" He stopped, then shrugged.

But his unfinished sentence sung through her mind. *No desire for anyone I care about to get in the way.* She shivered. The thought that maybe there was some sort of psychic link between them scared her almost as much as the thought of never seeing him again.

She glanced down at her hands for a minute. If she wanted him to open up, maybe it was only fair that she do the same.

"I've killed too," she whispered, not looking up—not even when his hand wrapped around hers and squeezed gently. She turned her hand and entwined her fingers in his, but resisted the temptation to cling tightly. It was time to be strong, time to be truthful about that night. She'd lied to everyone, including herself, for far too long.

"Brian, my husband, died in a fire—a fire I lit. I burned him, burned our home—burned everything that reminded me of our life together. And I have never regretted it." Even though the nightmares—and the fear that she might so easily kill again—had haunted her ever since.

The soft rattle of the wind buffeting the windows was the only sound to be heard for several long heartbeats. She waited tensely, not sure what sort of reaction she expected—or wanted—from him.

"You didn't mean to kill him. There's a difference." Though his voice was neutral, there was a hint of understanding and warmth in his expression that made her heart race. He understood, even if he didn't say as much. He too had lived the same hell.

She closed her eyes, blinking back the sudden sting of tears. For too long she had stood alone, afraid to tell anyone about that night, afraid that her gifts would forever isolate her. Maybe they still would. The full truth wasn't out yet.

"But I did mean to." She glanced down, watching his thumb gently caress her wrist. His gentle touch somehow soothed the sick churning in her stomach. Over six years had passed, yet the brutality with which Brian had attacked her still made her shake. And all because she had been out shopping rather than home to answer his call.

"He wouldn't stop hitting me," she whispered, unable to help the quaver in her voice. "No matter what I said or did, he just wouldn't stop. I wanted him to burn in hell. I screamed it at him and... and he did. And even if I had been able to restrain my fire that day, I wouldn't have. He deserved the death he got. In some ways, he was more of a monster than Eleanor ever could be."

"One death doesn't make you a killer, Maddie," Jon said softly. "You were acting in self-defense, nothing more."

"But what if I've killed twice?"

He met her gaze steadily. "Twice?"

She nodded and licked her lips. "Some mistakes I seem destined to repeat. I was barely six the first time. My father was hitting my mother and I just wanted him to stop. I lit a fire. He did stop, but by then, the fire had gotten out of control. My brother died in the blaze."

"Come here." He tugged her forward and into his arms. It felt like a homecoming. "You're not a killer, no matter what you think. You never could be."

She squeezed her eyes shut against the threat of more tears. In the midst of a nightmare she'd found a man she cared about—maybe even loved. And he would send her away from him without regret, simply because it was safer.

But being safe was something she no longer wanted.

She turned in his embrace and met his gaze. His face was so close that his breath washed warmth across her lips and sent shivers of desire thrumming through her body. "Don't send me away. I need to be here."

A slight smile tugged the corners of his mouth, and a hint of weariness momentarily warmed the coldness in his eyes. He reached up and gently brushed a stray curl away from her cheek, his touch trailing across her skin like fire.

"I have no choice. Eleanor will kill you in revenge for Hank, and that is something I just couldn't live with."

The catch in his voice made her heart sing. "Eleanor won't always be around."

"No. But someone like her will. You need a man you can

make a life with, someone with whom you can raise children and grow old. I'm not that someone, Maddie. I can't be. I chose my path a long time ago, and it's far too late to change."

She saw the pain in his eyes and knew being with her was his dream as well, whether or not he was willing to admit it. She pulled her gaze away from his and stared out the window. "All I've ever wanted in my life is someone to love and understand me," she said softly. "You wouldn't think something so simple would be so hard to find."

"Ah, Maddie." He leaned forward and kissed her forehead. He might well have been branding her, so deep did the brush of his lips burn. "If I hadn't given my heart to my work a long time ago, it would be yours. But I have no room in my life now for anything else. And certainly no desire for it to change."

She studied his face. There was an edge to his voice that made her wonder whom he was trying to convince—himself or her. But it was the determination in his eyes that told her it was pointless to argue with him.

How ironic that she'd gotten her wish—the chance to have him hold her one more time—only to discover that she wanted a whole lot more.

She looked across to her own bed. Half hidden by the growing darkness, it looked uninviting and solitary—like so much of her life. But it was a pattern she desperately wanted to break.

She had tonight, if nothing else. This was her chance to finally take a stand and do something *she* wanted to do, instead of merely drifting along, following the wishes and desires of others. And what she wanted, more than anything, was to lie in the warm security of Jon's arms for the rest of the night.

She leaned her cheek against his shoulder and ran her fingers across the golden hairs on his chest, placing her hand over his heart. Its unsteady rhythm matched her own.

"Sleep with me," she whispered softly.

His smile was something she felt deep inside. "Anytime. But I'm afraid sleeping is all I'm up to. I have to keep the leg as still as possible."

"Sleeping will do." Any time spent in his arms would be

better than nothing. And at least it would give her a memory to hold on to when she left in the morning.

All she had to do then was figure out how she was going to find Teresa without his help.

Sixteen

Jon jerked awake. For several minutes he stared into the darkness, listening to the wind howl past the windows. Maddie was pressed warmly against his side, her breath a whisper stirring the hairs across his chest. Nothing else disturbed the silence, yet something didn't feel right.

"What is it?" Her murmur ran heat past his chin as she glanced up.

Maybe the odd sound had been nothing more than his imagination. He ran his finger down her cheek then across the lips he longed to kiss. Maybe what had woken him was the ache of holding her so close and being unable to do anything about it. "Nothing. It's probably just the storm."

She made a sound close to a sigh, then jumped as a floorboard creaked. Her fingers clenched against his chest. "That nothing is moving around in the bathroom."

It certainly sounded as if *something* was. He placed his hand over hers and squeezed it lightly. "I'll go check."

Though he couldn't see the fear in her eyes, it ran like fire through her emotions. "What about your leg?"

"It'll be fine. Just wait here." He slid his arm out from under her and rose.

The darkness surrounded him, as heavy as a cloak. He limped forward, his leg stiff and awkward. But at least he could walk. A few hours ago that wouldn't have been possible.

The bathroom door creaked as he opened it. He cursed silently and hit the light switch. The sudden brightness made him blink, but nothing scurried into the corners of the room. He limped in and looked around. The small window was locked, and everything else seemed undisturbed. It had to be just the storm.

"Anything?" Her warm voice held a slight tremor.

He glanced back at her. She was lying in the bed with the blankets pulled up around her nose. All that was visible was the amber fire of her eyes, sparking brightly as they reflected the bathroom light. A sudden surge of desire caught him by surprise. How was he going to share the bed for the rest of the night and not touch her?

"It's just the wind," he said and switched off the light.

He hobbled to the end of the bed then stopped. She watched him steadily, and he could almost taste the desire beginning to stir the bright swirl of her emotions. He couldn't lie down with her again and not touch her. And he had a horrible feeling that if he *did* touch her, he wouldn't want to let her go.

He thrust a hand through his hair. "Maybe I should sleep in the other bed."

"Why?"

The slight huskiness in her voice sent heat racing to his loins and practically shot his good intentions all to hell. "It's safer, that's why," he muttered.

Safer for him, safer for her. Because she deserved more than he'd ever be able to give her.

The bed springs squeaked as she rose. She stopped in front of him—not touching him but close enough for him to feel the heat of her body, see the warm sparkle of desire in her eyes. It took every ounce of his control to simply stand there and not reach for her.

"I've spent most of my life seeking safety, and I'm tired of the chase. I'm not asking for a commitment, just the remainder of the night." She hesitated, and a hint of laughter ran through the emotive swirl surrounding her. "If you think your leg is up to it, of course."

The leg was up to it, he just didn't think his heart was. She wasn't like the other women he'd slept with. They'd been little more than temporary shields against the loneliness. He'd been able to walk away without remorse, his heart intact and untroubled. Maddie was a different prospect.

He reached out, gently cupping her cheek. She leaned into

his hand for a moment, then brushed a kiss across his palm. Heat shivered through his soul.

"I'm trying to be honorable here. It's something of a first for me."

"Then treat me as you treated the others. Just give me the night before you make me leave in the morning."

"I can't—"

"Hush." She leaned forward and kissed his lips, her mouth warm and soft against his. "Don't think," she murmured, "just feel. If only for this one night."

He groaned and pulled her into his arms. He'd never been a saint, and he certainly wasn't made of stone. And he just had to hope he had the strength to watch her walk away in the morning, because he certainly couldn't let her go right now.

Her mouth invited greater exploration. He tasted her deeply, urgently, and she matched his fire, making a rough, needy sound in the back of her throat as she wrapped her arms around his neck.

He scooped her up in his arms and walked the remaining few steps to the bed. A twinge of pain ran down his leg as he laid her down, but he ignored it and stripped off his shorts, lying down beside her.

"You're naked." She ran her hand down his chest to his stomach, then lower.

Trying to ignore the sensations flooding heat through his body, he skimmed his hand under her T-shirt and gently teased a nipple.

"You're not," he murmured and leaned forward, laving his tongue up her neck and around her ear.

A sigh that was close to a shudder escaped her lips. "Wait." She slipped the shirt over her head and tossed it onto the floor. Her panties quickly followed.

He ran his hand down the warm, silky length of her, imprinting every curve in his mind, from the gentle swell of her breasts to the lean roundness of her thighs. Claiming her lips again, he caressed the warmth between her legs until she grew slick, and he felt the tremors building in her body. He retreated, skimming his hand back up to her breast.

"The man is a tease," she said, a hint of laughter coiling through the huskiness of her voice. "But two can play that game."

Her tongue made a moist trail of fire down his chest. She traced the outline of his belly button for several seconds then went on, until he felt the wet heat of her mouth encase him. He groaned and arched upwards, fighting the fierce and sudden ache in his groin. Then her touch left him, trailing fire back up to his chest.

"Going to play fair now?" She raised up on her elbows and dropped dainty kisses on his lips and cheek.

He smiled and lightly nipped her lip. "Nope," he said, rolling so that she was beneath him. He caught her hands, linking his fingers through hers before gently drawing her hands above her head.

He took her nipple in his mouth, rolling it over his tongue and teeth, sucking deeply. She twisted beneath him, her small sounds of pleasure gnawing away at his self-control. He could hear her heart pounding a rhythm that was as erratic as the pulsing in his groin.

"Oh God, Jon," she whispered, kissing his hair, his ears, and his neck. "Touch me."

He pressed his knee between hers, nudging them apart. With his free hand he touched her, delving into her moistness, caressing the most sensitive part of her. She arched up to meet him, her soft cries becoming more urgent, more intense.

"Come on, my love," he whispered, and claimed her mouth, kissing her fiercely. She shuddered against him, breath ragged as she clung to him.

"I need you," she whispered and touched his hips, drawing him down towards her.

He joined her in one sure stroke. She urged him on, meeting every thrust with a small cry of pleasure that cut through his soul. Her breathing quickened again, then another shudder rippled through her body and broke what remained of his control.

"Maddie!" he cried, as the power of his own release tore through him. His arms collapsed, and he rolled sideways, not wanting to crush her with his weight. He lay still for several minutes, his chest heaving as he battled for breath.

"How's the leg?" she asked softly.

Eyes still closed, he reached down and clasped her hand. Cold metal met his touch, and he realized she was still wearing his ring. He smiled and gently squeezed her fingers. "The leg's just fine." But as he'd suspected, the heart was an entirely different matter.

She turned towards him. He shifted his arm, pulling her in close. Her sigh whispered across his chest and stirred an ache deep inside him.

He kissed the top of her hair and stared into the darkness, listening to her breathing grow quieter. He was a fool—a fool who now had a huge problem on his hands.

Could he really let her walk out of his life in the morning?

***

A persistent noise woke Maddie some time later. Heart pounding in fright, she lay in the warm security of Jon's arms and listened. After a minute she realized it was simply a loose piece of roofing banging in the wind.

How often had she lain in her own bed listening to that same awful noise? And how often had she hoped it *was* an intruder, simply because it would have provided a brief respite from the intense loneliness of her life? Far too often, she thought grimly. It was odd how the isolation she'd so desperately needed after Brian's death had quickly turned into a prison from which she feared to break free.

In many ways, that fear still held her. But at least Jon had shown her it *was* possible to control her gifts and put them to good use. It was up to her now to find the courage to break free from her self-imposed exile.

She sighed softly and ran her hand across the warm plane of his muscular stomach. Meeting him had also shown just how badly she missed having someone to share the highs and lows of life with. And yet she'd been something less than honest in her admission earlier. She didn't want just anyone to love her. She wanted *him*.

But that was an unlikely dream.

She bit her lip against the sudden sting of tears. Part of her wanted to fight his decision, to try to make him stay. His touch and his eyes told her he loved her, even if *he* would never admit it. But she might as well try to restrain the wind. As much as he might love her, he loved his work more. He didn't want to give it up, and he didn't want her to be a part of it.

If she stayed, or tried to make him stay, she would end up hating herself as much as he'd end up hating her. Better to walk away now.

He stirred slightly, his fingers running across hers and squeezing them gently. "You okay?"

His voice was blurred with sleep, yet she could hear the concern in it. "Fine," she whispered. "Just got to go to the bathroom."

She moved away from his touch, her feet brushing against the clothes she'd stripped off earlier. She bent down to collect them then quickly padded to the bathroom.

Shutting the door quietly, she turned on the light. A breeze touched her bare skin, running icy fingers across her throat and squeezing tightly. She coughed and glanced across to the window. Some fool had left it open. A fine haze of rain misted in through the opening, and the coldness in the room suddenly grew more intense. Shivering, she quickly donned her T-shirt and panties then moved to close the window.

"I wouldn't bother, my dear," a harsh voice whispered behind her. "I'll only have to open it again."

Heart leaping in fright, Maddie jerked around. Ebony smoke curled lazily from the shower and formed the shape of a woman. Eleanor.

Impossible! Maddie wanted to scream, only her voice seemed frozen to the back of her throat. She licked her lips and slowly backed away, fingers trembling as she reached for the door. If she flung it open hard enough, Jon would wake...

Eleanor made a quick motion with her hand, and the ice encasing Maddie's throat settled across her limbs. She couldn't move, couldn't scream. Could only watch as Eleanor glided towards her with unnatural grace.

"Don't we just smell like a bitch in heat." Though Eleanor's soft voice held a hint of amusement, malice twisted her face—a face that suddenly looked sharp and old. "I do hope you enjoyed yourself, my dear. It's probably the last time that you will."

She reached up and ran a needlelike fingernail down Maddie's cheek. It might have been a knife, cutting deep. Tears stung Maddie's eyes, but she could do little more than flinch and blink them away. But deep in her soul the fires flickered to life.

"He should never have killed Hank," Eleanor went on, almost conversationally. "It took me a long time to find a man like him, someone trainable but with half a brain. Now I'll have to start all over again."

Maddie stared at her. The woman had to be mad—or very, very sure of her own abilities. Despite Jon's presence in the next room, Eleanor was making no attempt to speak quietly. Surely he would hear and come running...

As if reading her thoughts, Eleanor laughed. It was a high, insane sound that lashed at Maddie's ears and made every nerve ending quiver in fright.

"My dear, he sleeps the sleep of the well-sated. Besides, my little fog is swallowing any sound we make."

Maddie blinked, suddenly realizing the fine mist of rain she'd noticed earlier had thickened to become a barrier near the door. Jon wouldn't hear her, couldn't save her. Fear spurted through her body. She closed her eyes, trying to calm the panic tightly squeezing her heart. She wasn't entirely helpless, as Brian had found out.

And she didn't have to move to unleash her fire.

Watching Eleanor carefully, she reached deep down into that dark place in her soul where the flames lurked.

Eleanor's gaze narrowed, as if she felt the heat suddenly building. "But enough talk. There is much I have yet to do, traps I must arrange."

Eleanor reached out, grabbing Maddie by the arm. Clawlike fingers tore into her flesh as the mist near the door began to curl lazily towards them.

Terror slammed past fear and sliced through Maddie's heart. She couldn't let Eleanor take her anywhere. Couldn't let herself be used as bait to trap Jon. With a silent scream of denial, she stared at the hand holding her so tightly and let loose her fire.

Eleanor's flesh burst into flame, and Maddie's skin shriveled away from its touch. Eleanor screamed, a high-pitched sound of anger and pain. The mist responded to the noise, weaving and pulsing in frantic haste around the flames scorching Eleanor's fingers and arm. When it curled away, the flames were gone.

"You will pay for this," Eleanor hissed, holding up a blackened hand for Maddie to see. It looked like a twisted, broken paw.

Then the mist eddied again, and the ice holding Maddie immobile seemed to spread, splintering through her soul. Pain erupted through her body and she screamed. But the only sound she heard was the sharp note of Eleanor's laughter as the darkness encased them both and swept them away.

***

"Maddie?"

His question seemed to echo across the lonely silence. Jon sat upright in bed, heart pounding unevenly as he stared at the light filtering under the bathroom door.

"Maddie, are you okay?"

There was no answer to his question, and every instinct told him something was horribly wrong. He threw the blankets aside and ran across to the bathroom, flinging open the door.

The room was cold and empty. He took a quick glance behind the door then walked to the window. It was latched, and the cobwebs he'd noticed earlier still trailed across the corners, indicating it had not been opened.

He swung around and moved back into the bedroom. Where the hell was she? For one brief, horrible instant he thought she'd left him, had gone from his life without saying good-bye. Then he saw her canvas overnight bag, still on the chair where she'd flung it. The sick tension in his gut increased.

Eleanor had her. He was certain of that much, if nothing else. Somehow, the witch had crept into the room and spirited

Maddie away.

He swore and stalked across to the clothes he'd left lying on the floor. Something burned up his leg as he pulled on his jeans. With another curse, he dug his hand into his pocket. The ring he'd taken from Hank was burning hot. He dropped it quickly on the bed and stepped back.

Smoke curled up from the gleaming red eyes of the panther, gradually forming a wraithlike image of Eleanor. But it was an Eleanor who suddenly looked haggard and old—and very desperate.

"I have your woman, Shapeshifter."

Despite her appearance, Eleanor's voice was still smooth and warm. He wondered how much magic she was using to keep it that way. Wondered how badly Maddie had been hurt. "Maddie's not my woman, witch. Do what you want with her."

Eleanor's laughter was high and inhuman. "Lie to yourself if you wish, but please refrain from doing so to me. And I prefer to be called a sorcerer, not witch. So, shall we talk terms?"

He clenched his fists and somehow resisted the temptation to shatter the wraith's smug face. "I'll talk no terms with the likes of you."

Eleanor sighed. "This denial of yours is becoming tedious. I think I'll leave."

The mist wavered, losing shape. Fear for Maddie cut deeper into his gut. He had no doubt he could find her. His spirit was now linked so closely to hers he only had to fly around until her soul cried out to him. But he wouldn't find her quickly enough to prevent Eleanor from taking some form of revenge on her.

"No!" he said quickly, then cursed himself for a fool when he saw the flash of amusement in the wraith's dark eyes. "What do you want?"

"I want the boy," Eleanor spat. "And I want him before the night is over. Or you'll not see her again, Shapeshifter."

He stared at Eleanor and saw only death. If he or Maddie escaped out of this mess alive, it would be something of a miracle. "The boy has left with his parents. I have no idea where they've gone."

"Then you had best hurry and find out, hadn't you? Dawn is only two hours away."

Two hours in which to find the proverbial needle in a haystack. "And when I find him?"

"Take my ring with you. My mark is still on the child, and the ring will tell me when you have found him. I will contact you then to make the exchange."

He ran a hand through his hair. "I want Maddie alive or no deal, witch."

"Then hurry, Shapeshifter. The snow is threatening, and she wears only a T-shirt." The insane sound of her laughter echoed around the room long after her image had faded.

He stared at the ring for a long moment. If he made any attempt to find Maddie without first getting Evan, he had no doubt that Eleanor would kill her.

He grabbed his coat and Maddie's bag and headed for the door. He only had one hope of finding Evan quickly. He just had to pray the FBI agent was in a mellow, helpful mood.

Seventeen

"Well, well, well." Mack leaned his chair against the wall and looked more like a smiling shark than ever. "This *is* an unexpected pleasure. I'd anticipated having to issue a warrant to get you in here."

"Cut the crap, Mack. I need your help." Unable to stay still, Jon began pacing the width of the small office Mack had obviously claimed as his own.

Mack's chair hit the floor with a thump. "What's happened?"

"Eleanor has taken Maddie hostage again. She'll exchange her for Evan." Jon swung away from the intensity of Mack's gaze and stalked across to the window. Ten minutes had passed, ten minutes in which anything could have happened to Maddie. He gazed down at the empty street, watching the rain pelting across the pavement. Imagined it doing the same to her pale skin.

He closed his mind to the image and swung back around. "I need to know where the kid is Mack." His voice was almost savage, but he didn't care. "He's my only hope of getting her back alive."

Mack eyed him neutrally. "You can't exchange one death for another."

"I don't intend to." He ran a hand across his eyes. They felt gritty and sore, as if he hadn't slept in a week. But this was a nightmare only just beginning. He dug the ring out of his pocket and showed it to the agent. "This belongs to Eleanor. Through it, she will know when I find Evan. Only then will she tell me where the exchange will take place."

The big man leaned forward and studied the ring. "It's

magical?"

"Yes." He bit down on his impatience and flipped the ring in his palm. "Through it she used to track Hank's movements. Now she'll track mine."

Mack leaned back in his chair and regarded him evenly. "I gather, then, that Hank is dead."

"Yes." He hesitated, then shoved the ring back into his pocket. "If you hurry, you'll find what's left of his remains up near Castle Peak."

Mack frowned. "How did he die?"

"Does it really matter?" He slammed his palms down on the desk and glared across at Mack. "He's dead. And Maddie will be, too, if we don't get a move on here."

Mack continued to regard him steadily. He briefly considered throwing the FBI agent against a wall or two to shake the information out of him, but past experience told him it wouldn't make a difference. The big man would budge only when it suited him.

"What if I tell you that I don't know where he is?" he said softly.

Jon snorted. "I'd call you a damn liar."

Mack grinned—all teeth and no emotion. "Have you considered the prospect that Eleanor will come for you and the boy once you find him? That Maddie may be dead right now, anyway?"

"Maddie's alive." He could feel it in his heart, in his soul. If she died, he would know. If she died, there would be nothing left but the need for revenge. "Eleanor won't come to us personally when I reach Evan. She'll do so by spirit. She wants me to witness Maddie's death. She wants to make sure I suffer."

"And you are suffering, aren't you? What if this is all part of her game?"

"Damn it, just tell me where the kid is!"

"No." Mack's quiet statement cut through his heart like a knife.

Jon stared at him. "What do you mean, no?"

"I mean no, I won't give you the boy." He hesitated, then rose quickly from the chair, as if he could feel the anger building on the other side of the desk and wanted to escape its path. "Not unless I come with you."

Jon laughed harshly and pushed away from the desk. "You're insane."

"And you're a hairsbreadth away from a murder charge!"

Jon slammed his palms back onto the desk. The force of his blow made the whole desk shake. "You can't charge me for killing someone who was already dead!"

Mack stared at him. "What in hell do you mean by that?"

He sighed in irritation and pushed away from the desk. He really didn't want to get into all this right now. It was only wasting precious time. "The thing masquerading as Hank Stewart wasn't born in this lifetime. It wasn't born in your grandfather's lifetime. It clung to life through the blood of others, and through Eleanor's magic."

The FBI agent blinked. It was the only indication that he was even listening. "You're saying he was some form of zombie?"

"Sort of." What Hank had been he didn't really know. And he didn't really care. The man was dead and could no longer hurt Maddie. That was all that mattered.

"But...zombies are shambling creatures with no brain or emotion. Hank was *human.*"

Jon shook his head. "You've been watching too many horror movies. Now, tell me where Evan is."

"I don't think it's a wise move-"

"What's not a wise move is all this screwing around! Because believe me, if it costs Maddie her life, there won't be a prison on this Earth strong enough to hold me—or keep me away from your damn throat."

If Mack was in any way intimidated by the threat, he didn't show it. "As I was saying, I don't think that's a wise move—unless I come with you."

Jon watched in silence as Mack dragged his coat off the back of the chair and quickly donned it.

Finally, the FBI agent met his steady gaze and gave him another bland smile. "But I do think I finally have an answer for the question I asked yesterday."

Jon raked a hand through his hair. Somewhere along the line he'd obviously lost the point of their conversation. "What question?"

"You really do care for this woman, don't you?"

He avoided Mack's knowing gaze and studied the storm-held night beyond the window, wondering how cold it was getting up in the mountains. Was it was snowing up there yet? "Yes. I really do. But I can't let you come with me, Mack. Eleanor's too dangerous."

"I agree."

He looked back in surprise, but Mack's gaze was determined.

"From what I can gather, she's got the better of you twice now. A third time might be unlucky for everyone."

He was fighting a losing battle, and he knew it. Still, he had to try one more time. "You've never met her like. You have no understanding what you're about to go up against."

Mack gave him a wolflike grin. "I've never met *your* like before, either, but I've survived our ten year association."

Jon glanced at his watch. Twenty minutes gone. "You'll slow me down. I can fly faster than you could ever drive."

"Which is a point I'd like to discuss on our way. Come along, son. We have no time to waste."

Jon smacked the wall in frustration. No one seemed to be listening to common sense these days—especially when *he* was speaking it. But with Maddie's life now on the line, he could think of no other human he'd rather have at his back than Terry Mackeral. With a final glance at his watch, he followed the FBI agent out the door.

***

"We're running out of time."

"I know." If Mack was at all concerned, Jon certainly couldn't see it. "We're almost there."

Jon turned his gaze to the skyline. Dawn was beginning to creep through the darkness, spreading red fingers of light across the stormy skies. An hour and a half had passed. And there was snow up on the mountain peaks.

Maddie was still alive, but he wasn't certain of anything

more than that. He rubbed a hand across gritty-feeling eyes. This was exactly the situation he'd spent half his life trying to avoid—someone he cared about getting caught in the line of fire. It was the reason he'd walked away from his family, the reason he'd tried to convince himself his heart could only belong to his work.

And it was the reason he would continue to push Maddie away from him once they'd rescued her. He couldn't let her go through this type of hell a second time.

Mack slowed the car and turned into a driveway. The headlights picked out a small cabin not far from the road.

"Place belongs to a friend of mine. Evan and his family were only here until this morning, then we were moving them interstate."

At least the police weren't taking any chances with Evan's safety. "I just need to talk to the kid."

Mack nodded. "And the ring?"

"Will let us know what Eleanor plans next." He climbed out of the car as soon as it stopped. The wind moaned through the trees, and its touch was bitterly cold. And Maddie was out in it, wearing only a T-shirt.

He slammed the car door shut and stalked up to the front door. Mack caught his arm only feet away and pulled him to a halt. "The father's a cop with a trigger temper. Best let me handle this."

He nodded and stepped away. Mack thumped on the door. The only reply was the unmistakable sound of a rifle being loaded.

"Who is it?" a voice called.

"FBI. Open the door, Steve."

"Put your badge against the window."

Mack muttered something under his breath, then glanced back at Jon. "The man can be a pain in the backside, but it's good to see he's being this cautious."

Jon bit down on the urge to smash past Mack and the fool with the gun. "Caution won't save Evan or Maddie. Hurry up."

Mack slapped his badge against the window. After a

moment, the door opened.

"Who's your friend?" the bear-like figure asked, pointing the rifle in Jon's direction.

Mack pushed the weapon aside. "He's helping with inquiries. We need to talk to your son, Steve."

The big man shook his head. "He's asleep, and I don't want to wake him."

Mack's sharklike smile flashed briefly. "Neither do I, but we have no choice. Which room?"

"Second on the right down the hall." Steve eyed Jon with distrust then swung his gaze back to Mack. "I'm coming with you."

"Fine. Just don't interfere, or I'll have you hauled up on charges so fast your head will spin."

Steve blinked in surprise, then nodded. Jon glanced at his watch again as they walked up the hall. Twenty-five minutes left.

Mack knocked lightly on the door, then opened it up and switched on the light. Evan shot up in bed, his face screwed up in fright.

Steve pushed past them both and walked across the room, placing a reassuring arm around his son's shoulders. "It's okay, Evan. The police just need to talk to you again."

Evan nodded, but his wide, amber gaze was aimed directly at Jon. "Why haven't you rescued her? You promised."

Jon ignored Mack's raised eyebrow. The teenager's gaze was full of fear. He knew, or at least suspected, why they were there. "I did. Eleanor took her again." He hesitated, then added softly, "She wants to exchange Maddie for you."

The teenager shrank back into his father's arms. Steve held him tight and glared at the two of them. "You can't seriously be thinking of complying."

"Of course not." Mack's voice held a soothing note. "But we do need Evan's help to locate his aunt."

"For God's sake, he's just a kid. Why don't you leave him alone?"

There was a desperate edge of denial in Steve's voice, and his fear curled through the room. Jon smiled grimly. Steve didn't want his son to be different. Didn't want him to be gifted, like his aunt.

But it was fools like Steve who had put Maddie through hell for so long. Anger shot through him, but he held it in check. "Like it or not, your son has inherited psychic abilities similar to his aunt's. Denying it won't change anything. It might even make it worse." Might eventually make him kill someone because he'd been forced to deny his gifts too long. "But that's not what we're here for, either."

"I can't find her," Evan said, a tremor of fear running through his soft voice. "There's some sort of wall between us."

"I don't want you to find her." Jon took the ring out of his pocket. The light sparked the panther's eyes to life, shooting pale red rays through the room. "This ring belongs to Eleanor. If you touch it, she'll know we've found you and will tell us where to meet her."

Evan shrank back against his father again. "She'll come here?"

"Only as a wraith, a ghost. She won't be real, and she won't be able to hurt you."

"This is ridiculous," Steve growled. The fear in his eyes was almost as bright as the fear in his son's eyes.

"Be quiet or leave." Mack moved to stand halfway between the two of them, as if he feared some sort of confrontation. "Go ahead, Jon."

Jon kept his gaze on the teenager. After a moment, Evan nodded and held his hand out. Jon placed the ring in the middle of Evan's palm, and the boy closed his fingers around it. Nothing happened for several heartbeats, then smoke began to curl through his fingers.

Evan yelped in surprise and would have thrown the ring away if Jon hadn't clamped his hand around the teenager's.

"It's okay," he soothed. "It's only smoke. It won't hurt you."

Evan licked his lips and nodded. It was a gesture so reminiscent of Maddie that Jon's gut twisted painfully. Time was running out, and he was no closer to finding her now than he had been nearly two hours before.

The smoke twisted and turned and finally found shape. Eleanor's malevolent gaze swept across the four of them. Steve and Mack made surprised noises, but Jon kept his eyes on the wraith—just in case it tried anything.

"I've kept my end of the bargain, Eleanor."

She smiled. It might well have been a cat snarling. "So you have, Shapeshifter. And just in time. Your poor, dear girlfriend was turning a little blue."

It felt as if someone had grabbed his heart and squeezed tight. "The deal's off if she's dead, witch." His voice sounded amazingly detached considering he was barely resisting the urge to smash the wraith's face in. Not that it would have done him any good. The wraith was as insubstantial as a ghost.

"Oh, she's not dead. Not yet." The wraith eyed him in amusement. "Come to the old cave up on Maxus Peak and see for yourself. Just be here by sunset with the boy or she'll pay, Shapeshifter."

"We'll be there."

He watched the wraith dissipate then uncurled Evan's fingers from around the ring and took it back. Though he didn't think it was possible for Eleanor to transport the kid away from them using the ring, he wasn't about to take any chances.

Evan stared at him, fear in his eyes. "You're not going to make me go with you, are you?"

Jon smiled. "No." Not when Maddie had worked so hard to free him. "But I do need a lock of your hair."

"This witchcraft business is getting a little out of hand," Steve muttered uneasily. "I really think you had both better leave."

Jon kept his gaze on the teenager. In some ways, the son was much wiser than the father. "Eleanor has placed her mark on you, so I have to convince her I have you with me. If I tie a lock of hair around the ring, she might be fooled long enough for me to rescue Maddie."

"Enough-" Steve lurched to his feet.

Mack stepped forward and placed a calming hand on the big man's arm. "If you want to save both your son and your sister-in-law, go get the scissors, Steve."

Steve hesitated, then glanced down at his son and nodded. But Jon could tell by the flashes of red that ran through his aura that it wasn't for Maddie's sake that he complied. If Evan hadn't been involved, Steve would have let Maddie rot in hell before he helped her.

Jon wondered how the fool was going to cope with a son who had inherited the same abilities that he hated—and feared—in Maddie.

He stood up and walked across to the window, but it looked south, not north. He couldn't see the mountain that held the witch and Maddie.

"Don't think you're going up there alone," Mack stated quietly.

Jon closed his eyes. He just wanted it all over with, one way or another. But Mack was right. He couldn't go up there alone. Not if he wanted Maddie to walk free from this mess.

"Fine," he said remotely, watching the wind whip the branches of the old pine. "It's not a good day for flight, anyway." But it sure as hell was a good day to kill.

***

The little man was back in her head, pounding away on his infernal drums. Maddie shook her head, but that only made the pounding increase. Sweat broke out across her forehead and bile rose up the back of her throat. She swallowed heavily, but the metallic taste in her mouth made her stomach turn. She groaned and squeezed her eyes shut, waiting for the rolling sensation to go away.

After a while she became aware of a breeze running chill fingers past her legs. She shivered, suddenly realizing her whole body felt cold—so cold her bones ached with it.

She opened her eyes. The light of a nearby torch flickered off the red-brown walls, making the shadows beyond the flame appear more threatening. Somewhere beyond that, lost in the darkness, came the steady drip of water. Beyond that again, the distant howl of the wind.

She shifted slightly, and pain lanced through her brain. Tears stung her eyes. She brushed them away with the heel of her hand, then stared at the huge metal bars about ten feet away. They rose from the rock floor to the ceiling and looked as old as time itself. This wasn't a hastily prepared prison, she thought with a cold feeling of dread. This was a prison Eleanor had used many times before.

Turning carefully, she studied the darkness behind her. A figure suddenly loomed, eyes gleaming in the flickering torchlight. Maddie yelped and edged back in fright. The figure did the same, and Maddie stared in surprise.

It wasn't Eleanor. The scream had sounded too young, and the body shape was wrong. Her heart did a quick leap of joy. It couldn't be, surely...?

"Teresa?" she questioned softly.

"Yes." The reply was timid, and the girl's voice hoarse, as if she hadn't spoken for a while.

Aware the slightest wrong movement could frighten the girl back into hiding, Maddie kept her voice low. "Are you okay?"

The teenager edged forward. She was tall and slender, with long, matted brown hair. Her face was gaunt and pale, and dark shadows ringed her eyes. It wasn't hard to guess she'd been Eleanor's guest for quite a while. "Are you a prisoner, too?

Maddie nodded. "I'm afraid Eleanor doesn't like me very much."

The teenager stared at her. "Is that her name? I've only seen her when she comes to check if I'm still asleep."

Which suggested the teenager had been awake for a while. Maddie wondered whether the fact that Teresa was now awake was an oversight on Eleanor's part or intentional. "How often does she do that?"

Teresa shrugged. "Regularly. She took my watch, so I can't really say what time."

If the witch checked regularly, she'd no doubt be back soon. Maddie shivered and rubbed her arms briskly. The movement sent the madman in her head into a frenzy of activity.

"I'm cold, too," Teresa said, edging closer.

The nightgown she wore wasn't much longer than Maddie's T-shirt and certainly didn't appear any warmer. "I'm told that two people hugging is a good way to keep warm," Maddie replied softly. "Want to try it?"

The teenager hesitated a second, then rushed forward and collapsed into her embrace. Maddie rubbed her hands up and down the girl's half-frozen arms and wondered how in the hell she was going to get them both out of Eleanor's cage.

"Where are we?" Teresa clung to her tightly, as if afraid to let her go.

"I don't know." She leaned her head back against the wall and studied the cavern beyond their prison. They were somewhere in the mountains, obviously, but more than that she couldn't guess. But wherever it was, it was a stronghold Eleanor had well prepared. Fear stabbed through her heart, and she closed her eyes. Jon would come for her, no matter how many traps Eleanor set for him. And he would die because he was only one man, and he couldn't fight Eleanor and protect *her* at the same time.

She should have listened to him, should have left when she had the chance, instead of lingering that extra night.

And yet, given the chance to do it all over again, her choices would remain the same. Maybe it was selfish, but if she had to die, then she wanted it to be with the memory of Jon's touch still burning across her skin.

Teresa shifted and glanced up. Her eyes were brown and slightly unfocused. Drugged, Maddie thought, and wondered if it might explain her own unnatural calm.

"How are we going to get out of here?" Teresa asked.

Another question she couldn't answer. Maddie smiled grimly and brushed a limp strand of hair away from the girl's eyes. "I'll find a way." She ran her hands up and down the teenager's arms for a minute, then frowned. "Did you wake up on the floor, or a bed of some sort?"

"A bed. Why?"

"Just curious. Come on, show me."

The teenager rose unsteadily. Maddie climbed to her feet then clung on to the wall as the darkness spun around her. The spinning eased after several deep breaths but didn't entirely go away. She rubbed the sweat off her forehead and wondered what in hell was wrong. Her skin was so cold that everything ached, and yet inside, it felt as if she were burning up. Her head alternated between a pounding ache and a weird, spaced-out sort of sensation, and she wasn't entirely sure which she preferred.

"This way," Teresa said softly.

Walking a few feet had them back into darkness. Another step had her legs bumping into the wooden bed frame. Maddie bent down and swept her hand across the surface. Rough wool met her touch. A blanket. She picked it up, then reached out and caught Teresa by the arm. "Here, wrap this around you."

"It smells," she muttered, but pulled the blanket around herself nevertheless.

The only smell Maddie could make out was unwashed teenager. "I want you to do me a favor, Teresa."

"What?" There was suddenly a great deal of wariness in the girl's voice.

Which was understandable, considering they were both strangers. The kid might *want* to trust her, but she wasn't a complete fool. "If we hear someone coming, I want you to lie down on this bed and pretend to be asleep. No matter what happens, I don't want you to move or make a sound. Can you do that?"

"Yes." Something in her voice suggested it was a charade she'd already played.

"And if you get the chance, I want you to run as fast as you can out of this place and head down the mountain. Okay?" If this was the same place where Hank had stopped earlier, then there'd be a road for the teenager to find and follow. "A friend of mine should be outside soon, and he'll help you."

"What's his name?"

"Jon." Maddie closed her eyes briefly against the sudden ache in her heart. "Come on, let's get back to the light."

They shuffled back to the bars. Maddie leaned her forehead against them, trying to ignore another wash of weakness. After several deep breaths, she studied the cavern once more.

It was hard to make out any distinct shapes in the uneven light of the sputtering torch. The breeze shivered past her legs, and the smell of snow, citrus and death was heavy in the air.

Her stomach rolled again. She clung to the bars and licked her dry lips. When the world stopped spinning again, she glanced up at the torch. The flames were bending to her right, following the lead of the wind.

"That's the way to run, Teresa," she said, pointing to the left of the cavern. "That's where the breeze is coming from, so there has to be some sort of exit."

The teenager nodded. "She never leaves the door unlocked, though."

"She only needs to get careless once." And the chances of that happening were greater now that everything seemed to be going Eleanor's way.

The sharp rattle of a stone bouncing across the cavern's floor made them both jump in fright.

"Go," Maddie whispered.

Teresa scooted across the darkness and disappeared. Maddie dropped to the floor and half closed her eyes, feigning a look of pain. Which wasn't all that hard, given the sick churning in her stomach.

The footsteps drew closer and changed from the click of claws to the sharp tap of boot heels. Maddie opened her eyes slightly.

"How nice. You're awake," Eleanor drawled as she stopped next the metal bars. "How are you feeling?"

There was no hint of scarring on Eleanor's right hand, no sign that she's ever been burned. And yet, as she dug into her pocket and produced a key, her movements were awkward and stiff.

Had she healed herself with magic, or was she simply presenting an unscarred front? "Does it really matter how I feel?"

Eleanor smiled. It might well have been Death smiling at her. "Of course it matters. Wouldn't want you dying before the boyfriend gets here."

The hint of malice in Eleanor's sharp features ran dread

through Maddie's soul. Sweat broke out across her forehead, despite the chill in the cavern. Something was wrong. Not with the situation, but within herself. She licked her lips again and glared up at Eleanor. "What have you done to me?"

Eleanor's laugh was high and unstable. "Let's just say you won't be lighting any funeral pyres for a while—except maybe your own."

Maddie stared at her and repeated, "What have you done to me?" The question was little more than a soft croak, her voice almost strangled by fear. Had Eleanor torn away her firestarting abilities, leaving her no weapon to fight with?

Eleanor smirked. "I've looped your gifts. Try using them on me, and they'll backlash against you." She stopped and studied Maddie critically. "And I'd say that is already happening. Feel a little hot, my dear?"

Maddie resisted the temptation to mop her brow. To be killed by her own fires just when she was beginning to understand them had to be one of the great ironies of all time. "Where's the other teenager?"

"Oh, sleeping close by." She leaned down and carefully slid the key into the lock, her movements awkward. "Come along, my dear. We have much to arrange."

"I'm not going anywhere with you." It sounded almost childish, but Maddie didn't really care. If she couldn't fight, she had to delay. The more Eleanor concentrated on her, the greater chance Teresa had of escaping.

Eleanor sighed. It was a dramatic sound that didn't fit the evil in her dark eyes. "I really haven't the time to play right now. Up."

She made a motion with her right hand, and something whispered across Maddie's neck and jerked tight. She gasped and raised her hands to her neck. There was nothing there but a whisper of icy wind entwining her throat. Panic and terror surged, and sweat dimpled her skin. Maddie briefly closed her eyes and struggled to breathe normally. If she lost control of her gifts, she'd kill herself. And that was one amusement she had no intention of providing the witch.

Eleanor made another pulling motion with her hand, and

the wind became a ring of ice that bit deep into Maddie's neck and wrenched her forward.

"Up," Eleanor repeated.

The leash pulled so tightly against her throat she could barely breathe. She scrambled to her feet and the tightness eased, allowing her to drag in great gulps of air. But the sudden movement made the drummer in her head go crazy. Dizziness hit her. She reached for the wall, trying to steady herself.

Eleanor gave her no time to recover, yanking on the leash again. "Come, my dear. The day passes us by, and we have bait to lay."

Her feet felt frozen and half-numb, and her legs were so wobbly they didn't seem strong enough to support her weight. But as she stumbled through the doorway, a fierce sense of elation ran through her. Eleanor continued to force her forward and didn't stop to re-lock the door.

There was still a chance to fulfil her promise to Evan. All she had to do was keep Eleanor occupied long enough for Teresa to slip away.

Eighteen

"Is now the right time to admit that I don't really know that much about witchcraft?" Mack hauled his coat collar up around his neck, leaned his hip against the car, and shoved his hands deep into his pockets.

Jon smiled grimly. The FBI agent looked like a man suddenly facing the gates of Hell. And it was probably a fair estimation of what awaited them.

"Eleanor's not really a witch. She's a sorcerer. Next step up the ladder." He stopped carving the end of the small white-ash branch and held it up to the light. A few more cuts, and his makeshift dagger would be ready.

Mack turned and studied the trees, his face giving little away. But Jon could feel his unease, saw the shadow snaking through the FBI agent's usually confident aura.

"You suddenly don't seem in so much of a hurry," Mack said.

Jon made a few final cuts along the limb, then put it down to join the other half dozen near his feet. "That's because I know what Eleanor is capable of, and I have no intention of going up there unarmed." Which is why he'd made Mack detour past the cabin they'd found Evan in on their way up here. He needed the supplies locked in the back of his truck.

Mack patted his shoulder. "I have a gun, you know. And backup is on its way."

"Eleanor can change shape quicker than you can shoot." He stood up and flexed his leg. The knife wound throbbed in protest, but he could move around fairly normally, and that was all that mattered. "As for your backup, they have five minutes, then I'm off."

"Don't be a fool, Barnett. You can't go after this woman alone if you want the kid or your Maddie to survive."

Your Maddie. The phrase whispered through his mind, soothing the lonely ache in his soul. Only she wasn't his Maddie and never could be. He angrily snatched up the white ash daggers near his feet.

"Take these and keep them safe," he said, handing Mack four of the weapons. "They'll protect you from Eleanor when all else fails."

Mack raised a skeptical eyebrow. "And how will these crudely carved bits of wood do this?"

"They're made of white ash. It's an ancient wood deadly to shapeshifters." He dragged his black bag off the car hood and rummaged around inside until he found the small metal medallion Seline had given him.

"So white ash can kill you?"

Jon glanced up sharply. "Yes, it can. Why? Plan to use it when this is all over?"

Mack gave him his sharklike grin. "Arrest you, maybe. Kill you, no." He hesitated and glanced past Jon. "The cavalry just arrived."

Jon looked over his shoulder and saw the three police vehicles pull to a halt. Mack strode across to the first car and began a hurried conversation with the driver. Jon listened for a few moments, then turned his attention back to the medallion in his hand. Looped with a shoelace, and so black with age that he couldn't make out the markings that surrounded the blue-green stone at its heart, it certainly didn't look like an amulet that would protect him from the worst of Eleanor's magic. But Seline had assured him it would work, and she usually didn't promise what she couldn't give.

He slid the amulet around his neck, then bent and placed two of the white ash daggers in his boots. The third he slid into the loop he'd sown inside his jacket.

His gaze ran back to the mountain peak lost in the mist and the trees above them. Maddie was up there somewhere, cold and alone and probably terrified. His fault, no one else's.

He dragged up the zipper on his jacket and marched across

to Mack. "Time to get moving."

Mack raised an eyebrow in surprise, but nodded. "How do you want to play it?"

"Send four men up the trail by that pine. The others follow the trail to our right." Both trails were little more than wild goose chases, but they would keep the policemen from interfering too soon. And probably keep them alive in the process. He met Mack's knowing gaze steadily. "You and I will take the trail near the creek."

"You know the drill," Mack growled to the men. "Let's move." Jon turned and walked across to Mack's car, grabbing Maddie's backpack from the back seat. She'd need something warm to change into once he'd rescued her. The soft hint of roses spun around him as he put it on.

"Hope you know what you're doing." Mack's gaze was on the shadow-wrapped trail ahead of them.

"So do I," Jon muttered grimly. Because if he didn't, they were all dead meat.

***

The flames burned high but without any heat. Grayish-green smoke rose, curling lazily towards the stormy sky but fading into the mist long before it reached the treetops.

But the illusion of heat was better than nothing. Maddie huddled a bare foot away from the fire, stamping half frozen feet in an effort to keep warm. Mud squished up between her toes and splattered up her legs. It felt clammy, reminding her of Hank's touch. She licked her lips and thrust the image away. At least the mud protected some of her from the wind's sharpness.

Across the clearing, the entrance to the cave sat in darkness. There had been no movement in those shadows as yet, and Maddie hoped Teresa hadn't gone back to sleep.

"They're close. I can feel them." Eleanor's whisper held a hint of excitement. "They have the child."

A sick sensation rose to the back of her throat. She briefly closed her eyes and tried to swallow it away. Surely Jon wouldn't risk Evan's life to save hers.

She had a sudden image of the harsh, almost savage look

in his eyes when he'd left her to find Hank, and ran a shaking hand through her matted hair. In some ways, it was frightening to realize she just *didn't know* what he was capable of.

She stared at Eleanor. The pale orange and blue flames made the sorcerer's sharp features look almost skeletal. "Why do you need Evan? You have Teresa—isn't one child's death enough?"

Eleanor's gaze didn't waver from the luminous star she was drawing in the mud, but her contempt whipped around Maddie, as sharp as a slap.

"Once it was, but now my need is greater."

"Is that why you've taken so many children over the last year or so?"

Eleanor gave a quick nod, her attention still on the star. "Once upon a time I only had to sacrifice every six months. Now it is every month."

Maddie wondered why her need had become so desperate that she now had to kill two children a month. And where had Hank fit into all this? Eleanor stood up and brushed the mud from her hands. The star at her feet glowed fiercely for several seconds, then quickly faded. She smiled and turned her attention back to Maddie.

"Now, for the final trap."

Maddie took a step away from the flames—and Eleanor. The invisible band pinched hard against her throat, and it became difficult to breathe again. Sweat trickled down the side of her face. She didn't need Eleanor's fire to provide any heat—she had her own. And it was a fire that was steadily growing.

"Don't," she gasped, more as a reminder to herself than a plea to Eleanor. The squeezing eased, regardless, and Maddie licked cracked lips. She had to keep Eleanor talking. Had to hope Teresa had found the courage to leave the cell and escape. "I just want to ask a question."

Eleanor smiled. It seemed to sharpen her features and make her look more like a cat than ever. "We have some time up our sleeve. Ask away."

"Just tell me why you're doing all this? Why do you, an

obviously beautiful and powerful young woman, need teenagers?"

Eleanor's dark gaze glittered with amusement. "Flattery earns you a few more minutes of freedom. As to the children, they are literally my life, my bloodline."

Maddie frowned, not sure whether the fuzzy ache in her head or the fire racing through her veins was responsible for her total lack of comprehension. "I'm afraid I don't understand."

"Then let me demonstrate."

Eleanor waved her hand. The smoke drifting across the clearing spun towards her, encasing her body from sight for several seconds. When it disappeared, Eleanor was gone, replaced by a withered, hunched-back figure.

"This is my true self." The crone's voice was high and shaky, but undoubtedly Eleanor's. Something in its tone still whispered of seduction and evil.

"This is how I will look by midnight if I do not take the virgin blood I need to sustain my life and looks." The smoke performed its gentle dance, and the more youthful Eleanor reappeared. "As you might guess, I prefer my current form."

"Was Hank like you?"

"Hank lived through me. I was his life, his bloodline. Of course, even I couldn't protect the fool from a wound inflicted by silver. He really should have known better than to carry such a weapon."

Movement flickered in the darkness behind Eleanor. Maddie fought the sudden rush of excitement and terror. Teresa had found the courage to move out of the cell, but all Eleanor had to do was turn slightly, and she'd see the teenager as plain as day. "Surely a sorcerer can find a better way to sustain her looks than killing innocent children."

Teresa was easing around the edge of the cavern entrance, a ragged white shape framed in the cold fire's flickering light.

"There is nothing as powerful as blood magic, and only blood magic can sustain me now." Eleanor raised an eyebrow and studied Maddie critically. "How old do you think I am?"

The crone had looked at least a hundred years old, but

something in Eleanor's tone suggested the number was higher. Much higher. "I really have no idea."

Teresa crept past the entrance of the cavern and disappeared into the trees. Maddie didn't relax. Couldn't afford to when the woman standing opposite her could take the shape of a panther and easily catch the fleeing teenager.

"My dear, I am five hundred and twenty-two years old. Hold it well, don't I?"

Maddie blinked. Five hundred and twenty-two years old? No wonder the woman was mad—she'd watched the entire world change around her while she remained the same.

"What about Hank? How old was he?"

"He was younger by several hundred years. It took me a while to find a man who was both trainable and, shall we say, as bloodthirsty, as me."

The sound of a branch snapping whipped across the clearing, as sharp as a gunshot. Eleanor spun around and stared into the trees.

Maddie waited tensely, listening to the silence and hoping Teresa had the good sense not to move. After several long heartbeats, Eleanor turned back.

"As much as I have enjoyed our little chat, it's time to move. Our guests are approaching."

Something in Eleanor's dark gaze made Maddie retreat a step. Eleanor smiled and waved her left hand casually. Ice snapped across Maddie's skin and held her tight. She couldn't move, could only watch as Eleanor made another motion with her hand and encased her in a wide circle of fire.

"Now, for my masterpiece." The flames parted as Eleanor walked through them, like slaves bowing before their master. "But I'm afraid you won't be around to see it."

The witch waved a hand. Maddie's silent scream was lost as the darkness encased her mind.

* * *

"Don't move," Jon warned softly.

He knelt down and studied the trail ahead. Something didn't feel right.

He picked up the rock near his feet and lobbed it ten feet

ahead. There was a slight tremor in the bushes to his left, and a swoosh of air as an arrow imbedded itself into the tree trunk to their right. He watched it quiver lightly in the mottled light of the forest. White ash, just like the one that had landed him in the well. And, in an odd sort of way, sent him Maddie.

"Placed to injure, not kill," Mack commented softly.

Jon nodded and picked up another rock, lobbing it farther ahead. Another arrow thudded into a tree. "Just in case the first one missed." A third rock had no effect.

He glanced back down the trail and frowned. A whisper of movement told him they were being followed. Mack's men, probably. It certainly didn't feel like Eleanor. Besides, the witch wouldn't make any noise.

He turned his attention back to the trail ahead. He couldn't *feel* any more traps. "Looks safe to move on."

He rose and led the way forward. No more arrows thudded out of trees to greet them—in fact, the trail seemed entirely *too* easy. He'd expected Eleanor to play with him a bit more, yet he was over half way up the mountain and so far had only a few poorly placed arrows to contend with.

Worry snaked through his gut. Something was wrong.

Ahead, a branch snapped, a sharp sound that seemed to echo through the unnatural silence of the forest. He stopped quickly, listening. For several seconds there was no further sound, then he heard a soft, fearful sob. Even as hope rose, he squashed it. The sob didn't belong to Maddie—it was much too young sounding. Eleanor would have no doubt ensured the mountain was empty of human habitation—she certainly couldn't afford to have strangers wandering into the middle of her blood sacrifice, fouling the magic. Which meant the person he could hear just might be the kidnapped girl. From the sound of it, she was heading down the trail towards them.

"Trouble?" Mack asked quietly, his hand hovering near his gun.

"Someone's running towards us—someone who's frightened and unsteady on their feet. It just might be our missing kid."

Mack raised his eyebrow. "You can tell all this standing

here?"

Jon gave him a grim smile. "I can. And so can Eleanor, if she's as close as we are. Let's move."

They scrambled up the trail, ducking low-hanging branches and trying to make as little noise as possible. Jon leapt over a slime-encrusted rock, but his footing slipped coming down, and he landed awkwardly. A needle-hot lance of pain ran up his leg. He swore softly and limped on for several more steps then stopped and grabbed at his leg.

Mack did a quick sidestep to avoid running into him. "Problem?"

"Tore my damn leg open again." Blood was beginning to seep through his jeans and past his fingers. It was a smell that would attract a hunter like Eleanor, if she were anywhere nearby.

Mack took a handkerchief out of his pocket and held it out. "Here, use this."

He accepted it with a grunt of thanks, and quickly tied it around the wound, tightening it as much as he dared. A soft gasp made him glance up. Not ten feet away stood a thin, pale girl. He might have thought her little more than a wraith except for the heaving of her chest, the sharp tang of fear in the turbulent swirl of her emotions.

Mack's sudden stillness suggested the FBI agent had also spotted her.

Jon didn't dare move. If either of them did, he sensed she'd run. "Teresa?"

The girl nodded once, dark eyes wide as her gaze flitted between the two of them. "Is one of you Jon?"

"I am." He straightened carefully, the knot in his stomach suddenly more painful than his leg. To know his name the teenager had to have been talking to Maddie. Which meant Maddie had somehow helped her escape, but at what cost to herself? "This is Mack, from the FBI."

"You have to get me out here. She's up there, she'll come after me..." Teresa glanced quickly up the trail then took a few stumbling steps towards them. "Please, we have to get out of here."

Her gaze was wide and terrified, dark eyes glassy. Running on sheer terror, he thought, and shared a grim look with Mack. "You take her down. I'll continue on."

"You can't take on Eleanor alone and expect to win."

"I know." He raked a hand through his hair and glanced up the trail. Maddie was up there, somewhere. And he sensed her time was running out. "I know your men aren't far behind us. Take the girl to them then come back up. But remember, Eleanor is a shapeshifter. Don't trust any animal you see in this forest."

Mack raised his eyebrow. "Not even a hawk?"

"Especially a hawk," Jon said grimly. "I won't be shapeshifting to fight Eleanor, so it won't be me you see."

Mack nodded, then squatted, making himself a less formidable sight to the frightened teenager. "Let's get you down the mountain and see what we can do to find your mom and dad."

Tears misted the teenager's eyes. She edged forward, timidly taking Mack's hand when he held it out.

"Please, we have to hurry," she whispered, casting another fearful look up the mountain.

"Don't you worry about that old witch. Jon will take care of her."

His gaze met Jon's for a moment, and Jon smiled grimly. It wasn't hard to guess at the unspoken words in Mack's mind. *I hope.*

Mack and the girl headed back down the mountain. Jon gave the blood-soaked handkerchief a tug, testing its tightness, then glanced up the trail. Teresa hadn't looked strong enough to make it too far on her own. Eleanor and Maddie couldn't be far away. He just had to hope his leg would hold out until he got there.

Fifteen minutes later, he leaned against the twisted wreck of an old pine and struggled to see past the sweat stinging his eyes.

Maddie was a mere fifty feet away, but it might as well have been a thousand. She lay on the ground, arms outstretched. He couldn't see if she was tied. Couldn't see if she was awake or hurt. Could barely even see her through the ring of pale flame that surrounded her.

Trying to ignore the painful twist in his gut, he let his gaze travel around the clearing. There was no sign of Eleanor, but she had to be near. The taint of magic hung so heavily in the air it was making him sick.

Or was that fear?

His gaze was drawn back to Maddie. Had she moved? Did she know he was near?

He pushed away from the tree and wiped the sweat from his eyes. An almost expectant hush hung across the clearing. Beyond the strange colored flames, there was nothing that might indicate the trap that had to be waiting. He smiled grimly, his gaze drawn back to the trees on the opposite side of the clearing. Eleanor was there somewhere, waiting and watching.

Why make her wait any longer than necessary? The only way to discover what the witch planned was to walk straight into her trap—and hope Seline hadn't underestimated the amulet's power.

He dropped Maddie's pack near the base of the tree, then limped into the clearing. A shiver of anticipation seemed to run through the air. He listened for any sound that might indicate an attack, but kept his gaze on the figure lying in the center of the flames. Still no movement, no sound from Maddie.

He stopped three feet away from the flames. A tingle ran from the ground and up his body, and the amulet sprang to life, burning fiercely against his throat. He glanced down. He'd stepped into some sort of star drawn into the ground. *Magic.* But what had Eleanor intended it to do?

Laughter, high and unstable, shattered the silence. Eleanor stepped out of the trees, a predatory smile dominating her thin features.

"I thought you'd be a tougher catch, Shapeshifter." She brushed a long strand of hair away from her face with a hand that alternated between burned and unburned flesh.

He frowned. The burned hand was obviously Maddie's work, but why was the witch wasting energy to cover it up?

Vanity, perhaps? "Maybe you've overestimated me."

Eleanor's dark eyes were watchful despite her triumphant air. "Oh, I doubt that very much." She hesitated, her face surreal in the odd light of the pale orange flames. "Perhaps you'd best rid yourself of those white ash daggers you have in your boots."

Electricity raced up his legs from the ground, swirling around his body like a cord, yet never really touching him. He sensed it was somehow meant to make him obey. That he didn't surely had to indicate the amulet burning against his throat was working. He bent and slowly took out the two daggers from his boots, then tossed them to one side. For the moment, at least, it was better to let Eleanor think she had him in her power. He left the smaller dagger hidden in his coat. Eleanor didn't mention it, so maybe she couldn't sense it through the leather.

"Let Maddie go, Eleanor. She's of no use to you."

Eleanor was the image of a cat playing with its prey. "I can't set her free, Shapeshifter, but you can."

He raised his eyebrows, feigning unconcern despite the churning in his gut. "How, when you have me pinned to this spot?"

Eleanor's smile widened, which meant his guess was right. The star was meant to do nothing more than temporarily immobilize him.

"There's no fun in defeating an enemy who cannot move. You will be free soon enough."

Eleanor was too calm and Maddie too still. Sweat trickled down his back. The whole situation seemed out of whack and way beyond his control. "Then what will stop me from ripping out your heart, witch?"

"Oh, you can try, but the price will be your lover's death."

His gaze ran back to Maddie. Despite the chill in the air, her slender body was flushed with heat. It burned across her skin, beacon bright against the cold flames surrounding her. Sweat beaded her forehead and darkened her burnished hair. Even her T-shirt clung damply to her skin. The pale flames surrounding her held no warmth, so why was she so hot?

He met Eleanor's gaze and saw the uneasy mix of amusement and cruelty in the dark depths of her eyes. The witch wanted them all to pay—him for his interference, Maddie for burning her hand... His heart gave a sickening lurch. Maddie was a firestarter. The heat was *internal.*

He flexed his fingers. "Let her go, Eleanor, and I am yours."

Her responding smile was little more than a sharp snarl. Her form was blurring, shifting shape, becoming something less than human—but not quite catlike. "She has five minutes, Shapeshifter." Her voice was a purr, deep and menacing. "But to rescue her, you must defy my spell and then defeat me."

Blood trickled down his leg; its sweet smell seemed to hang heavily in the air. The craving in Eleanor's inhuman gaze grew stronger.

"What spell?" he asked, watching her form shiver and darken, becoming more catlike with every passing heartbeat.

"The flames, Shapeshifter. They will take the essence of your soul." Her sharp smile was little more than the snarl of a panther. "They will take your shapeshifting abilities from you."

"No..." The denial escaped before he could stop it. He was a *shapeshifter*—it wasn't just a gift, like Maddie's fire starting, or a product of magic, as were Eleanor's shapeshifting abilities. It was an integral part of *what he was.* It couldn't be ripped away without killing him.

"It won't destroy you, Shapeshifter." Her voice had become little more than a rough growl, her shape a breath away from the panther. She was retaining only enough humanity to speak. "That would be too easy. You must pay for the trouble you have caused me. Pay with pain."

Her paws hit the ground, and with another snarl, she sprang. Not away from the flames, but into them—straight at Maddie.

"No!" He leapt forward, hitting the flames. Pain ripped through his body, tore the scream away from his throat. For a frightening heartbeat there was nothing but emptiness, then he hit the ground and darkness invaded his world.

Nineteen

Maddie jerked awake. For several seconds she stared at the mist shrouded trees high above her and wondered where she was. She felt the damp ground pressing into her back, the caress of the cool breeze against her heat-fevered skin, and it only added to her confusion.

Then memory returned with a thump. She was burning up, killing herself because Eleanor had somehow looped her firestarting abilities. And because she didn't understand how to fully control them, she couldn't stop the fires raging deep inside from consuming her.

If she attacked Eleanor, she'd kill herself for sure.

Something black flew over her head. White teeth flashed a second before a snarl cut through the silence. The ragged sound of a gasp cut through the air—*Jon*. She didn't question her sudden certainty. He was here and in trouble because of her.

I have to help him. Somehow, I have to stop Eleanor. But her body refused to obey her need to move. Despite the heat flushing every pore, her limbs were locked in ice. She couldn't move, was barely able to breathe. The panther snarled again. A heartbeat later there was a guttural sound of pain. *Dear God, what's happening to him?*

She struggled to shift her head. Sweat ran down her forehead and stung her eyes. She blinked the moisture away and gritted her teeth. Her breath became a hiss of pain as the ice tightened around her neck.

*I have to move...*energy surged through her body, energy that burned with heat. Something splintered against her neck, and suddenly, her head and arms were free.

She twisted around, trying to see what was going on. Jon

and Eleanor were silhouetted against the brightness of the flames. Jon was on his back, struggling to hold the panther standing astride his prone body at arm's length. Blood soaked his jeans, and a bloody rent marred his left side. The panther was unharmed, toying with its prey.

Fire surged, burning through her veins. Maddie bit her lip hard enough to draw blood. *Attack me, and you will kill yourself,* Eleanor had told her. But maybe, just maybe, she could turn her fires on something else instead of the witch, and give Jon the chance to run.

She quickly scanned the trees above her until she found a branch that hung out far enough over the clearing. Half closing her eyes, she stared at the limb and reached down to the fires boiling through her body. The response was quick and deadly. The branch exploded into flame and, with a crack that ricocheted through the clearing, fell to the ground. The cat snarled in fright and leapt away from Jon. He scrambled awkwardly to his feet but didn't flee.

"Maddie, run!" he gasped. He stood between her and the panther, a bloodied warrior still ready for battle.

She could barely move, let alone run. And even if she were able to, she wouldn't have. He was ready to die defending her. She had nothing left to offer him but the same willingness to trade her life for his.

She glanced quickly at the trees and found another branch. The panther leapt again. Maddie aimed her fire at the branch, simultaneously croaking, "Jon, jump back!"

He heard and obeyed. The branch landed in a heap at his feet, trailing flaming leaves like confetti. The smell of burning pine was sharp in the air. The panther twisted away awkwardly and landed to one side of the stump. Its form shivered and darkened, then became Eleanor once more.

"My bait is awake, I see." Eleanor's voice was still a seductive drawl, despite the wisp of age beginning to take its toll on her features.

Maddie met her dark gaze and felt as if she were falling deep into its malevolent depths. It surrounded her, sapping her strength, her will. Eleanor was the essence of evil—a woman who had feasted on the blood of innocents down through the ages simply to preserve her looks and her life. They were fools to think they could ever beat her.

Once again, Jon moved until he stood between them. Maddie blinked, feeling like a sleeper coming out of a dream. Fear surged anew. Just for an instant, she'd been drawn into Eleanor's mind and had glimpsed the dark depths of her soul. It might well have been Hell's playground.

"Let her go, Eleanor."

His voice was flat, devoid of any sort of emotion. Yet Maddie could see his fear as sharply as she could taste her own. It was evident in the tightening of his shoulders, in the play of muscles across his back. But he was frightened for *her,* not for himself.

Eleanor smiled. "I know, I know. She means nothing to you."

Jon didn't reply. His fingers flexed and Maddie suddenly wondered why he didn't change into a hawk. His attack on Hank had shown how deadly his other shape could be—why didn't he use it now that Eleanor was back in human guise?

"I'm afraid you're missing the point, my boy. I don't want you dead. I want you suffering, *then* dead."

Jon's back blocked most of Eleanor from Maddie's sight, but her evil reached out nevertheless, swirling ice around her. The cord whipped back around her throat, pulling tight. Pain eddied and hovered close, and darkness was suddenly only a heartbeat away.

"I've already taken your soul," Eleanor continued, her voice venomous. "Next I'll take your heart, then finally, your life."

I've taken your soul... Was it only last night that Jon had said his soul was a hawk? Was that why he didn't shift shape? But how could Eleanor rip such a vital part of his being away from him?

The thought fled as the ice around her neck pulled tighter. Stars danced before her eyes, and every breath suddenly became a battle of survival.

"Do your worst, witch."

His voice seemed to come from a million miles away, yet it contained a hint of callousness that shook her. Energy ripped through the air, as hot as the fires in her soul. She licked cracked lips and tried to concentrate on his back. His muscles flexed beneath his jacket as he crossed his arms and waited. Why didn't he *do* something? Couldn't he sense the energy building up around them, a trap ready to fall?

Eleanor's laughter clawed at the air. Flames burst to life around him, bright and surreal. He didn't move, didn't fight. All too quickly he was lost to the consuming hunger of the fire.

Panic surged through Maddie. Without thought, she gathered her fire and aimed it at Eleanor. The witch screeched in surprise and pain. A heartbeat later, Maddie screamed in agony as the fire rebounded and consumed her consciousness.

Maddie's scream tore past the spell holding Jon captive. The bright flames danced frantically around him but never touched—and yet the amulet hadn't protected him fully. Or maybe it just couldn't handle anything more than one attack at a time. Maddie's agony knifed through his brain. He was so attuned to her he could feel her pain, feel her struggle to breathe, to survive, through every pore in his skin. He tore the dagger from his coat and lunged through the flames at Eleanor. Her form was shifting, merging into that of the panther. She leapt away but not fast enough. He plunged the white ash dagger deep into her side, trapping her between human and panther shape.

She screamed and lashed at him. Claws raked across his face before he could smash her hands away, then she was on him, a writhing, screaming mass of humanity and cat and inhuman strength.

They hit the ground locked together. Eleanor took the impact of both their weight but didn't seem to feel it. He grabbed her arms, holding her claws away from his face. Eleanor bucked and threw him high over her head. He hit the ground with a grunt, but scrambled up as the witch launched at him.

A gunshot resounded across the silence. Eleanor screamed

and twisted in midair. Blood plumed from her arm as the bullet tore through muscle and bone. She landed catlike, howling in agony, then sprang again—not at him, but at Maddie.

Jon threw himself between them. Eleanor twisted in midair, somehow avoiding him. He hit the ground near Maddie's feet and rolled, rising awkwardly. Pain burned up his leg, but he ignored it, spinning to meet Eleanor's next attack. She was on him in an instant, tearing at his face and his chest, her breath hot acid against his face. He wrapped his arms around her and held on tight. Needle-sharp fangs tore into his shoulder. Gritting his teeth and hissing in pain, he lifted her up off the ground and staggered away from Maddie.

Eleanor screamed in frustration, but it was a high, inhuman sound. She placed her paws against his chest and tore herself out of his arms, leaping away. Two gunshots cut through the air. Something burned past his ear, drawing blood. Eleanor jerked. Blood and gore sprayed across the air as her body shuddered then dropped to the ground.

She had to be dead. There was nothing left of her head but a bloody pulp.

The ring of flames around them died, and across the clearing, Jon saw Mack climb to his feet.

He gave the FBI agent a brief nod, then turned and went back to Maddie. Kneeling down, he lifted her head onto his lap and touched her neck, feeling for a pulse.

Nothing. "Oh God, *no.*" Sudden fear stabbed through his heart. She couldn't die. Not now. He shifted his fingers on her neck, desperate to find some sign of life. He could live without his soul, but he couldn't survive without his heart. Without *her.*

Life shuddered under his fingertips. Her pulse was thready and weak, but there. Relief surged through him. He closed his eyes and leaned his forehead against hers. And felt the fire under her sweat-dampened skin, burning bright.

Eleanor was dead, but her magic still held Maddie captive. She was alive but dying—being consumed by the wrath of her own fires.

The amulet. It had protected him from worst of Eleanor's

magic. Even though he had yet to test his shapeshifting abilities, he sensed they were still very much a part of him. Maybe the amulet could undo whatever spell Eleanor had placed on Maddie.

Ripping it from his neck, he placed it around hers. The stone burned to life. Pale wisps of smoke spread out across her body until she was encased by it. She jerked, then shuddered. He placed his hands on her shoulders, gently preventing her from throwing herself around too much. Through her T-shirt he could feel the heat slowly dissipating from her skin. The amulet was working. He closed his eyes and sent a silent prayer of thanks to Seline.

"Jon?"

Her voice was little more than a harsh croak, but never had he heard a sweeter sound. He smiled down at her, not daring to speak. Because if he did, he sensed he might well ask her to stay, to never leave him again.

And despite everything that had happened in the last few minutes, or maybe because of it, he was more determined than ever to watch her walk away. She might own his heart, but he could survive without it knowing that she was safe and well out of harm's way.

"Where's Eleanor?"

He brushed a damp curl away from her eyes. "Mack shot her."

Surprise flitted through the bright amber depths. Like him, she hadn't expected Eleanor's end to be so simple, so *human.* "Then Evan's safe?"

"We all are."

She reached up and touched his cheek with a trembling hand. Her fingers followed the line of the cut stretching from his eye to his chin, then hesitated when she came to his neck and the steadily flowing tide of blood from his ear.

"You're hurt," she whispered, concern and love evident both in her gaze and the emotive swirl surrounding her.

It hurt him more than any wound could—simply because it was something he was willing to give up, something he would never have again. He took a deep breath and tore his gaze away from hers, watching Mack walk across the clearing instead.

Her confusion rolled around him, as sharp as a knife. He ignored it and smiled at Mack grimly. "Nice shot."

Mack nodded, stopping near Maddie's feet to study them both with a critical eye. "Sorry about the ear."

Jon shrugged and stripped off his coat, wrapping it around Maddie. Now that her internal heat had disappeared, she was beginning to shiver. Her skin felt like ice; hypothermia was only a step away.

"It's a nick, nothing more. You called an ambulance?"

"Yeah. Looks like you both need one." Mack stopped to light a cigarette. "How, exactly, am I going to explain this?"

Jon glanced across at Eleanor's body. She was still more cat than human, trapped even in death by the white ash dagger. Like Hank, her body was beginning to disintegrate. By the time the coroner got here, there'd be little left. "Don't try. Report the facts and let them come up with their own conclusions when they see her."

Mack exhaled a long plume of smoke, then turned. Several men had entered the clearing, the paramedics among them.

"Help is here," Jon said, smiling down at Maddie.

Her fingers wrapped around his and held on tight. Her touch, though icy, ran heat through his soul. But it was the accepting gleam in the tears in her eyes that was almost his undoing.

"Promise you won't leave without saying good-bye," she said softly.

Such a simple request, and yet one that would take every ounce of his strength. It would be far easier to walk away now and never see her again. He stared at her face, trying to imprint every small detail in his mind.

"I won't leave without saying good-bye," he said, and felt some of the tension ease away from her body.

But even as the medical officers separated them, he wasn't entirely sure he spoke the truth.

Twenty

"Maddie, are you listening to me?"

Maddie jumped, then rubbed a hand across her eyes and smiled grimly. She hadn't heard a word Jayne had said in the last five minutes, but she wasn't about to admit that.

"How's Evan coping?" she said, fiddling with the phone cord in an effort to gain a few extra inches so she could rest back against the pillows.

Jayne's sigh was a sound of frustration. "You weren't listening."

She grimaced. "Sorry."

"Evan's fine...mostly. He's still not talking to Steve, though."

"I don't really blame him." Her stupid brother-in-law wanted to take Evan to a psychologist. He couldn't accept the fact his son was gifted, preferring to think there was something mentally wrong with him. He was so like their father it was scary. And in her case, the only winner from her experience had been the psychologist's bank account.

"The police *did* recommend it," Jayne said softly. "He's still having nightmares."

"Nightmares are natural, Jayne. It's only been three days since he escaped Eleanor's clutches."

Three days, she thought, in which she hadn't seen Jon.

She bit her lip, letting her gaze move to the window. A sparrow scooted busily from one tree branch to another, chirping cheerfully. She wished she felt an eighth of his happiness.

"Still, it can't hurt," Jayne murmured.

Anger flared. "Oh for God's sake Jayne, get real," she

snapped. "You know as well as I do that visiting the psychologist did nothing for me except make everything worse. Here I was, a kid with this amazing ability to see the future and light fires with just a thought, and that psychologist and our father made me feel like an abomination. Do you really want that for Evan?"

The phone hummed with silence for several seconds. Then Jayne sighed. "No."

"Then get a backbone and stand up for your son. He has gifts, Jayne, gifts that saved his life. Make Steve see that. Because if he doesn't, he'll push Evan away, and you'll both lose him."

She'd seen it in her dreams. Had seen Evan walking away. It was a future that could be prevented only if Steve saw the error of his ways and stopped acting like such an ass.

"You've seen this?" There was a fearful edge in her sister's voice. Jayne no longer questioned Maddie's abilities, but in some ways, she still feared them. And rightly so, perhaps. They were far more dangerous than Evan's ever would be.

Maddie sighed. "Yes."

"Oh God, I don't want to lose him. I don't want him to end-"

Jayne stopped speaking, but what she'd meant was clear enough. *Don't want him to end up like you.* Maddie smiled grimly. It wasn't something she wanted, either.

Jayne cleared her throat. "When are you getting out of the hospital?"

"Today."

"We're heading home in a couple of days. I'll call you when we get back."

"Fine," Maddie said and hung up.

The nurse bustled into the room, her smile as white as her uniform. "All dressed and ready to leave, I see."

Maddie nodded. Three days spent under constant observation, with no one to talk to but nursing staff and cops asking too many questions, was more than enough. It was time to escape and go back home.

And do what? It was a question that had nagged at her

since she'd awakened in the hospital—alone. She no longer needed a retreat. She was willing to face her past, ready to accept responsibility for her gifts. She just didn't want to do it alone.

"I'll be back in a few minutes, then," the nurse continued. "With the wheelchair."

She didn't bother answering—the woman had already bustled out the door. She stared out the window again. Where was Jon? It hurt that he hadn't bothered coming to see her, that he hadn't kept his promise and let her say good-bye. He'd simply left her clothes and her bag near her bed when she was asleep and had left the hospital. No one had seen him since, not even Mack.

She glanced down at the ring on her finger. For the first time she saw it was a hawk, etched over the shape of a heart. She twisted it around her finger gently and wondered why he hadn't even come back for the ring. He obviously valued it.

"Ready to go?"

The nurse's question jerked Maddie from her thoughts. She nodded a second time and hastily got off the bed, grabbing her bag and climbing into the wheelchair. The nurse wheeled her out of the room. Mack was waiting in the hall.

"Your truck is waiting out the front, but I can arrange a driver if you don't feel up to driving," he said, falling into step beside the chair.

"I appreciate the offer, but I'm fine." She held out her hand, and he shook it gravely. "Thanks for everything."

He smiled. "The police will be in contact if we need any further information."

She nodded. He'd already told her the case was basically closed. Eleanor's death had ensured that. "You heading for home now?"

"I have two weeks' vacation coming. Might stay here a while and enjoy some surf fishing."

Maddie smiled. "I wish you luck."

He nodded and waved her good-bye, heading off down another corridor. The front doors slid open, and the nurse wheeled her into the bright sunshine.

"Here you go," she said, stopping the wheelchair. "You take care of yourself now."

"I will. Thanks." Maddie climbed out of the chair and hefted her bag into a comfortable position on her shoulder. Lifting her face, she enjoyed the caress of warmth against her skin for several seconds. After all the rain and gloom of the past few days, it was a pleasant change. At least it meant the roads would be dry. She wouldn't have to worry so much about her brakes on the trip home.

She turned, wondering where her truck had been parked. Mack had said out front, but he obviously hadn't meant directly out front, because it certainly wasn't here. But it only took a second to find it, parked five spaces down. And Jon was leaning casually against it.

Her heart leapt in sudden hope—and almost as quickly, it died. His face and his stance told her he hadn't changed his mind. He still didn't want her in his life.

She swallowed, trying to ease the sudden dryness in her throat. Then she swung the pack onto her other shoulder and walked towards him.

"I'm glad to see you," she said, stopping several feet away from him. Far enough away to stop herself from reaching out to him, yet close enough to lose herself in the warmth of his wonderful blue eyes.

"I promised I wouldn't go without saying good-bye."

She nodded. She wasn't the only one who was keeping her distance. He stood with his arms folded across his chest, effectively keeping her at arm's length.

Her gaze ran down the scar that stretched from the bottom of his eye to his chin. It was little more than a pale line and certainly didn't mar the beauty of his features. "How are your other wounds?"

He shrugged. "I heal fast. All that's left is the odd scar."

"And your shapeshifting?"

His sudden smile held a warmth that made her heart ache. "My essence is a hawk. It's not magic, but what I am. Eleanor could never take that away from me."

She nodded and shifted her feet slightly. It was hard to

keep her distance, hard not to reach out and touch him, just one more time. Lord, they were acting like casual acquaintances, not two people who had battled against a common foe and won. And they certainly weren't acting like two people who had shared their hearts and their souls in one brief night of love.

But maybe that was for the best. He didn't want her in his life—didn't want anyone he cared about placed in danger. Even if she didn't like his decision, she understood it. She'd made the same resolution after Brian's death, and it had taken her six long years to see her mistake. Retreating had gained her nothing but loneliness. It wasn't until she'd met Jon that she had truly understood.

But his retreat was emotional rather than physical. Any decision to change had to come from him, from his heart, not from anything she said or did. She glanced down at her feet for a minute, blinking away the sudden sting of tears. She would *not* cry. This wasn't a good-bye—just a temporary break. And whether it took ten hours or ten years, she would wait for him to come back to her.

And he would come back. He might be able to defy his heart, but he couldn't defy destiny. They were *meant* to be together. Her dreams had told her that much.

She dropped the pack from her shoulder, pulled the ring off her finger and held it out to him. "This belongs to you."

His gaze didn't waver from hers. "Keep it," he said softly. "I have no further use for it."

She could see the turmoil deep in the depths of his blue eyes. It bolstered her hope that he would come back to her. She wrapped her fingers around the ring, holding it tight. "Then I guess this is good-bye."

He nodded. "I had your brakes fixed, by the way. Didn't want you driving off a cliff on the way home."

"Thank you." Her voice came out little more than a constricted whisper. She swallowed, trying to ease the ache at the back her throat.

He shifted against the car and recrossed his arms. She saw his fingers flex, then clench into a fist. "Take care of yourself,

Maddie."

"You too." She hesitated, wanting to kiss him, wanting to hold him, but knowing if she did, she would plead with him to let her stay with him. Biting her lip, she bent down and picked up her pack.

Everything she'd ever wanted in life stood a bare two feet away, and she was walking away from it. She licked her lips and forced a smile. "Don't be a stranger." *Don't let this good-bye be forever.*

He made no reply. Taking a deep breath, she tore her gaze from his and walked around to the driver's side of the truck.

The engine started the first time. Jon stepped away as she released the hand brake. She could feel his gaze on her, causing a hot ache that burned clear through to her soul. She bit her lip, battling the urge to get out, wrap her arms around him and never let him go. The gears ground sharply as she shifted them too quickly. She didn't care. She had to leave before he saw the tears on her cheeks.

She planted her foot on the gas pedal and sped out of the parking lot. Her last sight of Jon was through the rear view mirror—a lone, unmoving figure, watching her leave.

Epilogue

Maddie leaned back and wiped the sweat from her eyes. On summer days like this, the heat in the greenhouses became almost unbearable. She reached for the water bottle. It was almost noon. Evan and Jayne would be here soon to help her pack. She needed to go in and make lunch.

But not just yet. She turned, studying the empty greenhouse. Even though she'd sold the last of her roses over two months ago, their scent still lingered. All the tables and equipment had been stacked in the far corner and the building echoed. Somehow, it seemed sad.

Three days from now she would leave her haven and never come back. Sometimes she still regretted her decision to sell, but the place was far too big for one person to manage and always had been. It had just taken a long time for her to admit it—and a long time for hope to die.

She twisted around, studying her old ramshackle home. The roof still needed fixing, and the house needed a good coat of paint. Even so, it was a home designed for a family, a place for children to run wild and free. If not hers, then someone else's.

A year and a half had passed since she'd last seen Jon. Somewhere along the line, she'd stopped expecting him to appear on her doorstep. It still hurt, but it wasn't the agonizing feeling of loss it had been.

She took another sip of water, then sighed and sat cross-legged on the sandy ground again. A small circle of rocks was in front of her. In the middle of it were a rather dead looking match, a severely melted candle and a log. She relaced the match with a new one, sticking it into the sand so it stood upright.

Then she narrowed her gaze and focused on the log. Deep down inside her, the embers stirred to life. She reached for the flames, directing them to the log, trying to control their force. After several seconds, the log burst into flame.

Good. Narrowing the focus of her power, she glanced at the candle. The wick leapt to life, the flame leaping high. *Now for the hard one.* She licked her lips, then tightened her grip on the burning rush of energy and sent it toward the match.

The match became a fireball and exploded.

"Damn it to hell," she muttered. Big flames she'd learned to control, but the smaller flames were proving more fickle. But at least she'd learned *some* control. Enough, anyway, that she longer feared killing herself—or anyone else.

Sweat trickled down the side of her face. Time for a break, she thought, and poured the rest of her water over the flames, putting them out again. She rose and headed out into the bright summer sunshine. Shading her eyes against the sun, she stopped and squinted up at the sky. The hawk was back, gliding leisurely along the thermals.

She smiled. The bird had first appeared several months after her arrival back home, and she'd seen it intermittently ever since. Over the last few days, it had been visible almost every day. It wasn't Jon, just a hawk enjoying its freedom and the warm summer breezes. But deep down, she couldn't help thinking that maybe it was some sort of omen.

She might have given up hope, but she hadn't yet given up on a miracle.

The kitchen was cool and dark when she got inside. Sighing in relief, she stripped off her damp T-shirt and ran upstairs for a quick shower.

Ten minutes later she heard the back door slam. Maddie grimaced. Trust Jayne to be early. Grabbing her hairbrush, she leaned out of the bathroom doorway. "Be down in five! Help yourself to something to eat and drink."

The pantry door squeaked open, and she smiled. Evan, no doubt investigating what she had to eat. Jayne had been complaining that of late she just couldn't keep enough food in the house to feed him, and it wasn't hard to see why. He'd grown a good foot in the last year and showed no signs of stopping. He was already as tall as his father.

She frowned. Jayne and Steve had split up almost a year ago, and the change in her sister was amazing. She'd once again become the vibrant, outgoing personality who had dominated most of Maddie's childhood—only this time that personality was edged with compassion and warmth.

But Steve was making noises about wanting to get back together—something Maddie knew Jayne wanted. She just hoped that if Jayne did allow Steve back into her life, it was in her own time and under her own rules. She'd hate to see her sister retreat into her shell again.

One good thing had come from the split, though. Steve had stopped treating Evan, and to a lesser extent Maddie, as some kind of freaks who needed psychological help. He'd even begun reading up on psychic abilities in an effort to try to help his son understand and control his gifts. It was something none of them had expected. Evan was speaking to his dad again, and Maddie's dreams no longer warned of him walking away.

She ducked across the hall to her bedroom. Grabbing a T-shirt and some shorts, she quickly dressed.

Still brushing her hair, she padded down the stairs and along the hall. "Hope you picked up some more boxes, because I'm just about-"

The jeans-clad figure turned as she entered the kitchen, and Maddie came to an abrupt halt. Jon!

Her heart skipped several beats. Lord, how often had she dreamed of this happening? Every waking hour in those first few months of separation had been filled with the fantasy of walking into a room and finding him there. But it was a dream that had gradually died. Was she dreaming now?

"Hello, Madeline." His warm, velvet voice held a hint of uncertainty.

It was his uncertainty that convinced her he was real and a not just a figment of her imagination. She swallowed heavily, trying to stem the sudden rush of joy. "Nice to see you again."

Her voice sounded deceptively calm, given the turmoil in her heart.

He nodded and ran a hand through his hair. Slivers of sunshine seemed to dance through his fingers. His hair was a little shorter now, and lines of weariness shadowed the diamond brightness of his blue eyes. But everything else was the same, right down to the thigh-defining tightness of his jeans.

Maddie clenched her fingers around her brush. She wanted to reach out and touch him—wanted to feel the heat of his body, the touch of his lips on hers. Wanted it for real, and not just in her dreams. But the first move had to be his. He might have come back to say hello and nothing more.

"We need to talk," he said softly. "Please, come and sit down."

She didn't move. Moving would only take her closer to him, and that was a risk she dared not take. Not yet. "What do you want to talk about?"

He sighed and pulled his gaze from hers. "Can we start with an apology?"

Hope fluttered. She shifted her weight from one foot to the other and raised an eyebrow. "For what?"

"For being such an ass. For taking so long to get back to you."

"As good a place as any to start, I suppose." She crossed her arms and stared at him. "Why did you take so long to get here? Another couple of days, and I would be gone."

"I know." He glanced up, a slight smile tugging his generous lips. "Have you bought another house yet?"

"No." How did he know she'd sold her house? The sold sign out front had been moved several days ago, so he couldn't have seen it coming in. Her heart skipped several more beats— had he been keeping tabs on her all along?

His smile widened, then he turned and walked across to the window, opening the blind. "Won't you miss this place? It's so peaceful."

She frowned. Why was he discussing the damn house? "Of course I'll miss it, but I can't afford the upkeep on my own."

"Uh-huh." He leaned a hip against the sink and crossed his arms, staring out the window for several long minutes. "I often dreamed of owning a place like this," he said softly.

"Then you're about a week too late to buy it. Some woman named Seline Whiteshore bought it." She slammed her hairbrush down and walked across to the refrigerator. "Want something to drink?"

He shook his head, not bothering to turn around. She poured herself a glass of soda and dragged out a chair. Whatever he'd come here to say was obviously going to take a while.

His next question was another bolt from the blue. "Do you still have my ring?"

Maddie frowned and glanced down at her finger. *Damn.* She'd left it in the greenhouse. "Yes, I have it. Why?"

"Do you know the significance of it?"

"Of course I don't!" Why did he discuss the house and the ring instead of *them?* Had he come here as a friend, nothing more? She swallowed heavily, but her voice still came out a croak as she continued. "Didn't it belong to your father?"

"Not precisely."

He turned to face her. Something in his eyes made her breath catch in her throat.

"My father actually gave it to my mother, who then gave it to me when I was old enough."

She had no idea where all this was leading. "So?"

He smiled. "In our family, it has become known as the Heart of the Hunter. It is a gift that the first born son of each generation gives to the woman he loves."

It took several seconds for the meaning of his words to hit her. He was saying he loved her—*Wasn't he?* She licked her lips, refusing to let elation bubble free. After a year and a half of waiting, she had to be sure. Even if he *was* admitting he loved her, he hadn't actually mentioned any plan to *stay.*

"Do you want it back?"

His smile was rich and warm, but she could see the uncertainty in his eyes. "No, I don't want it back. It belongs to you, as does my heart." He hesitated, then added softly, "I love you, Maddie."

Tears stung her eyes. She blinked, pulling her gaze away from his. He'd finally said the words she'd longed to hear, so why was she suddenly crying?

"Why haven't you come back for me before now?" she whispered, staring at her hands, which were clasped together on the table.

He took a step towards her, then stopped. "I walked away because I didn't want to see you harmed, didn't want you to become a target for some madman after me."

"So why come here now and tell me you love me?"

"Because I can't survive without my heart anymore." He walked around the table and squatted next to her chair. He didn't actually touch her, but he was close enough for the heat and the tension in his body to wash over her.

She kept her eyes on her hands and didn't move. Could barely breathe.

"I can't walk past a rose without thinking of you," he continued softly. "Every time I see a beaten up old truck with squealing brakes I find myself hoping it's yours. You have been in my thoughts and my dreams every minute of every day this past year and a half."

"That doesn't answer the question." She raised her eyes to his. She could see the fear and love and loneliness in the depths of his bright gaze—echoes of everything she'd felt since they'd parted. She reached out, gently touching the faint scar on his cheek. "Why are you here now?"

"We'd barely known each other a week, Maddie. I kept telling myself that what we shared, what I felt, could be little more than an offshoot of the danger we shared. That you deserved the chance to get on with your life and sort out your emotions without me getting in the way." He raised his hand, capturing hers. His thumb traced the white mark where his ring usually sat. "It wasn't until I saw you were getting ready to leave here that I realized I had to tell you what I felt before you left the past—and me—behind you forever."

"You were watching me?"

"Not often—just enough to assure myself you were okay."

"Then that hawk outside was you?"

He hesitated, then grinned. It was a decidedly boyish grin that did odd things to her already trembling heart.

"That was me trying to gather the courage to finally face you."

She glanced down at their entwined fingers. He loved her, but was he really ready to have her stand by his side? Because if he wanted her in his life, it would mean his *whole* life—whatever the risks or dangers that might entail—or nothing at all. "But nothing has changed. You can't give up what you do, so where does that leave me?"

The blue eyes she loved so much were filled with uncertainty. He still wasn't sure of her reaction, of her feelings for him.

"I've wasted a year and a half trying to survive without you. I can't do that any more. I need you, Maddie." His voice husky, he continued. "I want to have children with you and watch them run wild in this big, old house. I want to wake up in the mornings with you in my arms and go to sleep each night the same way. I want to grow old with you, Maddie. I've no right to ask you to risk your life, to become a part of mine, but that's exactly what I'm asking. Share my life—and let me become a part of yours. Marry me, Maddie."

The tears stinging her eyes finally fell. He reached up, gently wiping them away with the soft pad of his thumb. His touch sent shivers of anticipation racing through her soul. This man's caress was hers to keep—forever.

"Is that a yes?" he asked, smiling gently.

"Oh God, yes!" With a sob, she fell into his embrace. He held her close. It was better than any dream. "I was so afraid you would never come back to me," she whispered against his chest.

"And I was so afraid that you might have come to your senses and not wanted me back." He brushed a kiss across the top of her head. "That's why it took me so long to finally face you. I just couldn't bear the thought that you might not love me."

She raised her head and gave him a mock glare. "It's a shame you couldn't have found the courage sooner. Then maybe I wouldn't have sold the house."

His smile sang through her soul. "Seline Whiteshore is my boss. She bought the house on my behalf. It belongs to us, and our children." He placed his hands on her shoulders and eased her back. "We have to do this properly."

She sniffed and stared at him, perplexed. "Do what?"

He smiled and reached into his pocket, producing the ring. "I saw you come out of the greenhouse without it," he said before she could ask. "And I can't do this without it."

"I hate it when you speak in riddles."

"Shush." His eyes gleamed, then he took a deep breath, and his expression became serious. "The Heart of the Hunter is only given once in every lifetime. Do you, Madeline Smith, accept the heart of *this* hunter?"

She smiled and leaned forward, gently tasting his lips. "Only if the hunter promises he's not going to spend our entire lives simply *talking.*"

"That is the something you can be very certain of." He gave her a smile as sweet and tender as any kiss and slipped the ring onto her finger. "That, and the fact that I love you."

"I love you, too," she whispered, and knew that no matter what life threw at them, they would remain together.

Forever.

COMING IN DECEMBER 2001

HEARTS IN DARKNESS

KERI ARTHUR'S
SEQUEL TO
DANCING WITH THE DEVIL

Life has never been so insane for Nikki James. There's another teenager missing. She has another vampire to contend with. Her partner and best friend Jake is in the hospital dying. And a madman is kidnapping the wealthy.

Just when it seems nothing else could possibly go wrong, Michael returns—but not for her. This time, however, Nikki has no intention of running from either the case or from what still lies between her and Michael. And she isn't going to let him run, either.

The last thing Michael Kelly needs is a confrontation with Nikki—especially when his control over his bloodlust is still so tenuous. But when a kidnapper steps up his agenda to murder, he's forced into a partnership with Nikki to keep her safe. Soon Michael discovers the biggest danger he faces may not be from his need to "taste" her, but from his desire to make her a permanent part of his life—a life that is sure to get her killed.

Nikki is determined to make Michael see that life apart is worse than death. But before she can make him see the light, a specter from Michael's past rises that could destroy any hope she has of a future with him. Because this time the threat isn't physical. It's a matter of the heart.

Nikki must compete with the woman—the vampire—for whom Michael gave up life.

Printed in the United States
73870LV00002BB/12